这样学习
英语口语最有效

李奇 编著

THE MOST
EFFECTIVE WAY
TO LEARN ORAL
ENGLISH

中国广播电视出版社
CHINA RADIO & TELEVISION PUBLISHING HOUSE

图书在版编目(CIP)数据

这样学习英语口语最有效/李奇编著. —北京:中国
广播电视出版社,2006.1
ISBN 7-5043-4416-8

Ⅰ.这... Ⅱ.李... Ⅲ.英语,美国—口语
Ⅳ.H319.9

中国版本图书馆 CIP 数据核字(2006)第 006090 号

这样学习英语口语最有效

编　　著	李　奇
特约编辑	周　壮
责任编辑	常　红
监　　印	赵　宁
监　　制	张曲波
出版发行	中国广播电视出版社
电　　话	86093580　86093583
社　　址	北京市西城区真武庙二条 9 号(邮政编码 100045)
经　　销	各地新华书店和外文书店
印　　刷	保定华泰印刷有限公司
开　　本	880 毫米×1230 毫米　　　　1/32
字　　数	300(千)字
印　　张	9.75
版　　次	2006 年 3 月第 1 版　2006 年 3 月第 1 次印刷
书　　号	ISBN 7-5043-4416-8/H·248
定　　价	22.00 元

前言

　　每个英语学习者都想以最快的速度提高自己的口语水平，但却苦于寻找好的学习方法。本书为读者提供了极其有效的学习方法，帮助读者迅速提高口语水平。

　　本书特色如下：

　　1. 精选各类最鲜活、最地道的常用美语，去粗取精，提纲挈领。内容与生活息息相关，透过不同论题，从不同层面为读者提供活用英语的妙方。

　　2. 采取中英文对照的方式，配合详尽的讲解、典型的例句和精心归纳的惯用语，帮助读者轻松迅速地熟记生活对话。真正达到学以致用的效果。

　　3. 活学活用配合情景式演练，形式生动活泼，让读者真正实现滔滔不绝、侃侃而谈说英语的梦想。

　　4. 每一章节都配有精选的会话练习，可用来巩固所学知识点。读者会发现说英语不再是难事！

　　希望本书能帮助读者找到学习英语的乐趣、增强征服英语的信心、提高掌握英语的效率！

编者

2006 年 1 月

English...

第 1 部

焦点对话整理分析
掌握趋势·突破自我

●归纳对话中最常用的焦点句型,深入分析语法结构,提供正确的对话方式及技巧,并透过例句加以印证,实际观摩演练,平时可活学活用,增加应对能力。

第 **1** 篇 是否问句(Yes－No 问句)的问与答

没有疑问词的问句,可以用 **Yes** 或 **No** 回答的问句称为 **Yes/No** 问句。

例:【问】Are you a student?（你是学生吗?）

　　【答】Yes, I am.（是的,我是学生。）

　　　　No, I'm not.（不,我不是学生。）

像这种问句一般是以 **Be** 动词、**助动词**(do, will 等)、**情态助动词**(can, may, could, would, should, might 等)引导。

例:【问】Do you like tea?（你喜欢喝茶吗?）

　　【答】Yes, I do.（是的,我喜欢。）

　　　　No, I don't.（不,我不喜欢。）

　　【问】Can you open the can?（你能把这罐罐头打开吗?）

　　【答】Yes, I can.（可以,我能打开。）

　　　　No, I can't.（不行,我打不开。）

➔ 心得笔记

▶**Yes－No 问句之特色**

❶句首有 be 动词或助动词。

❷中译结尾一般带"吗?"中英文句尾声调皆上扬。

❸回答时,一般先回答 Yes 或 No,故名 Yes－No 问句。

● 焦点整理 ●

1. 凡此类问句,标准回答是短句,如:Yes, I am. 或 No, I am not. 但天下事并非总是一成不变,故仍有变化,如:

请注意观察下列的回答句:

Betty:Can David play the piano?（大卫会弹钢琴吗?）

John：①Yes，he can.

②No，he can't.

③No，but he can play the guitar.（不会，但他会弹吉他。）

④Who knows?（谁晓得?）

⑤I'm not sure.（我不太确定。）

⑥Maybe，but I'm not sure.（也许会，但我不太确定。）

⑦I wish I knew this.（但愿我知道这事。→我不知道。）

⑧None of your business!（不关你的事。→不礼貌的应对。）

⑨Does it matter to you?（这跟你有关系吗? /重要吗?）

→ 心得笔记

没有疑问词的问句(Yes/No 问句)回答时，基本上是以 **Yes** 或 **No** 来回答，但是在英语会话中变化很多，以上九种答案均可，并且尚有未列出之答案。因此请同学们回答时，要看情况应对，要读活书。

● 焦点整理 ●

2. 凡短句回答，一定连贯，**Yes** 即肯定，**No** 即否定。

例：

$$
(\times)\begin{cases} \text{Yes, he isn't.} \\ \text{Yes, he can't.} \\ \text{No, I am.} \\ \text{No, he can.} \end{cases}
\qquad
(\checkmark)\begin{cases} \text{Yes, he is.} \\ \text{Yes, he can.} \\ \text{No, I am not.} \\ \text{No, he cannot.} \end{cases}
$$

[注意]▶长句回答，可以 Yes 连否定或 No 连肯定。

$$
\begin{cases} \text{Are you a student?} \\ \text{No, I am not. 或 No, I am a business man.} \end{cases}
$$

● 焦点整理 ●

3. 对于"反意问句"(*tag question*)，其回答仍与一般的"Yes—No"问句相同，对的是 **Yes**，错的是 **No**。

例：He is a good doctor, isn't he?（他是好医生，不是吗？）

Yes, he **is**.（是的，他是好医生。）

No, he **isn't**.（不，他不是好医生。）

●焦点整理●

4. 句中有连接词 **or**(或)时，回答时选出一个适当的答案即可，不必再用 **Yes/No.**

例：Are you a student or a clerk?　　I am a student.

（你是学生还是职员？）　　　　（我是学生。）

例：Did you buy a bicycle or a motorcycle?

（你买的是自行车，还是摩托车？）

I bought a motorcycle.（我买的是摩托车。）

●焦点整理●

5. 别人请客吃东西时，回答时应注意礼貌，接受时说 **Yes, please.** 婉拒时说 **No, thanks.** 或 **No, thank you.**

例：John：Do you want a cup of tea?（你要茶吗？）

Mary：Yes, please.（好的，麻烦你了。）

例：Tom：Will you come out with me for dinner this evening?

（今晚我们一起出去吃饭好吗？）

Jane：No, thanks.（不用了，谢谢。）

➔心得笔记

如果你很忙不能帮助别人时可说：I'm sorry. I'm busy now. 如：

John：Would you please go to buy some bread for me?

（请你为我去买些面包好吗？）

Mary：I'm sorry. I'm very busy now.（抱歉。我现在很忙。）

━━━━━ ●焦点整理● ━━━━━

6. **Yes** 的代用语常见的有:**Of course.** (当然。)**Sure(ly).** (当然,
一定。)**Certainly.** (当然,一定。)**Quite so.** /**Just so.** (正是如
此。)**That's it.** (就是那样。)**That's right.** (没错。)等。
No 的代用语常见的有 **Of course not.** /**Surely not.** /**Certainly
not.** (当然不。)**Not at all.** /**Not in the least.** (一点也不。)
Never. (从未。)**Nothing.** (没什么。)等。

例: { **Did** you come home last night? (你昨晚回家了吗?)
{ **Yes**(=**Of course**=**Certainly**),I did. (回家了。)

例: { Do you like the weather in Beijing? (你喜欢北京的天气吗?)
{ Not at all. (我一点也不喜欢。)

━━━━━ ●焦点整理● ━━━━━

7. **Do you mind**
   Would you mind } +V-ing? 表示"是否介意做某事?"

多半用否定句回答,表示不介意。

例: { Do you mind opening the window?
{ (你介意开窗子吗? 也可译成:请打开窗子。)
{ No,I don't mind. (不,我不介意。)

━━━━━ →心得笔记 ━━━━━

但是在极少的情况下也有表示"**介意**"做某事,而用 **Yes** 回答的。
例:【问】John:Do you mind my smoking here? 或 Would you
     mind if I smoked here? (你介意我在此抽烟吗?)

【答】Sue:Yes,I { do
              would } . I have a cold. (是的。我感冒了。)

非常实战测验

● 活学活用 ●

1. Tom：Don't forget tomorrow night at my home.

Bill：No, I won't. Do you mind if I bring a friend?

Tom：_____.

Bill：See you then.

(A) Yes, it's a good idea.

(B) No, you'd better not.

(C) Certainly, I do.

(D) Not at all. You're both welcome.

【答案】▶ (A)

【译文】▶ 汤姆：别忘了明天晚上要到我家喔!

比尔：不,我不会忘的。你介不介意我带个朋友去?

汤姆：_____

比尔：到时候见啦!

(A) 好啊! 好主意!　　(B) 不好,你最好不要。

(C) 当然,我介意。　　(D) 一点也不介意。很欢迎你们到我家。

● 活学活用 ●

2. Jane：Do you read much, Jack?

Jack：Yes, _____

Jane：What kind of books do you read?

Jack：Plays and stories.

(A) books are Greek to me.

(B) I like sports very much.

(C) whenever I have some spare time.

(D) I hardly read at all.

【答案】▶ (C)

【译文】▶ 简：　杰克,你常常看书吗?

杰克:是的,＿＿＿＿＿＿＿

简：　你看哪些书呢?

杰克:戏剧和短篇小说。

(A)我对书一窍不通。　　　　(B)我非常喜爱运动。

(C)只要我有些空闲的时间。　(D)我几乎不看书。

【讲解】▶ ①*Play* [plei] *n.* 戏剧

②*Greek*　　*n.* 希腊文

something is Greek to me

表示对……像读希腊文一样,一窍不通。

③*spare*　　*adj.* 多余的,空闲的

④*hardly*　　*adv.* 几乎不(用于否定句)

例:I hardly ever catch cold.(我很少感冒。)

●活学活用●

3. Pat：　Hello. I need to come in and take the test for my driver's license. What hours are you open, please?

Officer：Our downtown office is open from 8：00 to 2：00, and you can take the test anytime between 8：00 and 2：00.

Pat：　And it isn't possible to do it on the weekends, is it?

Officer：＿＿＿＿＿＿＿.

(A)Yes, I'm sorry.　　　　(B)No, I'm sorry.

(C)Yes, I would.　　　　(D)No, I don't.

【答案】▶ (B)

【译文】▶ 帕特:喂。我必须来参加驾照考试。请问你们什么时间开放?

官员:我们市中心的办公室从八点到两点开放,你可以在八点到两点任何时间参加考试。

帕特:周末考是不可能的,是吗?

官员：_____
　　（A)有可能的,我很抱歉。　(B)不可能的,我很抱歉。
　　（C)是的,我会。　　　　　(D)不,我不。

【讲解】▶"反意问句"的回答与一般的"Yes－No"问句一样,肯定用
　　　　"Yes",否定用"No"。"I'm sorry"是暗藏否定意味的句
　　　　子,故与"No"连用,表示"不可能"。

━━━━●活学活用●━━━━

4. Bob：Would you mind lending me your car tonight?
　　Ben：_____I have to study anyway,so I won't be using it.
　　（A)I'm afraid not.　　　　(B)I suppose so.
　　（C)Well, I guess not.　　　(D)Of course.

【答案】▶(C)

【译文】▶鲍伯:今晚借一下您的车子好吗?
　　　　本：_____反正我要读书,所以我用不着。
　　　　（A)我很乐意。　　　　(B)我想是(如此)。
　　　　（C)嗯,我想我不会介意。(D)当然介意。

【讲解】▶①鲍伯问对方是否会介意借车给他,而对方回答表示不
　　　　介意。所以选(C)。
　　　　②*I suppose so.＝I think so.*

━━━━●活学活用●━━━━

5. Kevin：The day after tomorrow is Alfred's birthday. Maybe
　　　　I'll buy him a tennis racket.
　　Ralph：Does he play tennis?
　　Kevin：_____He's putting on too much weight.
　　（A)Never mind.
　　（B)No, but he should.
　　（C)Surely, tennis is a good sport.
　　（D)Play tennis? He's a professional.

【答案】▶(B)

【译文】▶凯文：　后天是阿尔弗雷德的生日,也许我会买个网球拍送给他。

拉尔夫：他打网球吗?

凯文：＿＿＿＿＿他越来越胖了。

(A)不要紧。

(B)不打,但他该打了。

(C)当然,网球是一项不错的运动。

(D)打网球? 他是职业选手呐。

【讲解】▶①*The day after tomorrow* 后天

②*put on weight* 变胖,体重增加;*lose weight* 减轻体重

③*professional* 职业者;*amateur* 业余爱好者

━━━━━●活学活用●━━━━━

6. Mary：Would you like some ice cream?

Lucy：No, thanks.

Mary：Why not? Don't you like ice cream?

Lucy：＿＿＿＿＿

(A) No, I don't. But it's too fattening.

(B) Yes, I do. But I'd rather have a milk shake.

(C) Yes, I don't. And I think a coke is a better choice.

(D) No, I do. And on second thoughts, I like some now.

【答案】▶(B)

【译文】▶玛丽：你要不要来点冰淇淋?

露西：不,谢了。

玛丽：为什么不要? 你不喜欢冰淇淋吗?

露西：＿＿＿＿＿

(A)不,我不喜欢,冰淇淋太容易使人发胖了。

(B)是的,我喜欢。但我宁可要份奶昔。

(C)是的,我不喜欢,我认为可乐更好。

(D)不,我喜欢,但是重新考虑过后,现在我想吃了。

【讲解】▶①在 *Yes—No* 问句的答案中,"Yes＋肯定短句","No＋

● 活学活用 ●

10. David：_____

Mark：Yes. But he likes the publishing business better.

(A) Wasn't Bill trained as an engineer?

(B) Bill wants to become a lawyer, doesn't he?

(C) Bill will never go into politics, will he?

(D) Did Bill ever dream that someday he'd be working in Shanghai?

【答案】▶(A)

【译文】▶大卫：_____

马克：是啊，但是他比较喜欢出版业。

(A) 比尔不是受过工程师的训练吗？

(B) 比尔想成为一名律师，不是吗？

(C) 比尔绝不会踏入政治界，不是吗？

(D) 比尔曾梦想过有一天会在上海工作吗？

【讲解】▶① *publishing business*　出版业

② *train sb. as...*　把某人训练成……

③ *go into*　踏入，涉足

④ *someday* = some day　（将来）有一天

● 活学活用 ●

11. Jane：　　Can you pass me the ice cream?

Mother：_____

(A) Sorry, they are too heavy for me to carry.

(B) Sorry, they don't taste good.

(C) Don't you think they are delicious?

(D) Don't you think you've had enough?

【答案】▶(D)

【译文】▶简：　可以把冰淇淋递给我吗？

母亲：_____

(A)抱歉,它们太重了我拿不动。

(B)抱歉,它们不好吃。

(C)你不认为它们好吃吗?

(D)你不认为你已吃得够多了吗?

【讲解】▶①*pass*　传递

②*too*＋形容词(副词)＋*to do*～　太……以致无法……

━━━━━━●*活学活用*●━━━━━━

12. Judy:Jane,would you like some more salad?

　　Jane:＿＿＿＿＿＿

　　Judy:Here you are.

　　(A)Yes,please. It looks very delicious.

　　(B)Thank you. I've had plenty of it.

　　(C)Yes,please. It's really delicious.

　　(D)Thanks. But I really can't.

【答案】▶(C)

【译文】▶朱蒂:简,要不要再来点沙拉?

　　　　简:　＿＿＿＿＿＿

　　　　朱蒂:在这儿。

　　　　(A)好的,麻烦你了。沙拉看起来很好吃。

　　　　(B)谢谢你。我吃很多了。

　　　　(C)好的,麻烦你。沙拉真是好吃。

　　　　(D)谢谢。但我实在吃不下了。

【讲解】▶①由 *some more salad* 可知 Jane 已吃过沙拉,故选(C)。

　　　　②(A)表示"看起来"好吃,表示 Jane 尚未吃沙拉,与句意不合。

　　　　③*Here you are.* 在这里。(是拿东西给别人时所说的。)

　　　　④*have plenty of sth.* 吃多了某物

● 活学活用 ●

13. Mr. Smith：Excuse me, sir. I'm writing a research paper on
Chinese culture. Do you mind answering a few
questions?

Dr. Zhang：＿＿＿＿＿
(A)Certainly. (B)No, of course not.
(C)By all means. (D)Yes, please.

【答案】▶(B)

【译文】▶史密斯先生：对不起，先生。我正在写一篇关于中国文化
的研究报告。你介意回答一些问题吗？

张博士： ＿＿＿＿＿
(A)当然。 (B)不，当然不。
(C)当然。 (D)好的，请。

【讲解】▶①*by all means* 必定；当然。

②关于或论及……主题用介词 *on*。

③当 *mind v.* 用于疑问句时，注意句中是否用 *my*。

例：❶Would you mind *my opening* the window?

（你在意我把窗子打开来吗？）

❷Would you mind *opening* the window?

（你能为我打开那窗子吗？）

● 活学活用 ●

14. John： Don't you like to eat American food? （多选）
George：＿＿＿＿＿
(A)Yes, I don't like to eat American food.
(B)No, I like very much to eat American food.
(C)No, because American food is too expensive.
(D)No, I prefer to have noodles in a Chinese restau-
rant.
(E)No, American food is not really to my taste.

【答案】▶ (C)(D)(E)

【译文】▶ 约翰：你不喜欢吃美国食物吗？

乔治：_____

(A)是的,我不喜欢吃美国食物。

(B)不,我很喜欢吃美国食物。

(C)不喜欢,因为美国食物太贵了。

(D)不喜欢,我比较喜欢到中国餐馆吃面条。

(E)不喜欢,美国食物实在不合我的胃口。

【讲解】▶ ①(A)(B)皆文法错误,(A)中前面用 Yes,后面不能用否定；而(B)中前面用 No,后面不能用肯定。

②*to one's taste* 合某人的胃口

━━━━● 活学活用 ●━━━━

15. Sam：Brrr! It's cold! _____

　　Sue：It's hanging over there next to the door.

　　Sam：Next to the door? Oh, yes. Thanks.

　　(A)I'm dying for a cup of hot coffee.

　　(B)Have you seen my coat?

　　(C)Is the heater on?

　　(D)Why don't we get a heater for the apartment?

【答案】▶ (B)

【译文】▶ 山姆：哇! 好冷喔! _____

　　　　苏：　就挂在门旁边。

　　　　山姆：门旁边? 喔,找到了,谢谢。

　　　　(A)我很想喝杯热咖啡。

　　　　(B)你看到我的外套了吗?

　　　　(C)暖气开了吗?

　　　　(D)我们何不在公寓里装暖气?

【讲解】▶ ①*brrr*　呼气声　②*next(to)*　紧靠着……

③*dying for* ＝ look forward to　渴望

④*heater* n. 暖气；电热器　⑤*apartment* 公寓

第2篇　含疑问词的问句回答方式

一、*How* 的用法及其例句

●焦点整理●

1. How(如何)：是疑问副词,用来问①情况,方法　②健康状况　③对方意见,要求　④理由　⑤程度。

例：①**How** do you get to the office? By bus. (你怎么去上班的? 乘公共汽车。)

②**How** is your father? (令尊身体怎么样?)

He is very well, thank you. (他很好,谢谢你。)

③**How** do you feel about the project? (你觉得这个计划如何?)

It's very good. (很好。)

④**How** *is it that* you didn't come? (你怎么没来?)

Because I was sick. (因为我病了。)

⑤**How** fast can you ride this bicycle? (这辆自行车你能骑多快呢?)

About 50 kilometers an hour. (大约 1 小时 50 公里。)

●焦点整理●

2. How 的常用搭配引导的问句有以下几种：

①How old 问"几岁?"　②How long 问"时间多久?"或"长度多少?"　③How often 问"次数"。　④How soon 问"多久之后?"　⑤How far 问"距离"。　⑥How much 问"价钱"。

⑦How many 问"有多少?"　⑧How come 问"原因"。

例：①**How old** is your daughter?（你的女儿几岁了?）

　　She is five.（她五岁了。）

②**How long** will you be here? ⎫

（你将在这儿待多久?）　　⎬➡[问时间多久]

Five days.（五天。）　　⎭

How long is the belt?（这条皮带有多长?）⎫

About four feet.（大约四英尺长。）　⎬➡[问长度]

③**How often** do you go to the movies?（你多久看一次电影?）

　　Once a week.（一周一次。）

　　或 Two times a month.（一个月两次。）

　　或 Every six days.（每六天一次。）

④**How soon** can I learn to speak English?（学会说英语要多长时间?）

　　About three years.（大约三年。）

⑤**How far** is it from here to the nearest hospital?

（从这儿到最近的医院有多远?）

　　Three blocks.（三条街。）

⑥**How much** does it cost?（这多少钱?）

　　Five dollars.（五块钱。）

⑦**How many** students are there in your class?（你们班上有多少学生?）

　　Twenty-seven.（27 人。）

⑧**How come** you didn't attend the meeting?（你为什么没去参加会议?）

　　I forgot.（我忘记了。）

●焦点整理●

3. How 其他常用的惯用语有

　①**How are you?**

　②**How about＋N/V-ing...?**

　③**How ＋形＋主语＋动词！＝What＋a/an＋形＋N（＋主语＋动词）！**

例：$\Biggl\{$ Why not get up? It's nearly eight o'clock.
（你为什么不起床？都快八点了。）
Yes/OK. /All right. （好，我起来。）

三、*What* 的用法及其例句

━━●焦点整理●━━

1. 用以询问物、事或人。译成"什么"。

例：① （问人）What are they? 或 What do they do?

（他们是干什么的?）指职业。答语可说成：They are police-
men.（他们是警察。）

② （问物）What's that on the table? （在桌上的是什么东西啊？）

It's a teapot. （是一把茶壶。）

③ （问事）What's going on there? （那里发生了什么事？）

A car accident. （一场车祸。）

━━●焦点整理●━━

2. What～for? ＝For what～? ＝Why～?

为什么？→强调目的

例：$\Biggl\{$ What did you go to Hangzhou for? （你去杭州做什么？）
To visit my uncle. （去拜访我的伯父。）

━━●焦点整理●━━

3. What is wrong/the matter/the problem with ＋ 宾语？（有
……事/麻烦/问题等?）

例：$\Biggl\{$ What is wrong with you? （你怎么啦？）
I have a bad cold. （我得了重感冒了。）

●*焦点整理*●

4. 日期的问法：

What day? 问星期名称

What date? 问几月几号

例： ①What day will he come back?（他星期几回来?）

Friday.（星期五。）

②What date is it today?（今天几月几号?）

It's November 28,1998.（1998 年 11 月 28 号。）

●*焦点整理*●

5. What's he like? 问他的"人品、性格"。

What does he look like? 问他人"长相"怎么样。

例：$\begin{cases} \text{What is he like?（他的人品如何?）} \\ \text{He is honest and kind.（他为人忠厚善良。）} \end{cases}$

例：$\begin{cases} \text{What does your boyfriend look like?（你的男朋友长得如何?）} \\ \text{He is tall and strong.（他又高又壮。）} \end{cases}$

●*焦点整理*●

6. What do you think of/about～你认为……怎么样?

例： What do you think of this novel?（你觉得这本小说怎么样?）

It's very boring.（很无聊。）

●*焦点整理*●

7. What 的常用口语：

What's the problem? 有什么困难?

What did you say? 你说什么?（请再说一遍。）

What do you mean by that? 你那是什么意思?

What's new? 最近怎样? 有什么新鲜事?

What's on your mind? 你在担心些什么?

What can I do for you? 有什么我可以效劳的吗?

非 常实战测验 ●━━━━━━━━━━━━━

主题 1➡How 的用法

●焦点整理●

1. Receptionist：Hello，Kent Restaurant.

Ms. Lee：　　How late are you open today?

Receptionist：＿＿＿＿＿＿.

Ms. Lee：　　Oh，that's too bad.

(A)I'm sorry. We're closed now.

(B)You can come anytime.

(C)We're open very late.

(D)We open at 11：30 a. m.

【答案】▶(D)

【译文】▶接待员：你好，肯特餐厅。

李小姐：今天你们几点营业?

接待员：＿＿＿＿＿＿

李小姐：哦! 真是太可惜了。

(A)我很抱歉，我们营业时间已过。

(B)你随时都可以来。

(C)我们营业到很晚。

(D)我们 11：30 开始营业。

●活学活用●

2. Paul：How can I get to the Palace Museum from here?

David：You can take a number 304 bus in front of our school.

Paul：How often does the bus leave for the museum?

David：＿＿＿＿＿＿

(A)Early in the morning.

(B)In an hour.

(C)Ten minutes later.

(D)Every half an hour.

【答案】▶(D)

【译文】▶保罗：我从这里要如何才能到故宫博物院？

大卫：你可以在我们学校前面搭乘304路公共汽车。

保罗：公共汽车多久开往博物院一次？

大卫：＿＿＿＿＿＿＿

　　(A)一大早。　　　　(B)约一小时后。

　　(C)十分钟后。　　　(D)每半小时一次。

【讲解】▶①get to ＋地方：到……地方去。

②How often：问公共汽车的"班次"有多频繁。

━━━━━●活学活用●━━━━━

3. A：Would you like some more chicken?

B：Yes,please. It's realy delicious.

A：Well,I'm glad you like it. How about some more rice?

B：＿＿＿＿＿＿＿

(A)How nice! I'd like some more dessert.

(B)Thanks for the compliment.

(C)No,thanks. I'm already full.

(D)Many thanks. I can't eat any more rice.

【答案】▶(C)

【译文】▶A：要不要再吃点鸡肉？

B：好的,谢谢。真好吃。

A：哦,真高兴你喜欢吃这鸡肉。再来点米饭怎么样？

B：＿＿＿＿＿＿＿

(A)真棒！我想再来一些餐后甜点。

(B)谢谢你的称赞。

(C)不用了,谢谢,我已经吃饱了。

(D)多谢! 我吃不下米饭了。

【讲解】▶①$\begin{cases} \text{Would you like. . . ?} \\ \text{How about. . . ?} \end{cases}$ 两者都有"询问、劝进"的意思。

②compliement　*n.* 恭维

③rice 非 dessert［di'zə:t］*n.* 餐后甜点

══════ ●活学活用● ══════

4. Bob：How long have you lived here?

　Sue：_____

　　(A)Since the beginning of the year.

　　(B)1970.

　　(C)Not long ago.

　　(D)Only until the end of the year.

【答案】▶(A)

【译文】▶鲍伯:你住在这儿多久了?

　　苏:　_____

　　　(A)从年初到现在。　　　　(B)1970 年。

　　　(C)不久前。　　　　　　　(D)只到年底为止。

【讲解】▶*until* 指"到……为止",表示持续动作的终止点。

　　　虽然 till 是 until 的口语体,但在句首时通常还是用 until。

══════ ●活学活用● ══════

5. Mary：How long had you been studying before you gave up?

　Helen：_____(多选)

　　(A)I have studied for five years.

　　(B)Five years.

　　(C)I don't remember clearly.

　　(D)Before I gave up,I had been studying for five years.

　　(E)I had given up for five years already.

【答案】▶(B)(C)(D)

【译文】▶玛莉:在你放弃之前,你已经读了多久了?

海伦:_____

(A)我到现在已读五年了。

(B)五年。

(C)我记不清楚了。

(D)放弃前,我已读五年了。

(E)我已放弃五年了。

【讲解】▶①(A)的时态不对,gave up 发生在过去,I have studied for...则指到现在为止,故应改 have 为 had。

②(E)答已放弃五年,未针对问句所问的在未放弃前已念了多久。

主题 2 ➡ Who 等疑问词的用法

●活学活用●

(Joh,Bill,and Sue are at a party.)

John:Where do you work,Bill?

Bill: I'm in foreign trade.　1

John:I'm an English teacher.

Bill: And you,Sue?　2

Sue: I'm a flight attendant.

Bill: Really?

John:Yes,she travels all over the world.

1. (A)Do you speak English?

(B)Are you a worker, too?

(C)How do you like it?

(D)How about you?

2. (A)Do you know each other?

(B)Where have you been?

(C)What do you do?

(D)How are you?

●本文翻译●

（约翰、比尔和苏在宴会中。）

约翰：你在哪里工作，比尔？

比尔：我从事外贸工作。＿＿＿＿＿＿＿

约翰：我是一个英文老师。

比尔：苏，你呢？＿＿＿＿＿＿＿

苏：　我是空中小姐。

比尔：真的吗？

约翰：真的，她环游全世界。

1.【答案】▶(D)

　【译文】▶(A)你讲英语吗？　　　　(B)你也是工人吗？

　　　　　　(C)你觉得怎样？　　　　(D)你呢？

　【讲解】▶How about you？＝What about you？＝And you？　你呢？

2.【答案】▶(C)

　【译文】▶(A)你们彼此认识吗？

　　　　　　(B)你去哪里了？

　　　　　　(C)你从事什么工作？

　　　　　　(D)你好吗？

　【讲解】▶What do you do？　你从事什么工作？（询问职业的用法，注意用 what）

　　　　　　＝What do you do for a living？　＝What is your job？

　　　　　　＝What line are you in？　＝What field are you in？

●活学活用●

3. Wife：　　Why didn't you tell me?

　 Husband：＿＿＿＿＿＿＿＿

　　　(A)I guess I forgot.

　　　(B)I'm sorry you have to wait.

　　　(C)I thought I'd come by to say hello.

　　　(D)I'd love to，but I have to work until six.

【答案】▶(A)

【译文】▶太太:你(那时或以前)为什么不告诉我?

先生:_____

(A)我想我是忘了。

(B)很抱歉你必须等。

(C)我原以为我会顺路来打个招呼的。

(D)我很想,但我必须工作到六点。

【讲解】▶comy by:顺路经过

━━━━━●活学活用●━━━━━

4. Joe:　Why don't you tell me a few things about your country?

Ken:_____

(A)Because I can't tell you too many things at a time.

(B)I'm afraid so.

(C)Sure. What in general are you interested in?

(D)I don't know. That depends on how much you're interested in it.

【答案】▶(C)

【译文】▶乔:你何不讲一些贵国的事给我听?

肯:_____

(A)因为我没有办法一下子告诉你太多事情。

(B)我看恐怕如此。

(C)当然好啊! 大致说来,你对什么有兴趣?

(D)我不知道。那要看你对它的兴趣有多大。

【讲解】▶①*Why don't you V*?＝Please V

②*at a time*　一次,一下子

③*afraid*　恐怕,遗憾,抱歉

④*in general*　大致上

⑤*depend on*　视……而定

● 活学活用 ●

5. John：_____

Jack：In two weeks.

John：Are you going to Japan?

Jack：No，I'm going to Thailand. I went to Japan two years ago.

(A) How long have you been here?

(B) When are you leaving for Thailand?

(C) How long do you plan to stay in here?

(D) When is your vacation?

【答案】▶(D)

【译文】▶约翰：_____

　　杰克：两个星期后。

　　约翰：你去日本吗?

　　杰克：不，我去泰国。两年前我去过日本了。

　　(A)你到这里多久了?　　(B)你何时要到泰国?

　　(C)你计划在这里停留多久?　(D)你的假期何时开始?

【讲解】▶① $\begin{cases} in \text{ two weeks } 两周以后(用在表未来的时间) \\ after \text{ two weeks} \\ \text{two weeks } later \end{cases}$ 两周以后(用在表过去的时间)

② ***Thailand*** ['tailænd] *n.* 泰国

③ ***leave for*** 前往

● 活学活用 ●

6. Teacher：Why didn't you hand in the paper yesterday? (多选)

Student：_____

(A) I'm sorry I forget.

(B) I must apologize for it.

(C) Because I had not finished writing the paper.

(D) I thought I was supposed to hand it in today.

(E) Please forgive me. I promise to hand in my next paper in time.

【答案】▶(B)(C)(D)(E)

【译文】▶老师：你昨天为什么没交报告？

学生：＿＿＿＿＿＿＿＿

　　(A)很抱歉我忘记了。　　　(B)我必须为此道歉。

　　(C)因为我的报告还没写完。(D)我以为应该今天交。

　　(E)请原谅我。我保证下一次的报告一定准时交。

【讲解】▶①(A)的时态不对，该把 forget 改为 forgot.

　　②***hand in***　缴交；呈递

────●*活学活用*●────

7. Zhang San：When does the library open on Saturday?（多

选）

Wang Wu：＿＿＿＿＿＿＿＿

(A)Eight-thirty in the morning, if I remember correctly.

(B)It closes at six in the afternoon.

(C)It opens Monday through Saturday.

(D)I don't know. Why don't we check with the librarian?

(E)It is not open on Sunday, I believe.

【答案】▶(A)(D)

【译文】▶张三：星期六图书馆何时开门？

王五：＿＿＿＿＿＿＿＿

　　(A)如果我没记错的话，上午八点三十分就开门了。

　　(B)下午六点关闭。

　　(C)星期一到星期六都开放。

　　(D)不知道。我们为什么不向图书馆管理员查询一下？

　　(E)我相信星期天不开放。

【讲解】▶①***check with sb.***　向某人查询

　　②(B)***close***，答非所问。(C)答星期一到星期六，未针对所

　　问的 ***Saturday***。(E)答星期天不开，答非所问。因此答

　　案为(A)、(D)。

主题 3➡What 的用法

● 活学活用 ●

1. Sally：What do you plan to do after the exam?

Kathy：_____ How about you?

Sally：I'll take some computer lessons.

(A) You can say that again!

(B) I'm all for it.

(C) Nothing special.

(D) I've changed my mind.

【答案】▶(C)

【译文】▶萨丽：考完试你打算做什么呢?

凯西：_____那你呢?

萨丽：我要去上电脑课。

(A) 你说得没错!　　(B) 我全力支持。

(C) 没啥特别的。　　(D) 我已改变心意了。

【讲解】▶take＋课程名称＋lesson/courses：参加……课,上……课

● 活学活用 ●

2. Alice：Is there a garage sale in the neighborhood today?

Nancy：Yes. There's one on the next street. _____

Alice：Some old furniture, perhaps.

(A) What can I do for you?

(B) What do you plan to buy?

(C) What's the big idea?

(D) What's on your mind?

【答案】▶(B)

【译文】▶艾丽丝：今天附近有旧货拍卖吗?

南希：　有呀! 下一条街就有一个。_____

艾丽丝：或许买些旧家具。

(A)我能帮你做些什么? 　(B)你计划买些什么?
(C)你有什么主意? 　(D)你在想什么?

═══════ ●活学活用● ═══════

3. Mark：What sort of music do you like，Tony?

Tony：I like pop and disco best.

Mark：What about classical music?

Tony：＿＿＿＿＿＿＿

(A)Very much. 　(B)Not bad.

(C)I hate it. 　(D)I'd love to.

【答案】▶(C)

【译文】▶马克:托尼,你喜欢什么样的音乐?

托尼:我最喜爱流行音乐和迪斯科舞曲。

马克:那古典音乐呢?

托尼:＿＿＿＿＿＿＿

(A)很喜欢。 　(B)还不坏。

(C)很不喜欢。 　(D)我乐意去(做)。

【讲解】▶①马克问托尼对于古典音乐的看法,托尼表示不喜欢。

②答案(B)通常用来表示对他人的表现表示赞美之意。

③*pop* [pɔp] ＝ *popular music*　*n.* 流行音乐

④*classical* ['klæsikəl] *adj.* 古典的

⑤*would love to* ＝ *want to*　想要

═══════ ●活学活用● ═══════

4. John：Do you happen to have twenty dollars with you?

Jack：＿＿＿＿＿＿＿

John：I want to buy a notebook.

(A)How do you want it?

(B)How much?

(C)What for?

(D)When can you pay me back?

【答案】▶(C)

【译文】▶约翰：你身上有没有二十块钱？

杰克：＿＿＿＿＿＿＿

约翰：我想买一个笔记本。

(A)你希望二十块怎么给？

(B)多少钱？

(C)做什么用？

(D)何时可以还我？

【讲解】▶①(A)**How** 应改为 **Why**，但仍不合句意。

②**happen to**＋**V**　碰巧……

③**What for**？＝Why？为什么？（强调目的）。也可做 what～for？

④**pay back**　归还

● 活学活用 ●

5. Luke：＿＿＿＿＿＿＿

Mary：Fried shrimp balls.

Luck：Great. That's what I was hoping you were going to make.

(A)What are you making for dinner？

(B)What is it that you enjoy most？

(C)What are you doing over there？

(D)What's your order, Madam？

【答案】▶(A)

【译文】▶路加：＿＿＿＿＿＿＿

玛丽：油炸虾球。

路加：太棒了！正是我希望你去做的。

(A)晚餐你要做什么吃的？

(B)你最喜欢的是什么？

(C)你在那边做什么？⇒应改 doing 为 making

(D)你点什么吃，夫人？

【讲解】▶①*fried*　　*adj.* 油炸的,煎的

②*shrimp*　　*n.* 小虾

③*over there* 在那边

④*order*　　*n.* 点菜

━━━━━ ●活学活用● ━━━━━

6. Dan:Oh,what a nice photograph!

　 May:＿＿＿＿＿＿

　 Dan:The one above the sofa.

　 May:Oh, yes. Thank you. That's my parents when they

　　　　were young.

　　　　(A)Which one do you like best?

　　　　(B)Thank you. It's very kind of you to say so.

　　　　(C)Which one are you talking about?

　　　　(D)Yes,it was taken a few years ago, in the West

　　　　　　Lake.

【答案】▶(C)

【译文】▶丹:喔,好漂亮的照片啊!

　　　　梅:＿＿＿＿＿＿

　　　　丹:沙发上面的那一张。

　　　　梅:喔,是的,谢谢您。那是我父母年轻时的照片。

　　　　(A)你最喜欢哪一张?

　　　　(B)谢谢你。你这么说真好!

　　　　(C)你说的是哪一张?

　　　　(D)是的,那是几年前在西湖照的。

【讲解】▶①*photograph* ['fəutəgra:f] *n.* 照片

②*take a photograph*　拍摄照片

● 活学活用 ●

7. Steven：What is the matter with you?（多选）

　　Ann：＿＿＿＿＿＿

　　　（A）I'm not feeling well.

　　　（B）I'm tired and hungry.

　　　（C）Mathematics gives me headaches.

　　　（D）Yesterday it rained.

　　　（E）Rainy weather depresses me.

【答案】▶（A）（B）（C）（E）

【译文】▶史蒂芬：你怎么啦？

　　　　安：＿＿＿＿＿＿

　　　　　（A）我身体不太舒服。

　　　　　（B）我又累又饿。

　　　　　（C）数学让我好头痛。

　　　　　（D）昨天下雨了。

　　　　　（E）雨天让我感到沮丧。

【讲解】▶①***What is the matter*** ？ ＝ ***What is wrong*** ？（怎么啦？生病了？出什么问题了？）

　　　　②***depress*** ［di'pres］ *vt.* 使沮丧

● 活学活用 ●

8. Clerk：　　What can I do for you?（多选）

　　Mr. White：＿＿＿＿＿＿

　　　（A）I want a toothbrush and some toothpaste.

　　　（B）I want to buy a necktie.

　　　（C）Thank you，my health has been fine lately.

　　　（D）Do you have any fresh rolls?

　　　（E）At my age，people don't have illusions.

【答案】▶（A）（B）（D）

【译文】▶店员：有什么需要效劳的？

怀特先生：_____

　　(A)我想买支牙刷和一些牙膏。

　　(B)我想买条领带。

　　(C)谢谢你，最近我身体很好。

　　(D)你们有没有新鲜的小圆面包？

　　(E)我这个年纪的人不会有幻想的。

【讲解】▶①店员看到顾客上门时所说"请问你要买些什么?"除了
　　　　用"What can I do for you?"之外，还可说："May I help
　　　　you?"　"What can I serve you with?"等。

　　　②*roll*　　*n.* 卷状蛋糕或肉饼

　　　③*illusion* [i'lu:ʒən] *n.* 幻想

第3篇 一般情况会话

所谓一般会话就是如何对别人的话做出恰当的反应。

━━━━● 焦点整理 ●━━━━

1. 见面用语：通常以 **How,Hi** 开头,且以简短为宜。

例 ①
How are you? ＝ How are you doing? （您好吗?）
I'm fine,thanks. And you? （我很好,谢谢。您呢?）

②
How have you been? （您这一向可好?）
Very well,thank you. 或 thanks. （很好,谢谢。）

③
How are you getting on (along)? （您好吗?）
Not bad. What about you? （还可以,您呢?）

④
Hi,I'm glad to meet you. （您好,很高兴认识您。）
Hi,I'm glad to meet you,too. （您好,我也很高兴认识您。）

━━━━◆ 心得笔记 ◆━━━━

初次见面时以 **How do you do**? 或是 **Nice meeting you**. 开头为宜,回答亦同。

━━━━● 焦点整理 ●━━━━

2. 道谢的语句,以简单明了为原则,强调感激。

例：①
Thank you very much. （多谢）
Thank you so much.
Thanks ever so much.
Many thanks. Thanks a lot.

I'm very much obliged(grateful,indebted)to you.

② ⎰ （我非常感激您。）

I'm really very grateful to you.（我非常感激您。）

③ I don't know how to thank you.（我不知怎样感谢您才好。）

④ I appreciate it.（我很感激！）

⑤ You've done me a great service.（你帮了我一个很大的忙。）

━━━━●焦点整理●━━━━

3. 对辞谢的答语有下列几种：

①**You're welcome.**

②**Not at all.**

③**It's nothing.**

④**It's（my）pleasure.** →这些都可译成 不客气 。

⑤**Don't mention it.**

⑥**No trouble at all.**

其他的说法如下：

例：①Please don't thank me.（请不必谢我。）

②It's not worth mentioning.（这不足挂齿。）

③I thank you.（我也谢谢你。）

④It's the least I could do.（这是我应该做的。）

⑤It's quite all right.（不客气。）

━━━━●焦点整理●━━━━

4. 表示对不起或向人道歉时，最常用：

①**I'm sorry.** 对不起！

②**I'm awfully sorry.** 非常对不起。

③**I apologize.** 我向你道歉。

④**Excuse me.** 对不起！（客套语，常用于要走开、借过、插话、表示会议等场合，I'm sorry. 则表示已犯某种过失。）

其他的说法如下：

例:①I'm very sorry for what I've done.（我对我所做的事感到抱歉。）

②It was most thoughtless(stupid, rude)of me.（我太粗心[笨、粗鲁]了。）

③May I be excused please?（对不起,我离开一下就来。）

●焦点整理●

5. 接受道歉的人所回应的用语有：

①That's all right. 没关系。

②It's OK. 没关系。

③Don't worry about it. 不要挂在心上。

④Forget it. 算了。

⑤Never mind. 不必介意。

●焦点整理●

6. 请求帮忙时常以 May, Could, Will, Would 及 Can 开头。

例:①May I ask a favor of you?（我可以请你帮忙吗?）

②Could you do me a favor?（你能帮我的忙吗?）

③Will you please give me a hand?

（请你帮我一下忙好吗?）

④Will you help me?（帮一下忙好不好?）

⑤Would you allow me to use your typewriter?

（你的打字机借我用一下好吗?）

⑥Can I take this book?

（我可以拿这本书吗?）

●焦点整理●

7. 对请求之答语以简短有力为原则。

例:{
Yes, with pleasure.（好的,我很高兴[荣幸之至]。）
Yes, certainly.（当然可以。）
By all means.（一定,务必。）
}

━━━━ ● 焦点整理 ● ━━━━

8. 告别用语常用的有：

① **Good-bye!**　再见！　　② **See you later!**　回头见。

③ **See you then!**　到时再见。④ **See you tomorrow.**　明天见。

⑤ **So long!**　再见。　　　⑥ **Good night!**　晚安。

━━ → 心得笔记 ━━

通常别人对你说什么，你就可用什么作答。

━━━━ ● 活学活用 ● ━━━━

1. Alice：Guess what?

　John：_____

　　（A）What?

　　（B）Sure. What can I do for you?

　　（C）I'm glad you're having a good time.

　　（D）Really?　What a pleasant surprise!

【答案】▶（A）

【译文】▶艾莉丝：猜猜看发生了什么事？

　　　　约翰：_____

　　　　　（A）什么？

　　　　　（B）当然。我能为您做什么呢？

　　　　　（C）我很高兴你玩得愉快。

　　　　　（D）真的吗？多么愉悦的惊喜？

【讲解】▶①*have a good time*　玩得愉快，玩得尽兴

　　　　②*pleasant　adj.* 令人愉快的，快乐的

●活学活用●

2. Son：   Will it be expensive?
   Mother：_____
     (A)Oh, really?   (B)Okay. I understand.
     (C)Don't worry. I'll pay. (D)Oh, don't let me keep you.

【答案】▶(C)
【译文】▶儿子:那会很贵吗?
　　　　母亲:_____
　　　　　(A)哦,真的吗?
　　　　　(B)好的,我明白。
　　　　　(C)别担心。我会付账。
　　　　　(D)哦,别让我留住你。
【讲解】▶①*expensive*　*adj*. 昂贵的
　　　　②*keep*　*v*. 留住

●活学活用●

3. John：Good evening, Jane.
   Jane：Hi, John. I'm glad you could come.
   John：_____
   Jane：No, you're right on time.
     (A)It's my great honor, thanks.
     (B)You're welcome. Am I the first?
     (C)Thanks. Do you have the time?
     (D)I hope I'm not too late.

【答案】▶(D)
【译文】▶约翰:晚上好! 简。
　　　　简:　嗨! 约翰。很高兴你能来。
　　　　约翰:_____
　　　　简:　不,你正好准时到。
　　　　　(A)是我的殊荣,谢谢您。

(B)别客气。我是第一个到的吗？

(C)谢谢，现在几点钟？

(D)我希望没有来得太晚。

【讲解】▶①简回答对方说刚好准时到，以告诉对方并没有来得太迟。

②*right on time*　刚好准时到

③*Do you have the time*？＝*What time is it*？（现在几点了？）

━━━━━ ●活学活用● ━━━━━

4. Mr. Clement：　　I'd like a room.

　Hotel Receptionist：＿＿＿＿＿＿

　　(A)Certainly, there's plenty of room.

　　(B)Certainly. Have you ordered in advance?

　　(C)Sorry, sir, but the room isn't ready yet.

　　(D)Do you have a reservation, sir?

【答案】▶(D)

【译文】▶克莱门特先生：我想要间房间。

　　　　旅馆接待员：＿＿＿＿＿＿

　　　　　(A)当然可以，还有许多空间。

　　　　　(B)当然可以，您有预先订房吗？

　　　　　(C)抱歉，先生，这间房尚未准备妥当。

　　　　　(D)您有预先订房吗？

【讲解】▶①*receptionist*　接待员

②*room* 当不可数名词用时作"空间"解。因此 plenty of room 指"许多空间"，而非"许多房间"。

③*order*　订购（货物）；点（菜）

④*in advance*　预先

⑤*reserve*　*vt.* 预订

　reservation　*n.* 预订的东西（如房间、座位、票等）。

● 活学活用 ●

5. Doctor：　　　We're ready now. Sorry to have kept you waiting.

Mrs. Freeman：_____Do you have all the test results?

Doctor：　　　Yes, I've got all of them now.

(A) Pleased to meet you.

(B) None of my business.

(C) That's all right.

(D) You bet.

【答案】▶(C)

【译文】▶医生：　　我们现在准备好了,抱歉让您久等。

弗里曼太太：_____你有全部的检验结果吗?

医生:是的,我全都拿到了。

(A)很高兴认识你。　　　　(B)与我无关。

(C)没关系。　　　　　　(D)当然!

【讲解】▶① *keep sb. waiting*　使某人等待

② *none of my business*　与我无关

③ *You bet*. = You can be certain.　当然;包在我身上。

● 活学活用 ●

6. Lucy：I don't think we'll find a better buy than this.

Judy：_____

Lucy：Well, if you insist.

(A) Let's try at least one more place.

(B) You're right.

(C) It's a deal.

(D) We might as well order some.

【答案】▶(A)

【译文】▶露西:我想我们不会找到比这个更好的便宜货了。

朱蒂:_____

露西:好吧,如果你坚持的话。

　　(A)我们至少再试一家吧!

　　(B)你说得对。

　　(C)那就成交了。

　　(D)我们该订一些。

【讲解】▶ ① *buy*　便宜货,廉价品

　　　② *It's a deal.*　成交了;一言为定

　　　③ *might as well*～　最好……

═══════ ●活学活用● ═══════

7. Manager:This is a challenging job. Who wants it?

　　David:＿＿＿＿＿

　　(A)I'll take it.　　(B)It's a good idea.

　　(C)You bet!　　(D)No sweat!

【答案】▶ (A)

【译文】▶ 经理:这是一份富有挑战性的工作。谁想做?

　　　大卫:＿＿＿＿

　　　　(A)我愿意接受。　　(B)是个好主意。

　　　　(C)当然!　　　　(D)轻而易举!

【讲解】▶ ①*challenging* ['tʃælindʒiŋ] *adj.* 挑战性,引起兴趣的,

　　　刺激性的

　　　②*You bet* [bet]!(口)当然;的确!

═══════ ●活学活用● ═══════

8. Guest:I brought this painting from my country. I hope you
　　like it.

　　Host:＿＿＿＿＿

　　(A)It's a pity.

　　(B)No wonder.

　　(C)That's exactly what I want!

　　(D)Let's face it.

【答案】▶(C)

【译文】▶客人：我从我的国家带了这幅画，但愿你会喜欢。

主人：＿＿＿＿＿＿

(A)真可惜。　　　　(B)难怪。

(C)那正是我想要的！　(D)让我们面对它吧。

●活学活用●

9. Daddy： This is birthday present for you.

Daughter：＿＿＿＿＿＿

(A)What's the problem?

(B)Oh，what a surprise!

(C)I can't help it!

(D)I'm afraid so.

【答案】▶(B)

【译文】▶父亲：这是给你的生日礼物。

女儿：＿＿＿＿＿＿

(A)是什么问题呢？　(B)哦，真叫人惊喜的礼物！

(C)我没有办法！　　(D)恐怕会如此！

●活学活用●

10. Dr. Armstrong：Good afternoon，Mr. Goodman.

How are you feeling today?

Mr. Goodman：Not very well.

Dr. Armstrong：＿＿＿＿＿＿

Mr. Goodman：I have a sore throat，and my whole body

aches.

(A)What's the matter with you!

(B)You must have been ill.

(C)What can I do for you?

(D)What seems to be wrong with you?

【答案】▶(D)

【译文】▶阿姆斯特朗博士：午安，古德曼先生。今天觉得怎么样？

古德曼先生：　　并不很好。

阿姆斯特朗先生：_____

古德曼先生：　　我喉咙痛,并且全身也疼。

　　(A)你发什么神经啊!

　　(B)你一定是病了。

　　(C)有什么要我效劳的吗?

　　(D)你觉得哪里不对?

【讲解】▶①***What seems to be wrong with you***?

　　　　＝What is the matter with you?

　　　　＝What is wrong with you?

　　　　皆表示"你怎么啦?"但若用感叹号则表示"你发什么神
　　　　经啊!"此为责备之意,非问句。

　　　　②***sore throat***　喉咙痛

●活学活用●

11. Clerk：Can I help you,sir?

　　John：Yes. I want to buy a blue shirt,size fourteen.

　　Clerk：I have several in your size. _____

　　John：Yes,of course.

　　　(A)How do you like it?

　　　(B)Why don't you buy it?

　　　(C)Do you want to try on one of these?

　　　(D)They must be very cheap.

【答案】▶(C)

【译文】▶店员:先生,我能替你效劳吗?

　　　　约翰:是的。我想买件蓝衬衫,14 号的。

　　　　店员:有几件你的尺寸。_____

　　　　约翰:是的,当然。

　　　　(A)你觉得如何?

　　　　(B)你为何不买下它呢?

　　　　(C)你想试穿其中之一吗?

　　　　(D)它们一定非常便宜。

【讲解】▶①*How do you like it*?　你觉得如何;你还喜欢吧?

　　　　②*try on*　试穿

　　　　例:I tried on another hat.(我试戴另一顶帽子。)

━━━━━●活学活用●━━━━━

12. Mary:I wonder if I could use your telephone.

　　John:＿＿＿＿＿＿

　　　(A)I wonder how.

　　　(B)I don't know.

　　　(C)Well,of course.

　　　(D)No wonder,here it is.

【答案】▶(C)

【译文】▶玛丽:不知道能否借用一下电话。

　　　　约翰:＿＿＿＿＿＿

　　　　　(A)我想知道怎么做。

　　　　　(B)我不知道。

　　　　　(C)好,当然可以。

　　　　　(D)难怪,就在这里。

【讲解】▶①*I wonder*＋疑问词…　我想知道……(不知道……)

　　　　例:*I wonder if* I might ask you a question.

　　　　　(不知道可不可以问你一个问题。)

　　　　②(A)(B)未针对问题。(C)*Well,of course.*其语气就是

　　　　go(*right*) *ahead.*(尽管用吧!)故其答案为(C)。

　　　　(D)(*It's*)*no wonder*(that)...　……是不足为奇的

　　　　　例:(*It's*)*no wonder*(that)he didn't want to go.

　　　　　　(他不要去是不足为奇的。)

　　　　　未针对问题回答,故不选(D)

●活学活用●

13. Mary：Tom told me that you collect stamps.

　　John：_____

　　　　(A) Who told you that?

　　　　(B) I don't think so.

　　　　(C) Does he collect stamps?

　　　　(D) Yes，I do. Do you?

【答案】▶(D)

【译文】▶玛丽：汤姆告诉我你在集邮。

　　　约翰：_____

　　　　　(A) 谁告诉你的？

　　　　　(B) 我不认为是这样的。

　　　　　(C) 他集邮吗？

　　　　　(D) 是的，我集邮。你呢？

【讲解】▶(D)***Yes，I do***. 此 do 是助动词，代替 collect stamps。

●活学活用●

14. X：My father is not at home right now. (多选)

　　Y：_____

　　　　(A) Could you tell me when he will get home?

　　　　(B) Don't you remember I called this morning?

　　　　(C) May I leave a message with you?

　　　　(D) What can I do for you?

　　　　(E) May I take a message for him?

【答案】▶(A)(C)

【译文】▶X：我父亲现在不在家。

　　　　Y：_____

　　　　　(A) 你能告诉我他什么时候会回家吗？

　　　　　(B) 你不记得我今天早上打过电话吗？

　　　　　(C) 你能帮我留个话吗？

(D)我能为你效劳什么呢？

(E)我能为他传话吗？

【讲解】▶(A)用 *Could* 比用 Can 委婉。(B)(D)未针对问题；(E)答
非所问。(C)句中 *leave a message with* 意为"……传言
给……"

●活学活用●

15. Jack：Hello. Is this the Star Supermarket.

Voice：No. I'm afraid you've called the wrong number.

Jack： Is this three-two-one，double nine-three-one?

Voice：No. This is three-one-two，double nine-three-one.

Jack：_____

Voice：That's all right.

(A)Oh，I'm sorry.

(B)Are you sure?

(C)No！ That's impossible！

(D)May I speak to Dr. Edison?

【答案】▶(A)

【译文】▶杰克：喂，是星星超级市场吗？

声音：不。恐怕你打错了。

杰克：是 321-9931 吗？

声音：不。 是 312-9931。

杰克：_____

声音：没关系。

(A)喔，抱歉。

(B)你确定吗？

(C)不！ 那是不可能的！

(D)我可否和爱迪生博士讲话呢？

【讲解】▶①别人道歉时，可回答 *That's all right*. *Never mind*.
Don't mention it. *Not at all*. *Not in the least*. *Forget
it*. *It's nothing*. 等来表示"不要挂在心上！"

②**I am afraid**：❶"恐怕"＝**I fear** 用于推测不愉快的事
物；

❷"可惜"用于缓和语气。

例：❶**I'm afraid he won't come.**（他恐怕不来。）

❷**I'm afraid I can't help you.**（可惜我不能帮助
你。）

━━■●活学活用●■━━

16. Mary：You must be able to speak several languages.

John：＿＿＿＿＿＿

(A)French, I guess.

(B)No, neither.

(C)That's a problem.

(D)Yes, I'd say five.

【答案】▶(D)

【译文】▶玛丽：你一定能讲好几种语言。

约翰：＿＿＿＿＿＿

(A)我猜是法文吧。

(B)不，两种都不会。

(C)那是个问题。

(D)是的，我能说五种语言。

【讲解】▶①**must**＋原形动词——对现在肯定的猜测。

②(A)未针对问题，原问句用了 **must**，回答却用 **guess**。

(B)此句中的 **neither** 作"二者中没有一个"解，因此(B)
句意不对。

(C)更不切合问句的 **must** 之问法，也未具体的答出问
题。

(D)**I'd say**＝I should say 我的意思是说，我想

例：That is, I should say, true.（我想那是真的。）

●活学活用●

17. Simpson：I thought I would get stamps out of the machine，only I find I haven't any coins on me.（多选）

Neighbor：_____

(A)I'm afraid I haven't either.

(B)Machines are usually out of order.

(C)Some special stamps are very beautiful.

(D)Do you have a stamp collection?

(E)I'm awfully sorry I have no coins either.

【答案】▶(A)(E)

【译文】▶辛普森：我原想我会从自动售货机买到邮票的，可是我发现我没有硬币。

邻居：_____

(A)恐怕我也没有硬币。

(B)机器常出故障。

(C)有些特殊的邮票很漂亮。

(D)你搜集许多邮票吗？

(E)十分抱歉，我也没有硬币。

【讲解】▶①only 在此为口语，做连接词用，表"却……，然而……"。

②*collection* [kə'lekʃən] *n.* 搜集

③*awfully* *adv.* （口语）非常

常用口语

1. After you.　你先请(让对方先走)。

2. All sales are final!　货物售出,概不退换!

3. Allow me.　我来。(为他人效劳时的用语)

4. As you wish. ＝Anything you say.　悉听尊便。
   ＝Whatever you say. ＝It's up to you.

5. Any time.　①随时奉陪。
   　　　　　　②不客气(我随时效劳)。

6. around the corner　即将到来
   〈例〉:新年快到了。
   　　　The Chinese New Year is **around the corner**.

7. all thumbs　笨手笨脚
   〈例〉:他笨手笨脚的。
   　　　His fingers are **all thumbs**.

8. all mouth　光说不练
   〈例〉:你只会说而已。
   　　　You're **all mouth**.

9. all ears　全神倾听
   〈例〉:我洗耳恭听。
   　　　I'm **all ears**.

10. It's all set.　一切就序。

11. You are all wet. ＝You are completely mistaken.
    你完全搞错了;你完全误会了。

12. be afraid $\begin{cases} \text{of} +\text{N} & \text{害怕} \\ \text{that}+\text{从句} & \text{恐怕} \end{cases}$
    〈例〉:我恐怕不行。
    　　　I'm afraid I can't.

13. at one's service＝at one's disposal　为某人效劳

〈例〉：我随时效劳。

I'm *at your service* disposal.

14. A lot you know!　你知道的可真不少！

15. Baloney!　你吹牛。

16. Behave yourself!　放规矩点！

＝Mind your P's and Q's.

＝Watch your manners.

17. Better late than never.　亡羊补牢为时未晚。

18. Not bad.　还不错。

19. break the ice　打破僵局，化解误会

〈例〉：要化解凯莉和肖之间的误会可真难啊！

What a difficulty to *break the ice* between Carrie and Shaw.

20. Business is business!　公事公办！

21. Butter him up a little!　去奉承他几句吧！

22. It's a bargain.　买得物超所值。

23. beat aroud/about the bush　旁敲侧击，拐弯抹角

〈例〉：不要旁敲侧击；不要拐弯抹角。

Don't *beat around* the bush.

24. { bet you!　＝我跟你打赌！
   { You bet!　＝Of course.＝And how!　当然！

25. Don't boss me around!　别一直叫我做这做那的！

26. Don't blow it.　别搞砸了。

27. Beware of pickpockets!　谨防扒手！

28. blind date　（不知对方为谁的）约会

〈例〉：我通常是不会赴盲目的约会的。

Usually I don't go to a *blind date*.

29. Don't brush me off!　别敷衍我！

30. Be my guest.＝My treat.＝I'll treat.　我请客。

＝It's on me.＝The bill is on me.

31. Bingo.　猜中了，成功了。

32. Couldn't be better.　再好也不过了/很好/好的不得了。

〈例〉:甲:最近过得怎样?

乙:非常好。

A:How's life?

B:*Couldn't be better*.

33. Come on in!　进来吧!

34. Come on. ①快一点。(=Hurry up!)
②少来这一套。

35. Cheers! =Bottoms up! =Drink up! =Toast!　干杯。

36. call the roll　点名

〈例〉:安德森教授每次一上课就开始点名。

Professor Anderson always *calls the roll* at the beginning of the class.

37. complimentary fruit　免费水果

〈例〉:每个房间都有电视和免费水果。

Each room has a television and *complimentary fruit*.

38. No credit, cash only.　谢绝赊账。

39. The cap fits.　还可以。

40. Could be.　可能吧!

41. It's a close call.　真是好险啊!

42. a piece of cake　小事;简单的事

〈例〉:写英文信对我来说是小事一桩。

It's *a piece of cake* for me to write an English letter.

43. No comment.　不予评论。

44. Congratulations!　恭喜!

45. That is my cup of tea.　那正合我的胃口。

46. to cut class　逃课

〈例〉:彼得逃课去看电影。

Peter **cut class** to see movies.

47. You're so cool!　你好酷喔!

48. crocodile tears　鳄鱼的眼泪,引申为"假悲伤,假慈悲"

〈例〉:别假慈悲了。

Don't shed your *crocodile tears* for me.

49. Count me in.　算我一份。我也要加入。

50. No cheating.　不要作弊。

51. Charge it, please.　请记账。(指用信用卡等记账,不付现金)

52. It's duck weather.　下雨天。

53. Done！＝It's done.＝It's a deal.　一言为定。

54. Do as I say！＝Do as I told you.　照我的话去做。

55. Do something, please.＝Don't just stand there！
　　快想点办法。

56. Dear John letter.　绝交信。

57. Dear me！＝Oh, dear！　天啊！妈呀！

58. Excuse me a minute！　失陪一下。

59. It's an emergercy.　是紧急事故。

60. to fix something to drink　弄些喝的东西〔fix：烹煮东西〕
　　〈例〉：甲：要不要我弄点喝的？
　　　　　乙：好啊！
　　　　　A：Shall I **fix** us **something to drink**？
　　　　　B：Yes, please.

61. Don't be so fussy！　别太挑剔了。

62. First come, first served.　先来先享用；先来先接受服务。

63. It's free.　那是免费的。

64. Forget it.　算了；别提了；不用客气。

65. I'm flattered. [ˈflætəd] 我受宠若惊。

66. fly　*n.*　拉链
　　〈例〉：拉上你的拉链。
　　　　　Zip up your *fly*.

67. Fine with me.＝It's OK. with me.　好啊！我没问题。
　　〈例〉：甲：你今晚要是没事的话,一起吃顿饭如何？
　　　　　乙：好啊！
　　　　　A：If you're not doing anything tonight, how about hav-
　　　　　　ing dinner？
　　　　　B：*Fine with me*.

68. Don't fool around.　别鬼混。

69. Get lost. ＝Get away. ＝Go away. ＝Get out of here. ＝Go blow. ＝Beat it! ＝Out you go!　滚开;闪边!

70. Give it a shot.　让我们试试看。

71. sth. is Greek to sb.　（某人)不懂(某物)
〈例〉:我不懂。
　　　　It's **Greek to** me.

72. go too far　做得太过份了
〈例〉:你太过份了。
　　　　You've **gone too far**.

73. go for a drive　兜风
〈例〉:你喜欢去兜风吗?
　　　　Would you like to **go for a drive**?

74. I'll get it. ①我来接电话。
　　　　　　　②我来开门。

75. Be good.　别乱来。

76. get sb. wrong　误会某人
〈例〉:玛丽误会路克了。
　　　　Mary **got Luke wrong**.

77. I got it. ①我懂了。
　　　　　　②我成功了。＝I made it.

78. Go ahead.　请便。

79. How can I reach you?　我怎么和你联络?

80. How do you do?　你好吗? 幸会。
用在第一次见面时的礼貌用语,回答只要说 How do you do?
而不要加上 fine 或 thanks。第一次见面也可说:
It's nice meeting you. ＝It's nice to meet you.

81. How dare you!　你好大的胆!

82. How come?　怎么会这样呢?

83. Please help yourself.　请自便。

84. Hold it. ＝Freeze!　不准动!
＝Don't move! ＝Stay where you are.

85. Hold on,please＝Hang on,please.　请稍候。（电话用语）
　　＝Just a moment,please.＝A moment,please.

86. How say you?　尊意如何？

87. How could you?　你怎么可以那么做？

88. How can you be so sure?　你怎么会如此肯定呢？

89. How is everthing?＝How are you getting along?　近况如
　　何？

90. Have I made myself clear?　我的话够清楚了吧？

91. How about that?　怎样？不赖吧！（事情完成后，向对方夸耀
　　的用语）

92. have one's word　得到某人的保证
　　〈例〉:我向你保证。
　　　　　You *have my word*.

93. I'm together.　我没问题。

94. I've heard so much about you.　久仰。

95. I want to have a word with you.　我想跟你谈谈。

96. It stands to reason.　那是显而易见的道理。

97. Is this seat taken?　这个位子有人坐吗？

98. I should have known.　哎呀，我早该知道才对。

99. I'll be there.　我会准时到的。

100. Incredible!＝Terrific!　太棒了！

101. I'll take it.　我买了。（在商店中的用语）

102. I know what.　我有个好主意！

103. I got to go.　我得走了。

104. It depends.　看情况（而言）。

105. I've had enough.　我受够了。

106. It's a long story.　说来话长。

107. It's all over.　好了，都没事了。

108. I said no!　不行就是不行。

109. Are you kidding?　你在开玩笑吗？

110. Keep the change!　不用找钱了！

111. Let's go Dutch.　我们各付各的账吧。

112. Let's call it a day.　今天到此为止。

113. Let me see.　嗯，让我想想看。

114. Let's flip for it.　让我们丢硬币决定。

115. Don't let me down.　别让我失望。

116. Just look at you!　瞧你那副德行。

117. Lady first.　女士优先。

118. Long time no see.　好久不见了。

119. to miss the boat　错失良机

　〈例〉：他们坐失良机。

　　　　They *miss the boat*.

120. Don't make a scene!　别出洋相了!

121. My legs are going to sleep.　我的脚快麻死了。

122. You can't miss it.　绝对不会错失的;绝对找得到。

　〈例〉：邮局在街道的左边。经过杂货店就到了。

　　　　The post office is on the right side of the street.

　　　　Just past the grocery store. *You can't miss it*.

123. May I have your attention, please. 请注意! 请听我这里!

　　＝Look here!　＝Listen, please.

124. a matter of . . .　……的问题

　〈例 1〉：It's *a matter of* degree.

　　　　　那是程度的问题。

　〈例 2〉：It's *a matter of* money.

　　　　　那是钱的问题。

　〈例 3〉：It's just *a matter of* time.

　　　　　那是迟早的问题。

125. May I introduce myself to you? /Let me introduce myself.

　　请容许我自我介绍一番。

126. Mind your own bussiness.　少管闲事

　　＝Keep out of this!　＝Keep your nose out of this.

　　＝It's none of your business.

127. Many men, many minds.　十人十心。

128. Be a man.　像男人一点,好不好? (激励男性要有男子气概的用语)

129. Nonsense!　乱讲；胡扯。
　　＝What(a)nonsense!

130. No way. ＝Nothing doing!　＝No soap. ＝Not a chance.　不
　　行!

131. Not necessary.　不必了。

132. Not really.　不尽然,不见得。

133. Not that I know of.　没这回事。

134. Name it!　尽管说吧!

135. Never say die!　不要气馁! 不要灰心! 不要悲观!
　　＝Take heart!

136. Oh,my!　＝My goodness.　我的天啊! (惊叹语)
　　＝My God.

137. Oh,yeah?　喔? 是这样吗?

138. on the house　免费地(的)〔通常是经营者(店主)请客〕
　　〈例〉:店主请客。
　　　　　　It's *on the house*.

139. I'm on my way.　我马上到。

140. on earth＝in the world　到底,究竟(接于疑问词后)
　　〈例〉:你到底在干什么?
　　　　　　What *on earth* are you doing?

141. On the double!　快一点!

142. Or else what?　不然,你敢怎样?

143. Once is too often.　一次都嫌多。

144. pick up the tab　(口语)付清账款(for)
　　〈例〉:If you drive,I'll *pick up the tab* for the bowling.
　　　　　要是你开车,我就请客打保龄球。

145. Pardon?　＝I beg your pardon.　请再说一遍。
　　＝What did you say?

146. Post no bills!　禁止张贴。

147. A promise is a promise.　说话算数。

148. Don't pull my leg.　别扯我后腿。

149. potato 的用法：

①a small potato　无足轻重的人

〈例〉：没有人是不重要的,除非他自己也认为自己不重要。

No one is a **small potato**, unless he thinks he is.

②hot potato　敏感的事物

150. Don't play dirty games.　别要诈。

151. Don't push me.　不要逼我。

152. Quite so?　是啊！可不是吗？

153. ring a bell　使人想起……

154. That name rings a bell.　那名字听起来很熟悉。

155. run out of　用尽了,用光了

〈例〉：茶叶用完了。

We **run out of** tea.

156. Be reasonable.　讲理点。讲点理吧。

157. to stand sb. up　放(某人)鸽子

〈例〉：这次别再放我鸽子了。

Don't **stand me up** again this time.

158. So far so good.　到目前为止一切还好。

159. Say when.　够了就告诉我。(帮别人倒饮料时,要求别人告知"饮料够了"的用语)

160. Same here. ＝Me too.　我也一样。

161. Save your breath!　省点力气吧！别浪费口舌了！

162. Stay put. 饶了我吧！ ＝Don't move.　别动。
＝Stay where you are.

163. Sure is.　当然是。

164. spare 的用法：

①Spare me!　别再说了。不用细说了！

②spare time　空闲时间

〈例〉：你闲暇时都在做什么？

What do you usually do in **spare time**?

③spare 备胎

〈例〉：车后行李厢里有备胎。

There is a **spare** in the trunk.

165. say 的各种用法：

　　You can say that again.　你说得对极了。

　　在口语中表示赞同对方看法的用语还有：

　　You're telling me.　你说的对极了。

　　I couldn't agree(with you)more. 我完全同意你的看法。

　　That's the spirit.　你讲得对极了。

　　①甲：毅力乃是使人成功的因素。

　　　　乙：你说得对极了。

　　　　A：Perseverance is what makes people succeed.

　　　　B：*You can say that again*.

　　②艾米：　真正的好歌星是不需要靠关系的。天份和不断的
　　　　　　练习才重要。

　　　　巴巴拉：你说得对极了。

　　　　Amy：　A really good singer doesn't need any connections.
　　　　　　　Talent and constant practice are the most impor-
　　　　　　　tant things.

　　　　Barbara：*That's the spirit*.

166. see 的各种用法：

　　①See? I told you so.　相信了吧？早跟你说过了,你偏不听。

　　②See you.　再见。

　　③I see things,not people.　我论事不论人。

　　④I see.　我明白了。

　　⑤I'll see.　我考虑看看。

　　⑥I'll see you dead first.　那种事情我绝不同意。

　　⑦We'll see about that!　咱们走着瞧!

　　⑧You ain't seen nothing yet.　好戏还在后头。

　　〔注：(口语) ain't = am not, are not, is not, has not, have
　　not〕

167. Sensational.　棒极了。

　　＝Terrific!

168. Be smart.　放聪明点。识相些。

169. Don't be so sure!　别太自信了!（世事难料）

170. Don't be silly!　　别傻了!

171. So that is!　　原来如此!

172. So what!　　有什么了不起的!
 ＝Big deal!

173. a slip of tongue　　说溜了嘴
 〈例〉:说溜嘴可能会造成误会。
　　　　A slip of tongue could leads to a mistake.

174. slip one's mind　　忘记了

175. Shame on you.　　不要脸!

176. It served him right.　　他活该!他自作自受!

177. take a person by surprise　　使某人大吃一惊
 〈例〉:甲:我们现在就去北海公园玩好不好?
　　　　乙:你别吓我了!明天要期末考试!
　　　　A:How about take a trip to Beihai Park right now?
　　　　B:Don't ***take me by surprise***. Tomorrow we have the
　　　　　final exam.

178. There goes everything.　　一切都完了。

179. take a leak　　去小便(同辈用语)
 〈例〉:对不起,我去上一下厕所。
　　　　Excuse me,I have to ***take a leak***.

180. Take it easy. ＝Don't sweat it. ＝Easy!　慢慢来,放轻松。

181. That's it.　　那就对了。

182. Time is up.　　时间到了。

183. take a rain-check　　改天;延期
 〈例〉:因为下雨,所以野餐延期了。
　　　　The picnic ***took a rain-check*** because of the rain.

184. There you go again!　　你又来(这一套)了。

185. I'm telling you for the last time.　　这是我最后一次警告你。

186. It was a tie.　　平手。

187. Thank God it's Friday.　　周末又到了。
 ＝T. G. I. F

188. Are you telling me?　　用得着你说吗? 你在教训我吗?

189. take chances　冒险

〈例〉:不要冒险。

Don't *take* any *chances*.

190. That's about it.　就这么多了。

191. That's more like it.　那还差不多。

192. Today isn't my day.　我今天真倒霉。

193. Don't take it so hard!　别太难过了,看开一点。

194. What's the matter with you? ＝What's wrong with you?

你怎么搞的?

195. window shopping　逛街(只看不买)

〈例〉:我星期天常和朋友去逛街。

　　　　　I often go *window shopping* on Sundays.

196. Who is it?　谁呀?

197. Wash your mouth out(with soap).你嘴巴放干净一点。

198. Watch your tongue.　不要胡说八道。

199. What a pity!　好可惜啊!

200. What could be worse?　还会有更糟(的事)吗?

201. Way to go! ＝Well done!　干得好!

202. What say? ＝What do you say?　意下如何?(你有何意

见?)

203. What's that long face for?　为何摆张臭脸?

204. What else is new?　那有什么稀奇的?

205. Want to make something of it?　怎么,想打架是不是?

206. Who cares?　谁管他啊? 我才不在乎呢?

207. When's chow?　何时开饭啊?

208. Where were we?　我们刚才说到哪儿了?

Where was I?　我刚才说到哪儿了?

209. Who are you?　你算老几?

210. Who knows?　谁知道啊!(没人知道之意)

＝God knows.

＝Heaven knows.

211. Hey,you know what?

嘿,你知道吗?(欲告诉别人某事的开头语)

212. What brings you here?　什么风把你吹来的?

213. What's up?　怎么啦? 发生什么事?

214. You don't say (so).

　　①(用上升调)不会吧,未必吧! 不至于吧!(表疑问)

　　②(用下降调)真的!(表惊讶,讽刺)

215. You too.　你也是。彼此彼此。

216. You got me!　你问倒我了。你难倒我了。

217. You're telling me!　这还用你说?

English...

第 2 部

情景对话活用归纳
焦点追踪，必胜锦囊

●系统地归纳日常生活对话 21 篇。采用中英对照方式编排，不仅能帮助您解除理解及记忆上的困扰，更有助于您迅速举一反三。例题灵活，解说详尽，足以激发潜力，增强实力。

Openings and Closings
招呼与道别

第**1**篇

情景对话精选

（一）
A：How are you doing?
B：Pretty well. Thank you.

甲：最近好吗?
乙：很好。谢谢。

（二）
A：How are you getting along?
B：Fairly well. Thank you.

甲：最近好吗?
乙：很好。谢谢。

（三）
A：What's new?
B：Nothing much.

甲：最近有何新鲜事?
乙：没什么。

（四）
A：How's life?
B：Couldn't be better.

甲：最近怎样?
乙：很好。

1. ➡"打招呼"常用语句
①"各种不同时间见面时打招呼"常用语句：
❶Good morning(afternoon,evening).
❷Hello.
❸Hello there.
❹Hi.
②"问候对方"常用语句：
❶How are you today(this morning),John?
❷How do you do?
❸How are you doing?
③表"身体不适"常用语句：
❶Not too(very)well.

❷I have a headache.

❸I have a cold.

④"听到对方生病时"常用语句：

❶I'm sorry to hear that.

❷That's too bad.

2. ➡"询问对方近况"和"老友重逢时"常用语句

①"询问对方近况"常用语句：

❶How are you getting along?

❷How have you been?

②表"老友重逢时"常用语句：

❶It's nice to see you again.

❷I'm glad to see you again.

③表"好久不见"常用语句：

❶You're quite a stranger.

❷I haven't seen you for ages.

❸It's a long time since I saw you last.

3. ➡"道别"、"祝旅途愉快"、"请辞"和"要对方保重"常用语句

①Good-bye. /Good luck. /So long. /Good night. /Good day.

②Have a good time. /Have a nice trip. /Have a good vacation.

③表"认识对方而感到高兴"常用语句：

❶It's nice meeting you.

❷I'm glad to have met you.

④"道别"常用语句：

❶I'll be seeing you.

❷See you again tomorrow.

❸See you later.

⑤"请对方保重"常用语句：Please take(good)care of yourself.

⑥"请人再来玩"常用语句:

❶Please come and see me sometime.

❷You must come again.

非常实战测验

●活学活用●

1. Jane: Hello, Tom. How are you?

Tom:＿＿＿＿＿＿

(A) I'm fine, thanks. How do you do?

(B) Thank you. How do you do?

(C) I am a new student.

(D) Fine, thanks. How are you?

【答案】▶(D)

【译文】▶简: 哈啰,汤姆,你好吗?

汤姆:＿＿＿＿＿＿

(A)我很好,谢谢。久仰。

(B)谢谢。久仰。

(C)我是新学生。

(D)很好,谢谢。你好吗?

【讲解】▶(A)对方用 *How are you*? 问,反问对方时仍用 How are you?

(B)*How do you do*? 用在第一次见面时的礼貌用语,回答只要说 How do you do? 而不要加上 fine 或 thanks。

(C)句的答话"我是个新学生。"与句意不合。

(D)*How are you*? 是已经认识的朋友见面时的寒暄话,正确回答方式应是答案(D)。

●活学活用●

2. John：Excuse me. I've got to go now.

Paul：But it's only 9：30.

John：Yes. But I have to check in one hour before departure time，11：45.

How much more time does John have before he checks in?

(A)75 minutes.

(B)One hour.

(C)Half an hour.

(D)Two hours and fifteen minutes.

【答案】▶(A)

【译文】▶约翰：对不起，我现在该走了。

保罗：但现在才九点半呀！

约翰：没错，但我必须在出发时间 11：45 前一小时签到。

约翰在签到前还有多少时间?

(A)75 分钟　　　　(B)一小时

(C)半小时　　　　(D)两小时十五分。

【讲解】▶**check in** ①签到(到达并办理登记)②登记

got to 必须＝**have(got)to**

现场会话 实战复习测验●

1. Jane： Have you really got to leave now?

Roger：_____

(A)Yes, I did. Very much indeed.

(B)Oh, I'm so pleased.

(C)Yes, I have to. I'm afraid.

(D)Really? Thank you.

2. Tom：How are you, Bob? (多选)

Bob：_____

  (A)Same as usual.

  (B)Fine，thanks.

  (C)You are welcome.

  (D)Not at all.

  (E)Of course not.

3. Mr. Smith：Well，I'm afraid we must go now. Thank you very much for the wonderful evening.

  Mr. Brown：_____

  (A)Yes，please.

  (B)Oh，I'll be expecting you then.

  (C)I enjoyed the evening very much indeed.

  (D)We enjoyed having you over.

4. As Jack is leaving a party he thanks his hostess as follows：

_____

  (A)Thank you for the inviting.

  (B)Thank you. I'm glad I could stay so long.

  (C)Thank you. I had a very good time.

  (D)Thank you for the nice party. I expect to come again.

5. Mr. Brown：What a surprise! I haven't seen you for ages. How've you been?

  Mr. Smith：_____It's good to see you.

  (A)I couldn't be better.

  (B)I just came back from Guangzhou.

  (C)Yes，I have been doing my work at home.

  (D)I'm helping my elder brother.

6. Mary：I must be leaving now. Good-bye.

  John：_____

  (A)So long.

  (B)I have an engagement.

  (C)Have a good trip.

  (D)Pleased to see you.

7. X：Glad to see you all.

　Y：It's been a long time since you dropped in, George,

　　_____

　　(A)didn't you?　　　　(B)isn't it?

　　(C)don't you?　　　　(D)hasn't it?

8. X：How are you?（多选）

　Y：_____

　　(A)Never better.

　　(B)I'm a bit under the weather，I'm afraid.

　　(C)Glad to know you.

　　(D)Thanks，all the same.

　　(E)Fine，thanks. How are you?

9. A：Sorry，it's getting late；I have to go now.

　B：_____

　　(A)So long.

　　(B)See you tomorrow.

　　(C)Good night.

　　(D)Good evening.

解题关键分析

1.【答案】▶(C)

　【译文】▶简：　你现在真的必须离开吗?

　　　　　罗杰：_____

　　　　　(A)是的,我的确是的。

　　　　　(B)喔,我好高兴。

　　　　　(C)是的,恐怕我必须离开了。

　　　　　(D)真的? 谢谢。

2.【答案】▶(A)(B)

　【译文】▶汤姆：你好吗,鲍伯?

　　　　　鲍伯：_____

　　　　　(A)老样子。　　　　　　　　(B)很好,谢谢。

(C)不客气。　　　　　　　　(D)不客气。

(E)当然不。

3.【答案】▶(D)

　【译文】▶史密斯先生:嗯,我恐怕我们现在得走了。非常谢谢你
　　　　　　　提供这么棒的夜晚。

　　　布朗先生:　_____

　　(A)是的,请吧。

　　(B)啊,我将期待你再来。

　　(C)今晚我确实很高兴。

　　(D)我们很喜欢你们过来。

4.【答案】▶(C)

　【译文】▶当杰克正要离开宴会的时候,他感谢女主人如下:

　　_____

　　(A)谢谢你的邀请。(应改为 Thank you for the invi-
　　　　tation.)

　　(B)谢谢你,我很高兴待了这么久。

　　(C)谢谢你,我玩得很愉快。

　　(D)谢谢你这么美好的宴会,我期望再来。(后半句不
　　　　符合正常人说话的礼貌,故不选)

5.【答案】▶(A)

　【译文】▶布朗先生:　真叫人惊讶! 我好多年没见到你了,你好
　　　　　　　吗?

　　　史密斯先生:_____能见到你真好。

　　(A)我再好不过了。

　　(B)我刚从广州回来。

　　(C)是的,我一直在家做我的工作。

　　(D)我正在帮我的哥哥。

6.【答案】▶(A)

　【译文】▶玛丽:我现在必须离开了。再见!

　　　约翰:_____

　　(A)再见。

　　(B)我有个约会。

　　　　　(C)祝你旅途愉快。

　　　　　(D)很高兴见到你。

7.【答案】▶(D)

　【译文】▶X:很高兴见到你们大家。

　　　　　Y:乔治,从你上次来看我们到现在已经很久了,

　　　　　　　_____

　　　　　(A)不是吗?　　　　　　　(B)不是吗?

　　　　　(C)不是吗?　　　　　　　(D)不是吗?

　【讲解】▶Y 答句中的 It's 是 It has 的缩写,故反意问句应为 hasn't it?

8.【答案】▶(A)(B)(E)

　【译文】▶X:你好吗?

　　　　　Y:_____

　　　　　(A)再好不过了。　　(B)恐怕我有点不太舒服。

　　　　　(C)很高兴认识你。　　(D)谢谢你,完全一样。

　　　　　(E)很好,谢谢。你好吗?

　【讲解】▶*under the weather*　〔口〕身体不适

9.【答案】▶(A)(B)(C)

　【译文】▶A:抱歉,时间不早了,我得走了。

　　　　　B:_____

　　　　　(A)再见。

　　　　　(B)明天见。

　　　　　(C)晚安,再见。

　　　　　(D)晚安。

　【讲解】▶"Good night!"含有"道别"之意,而"Good evening!"只是单纯的招呼用语。

Making a Phone Call
打电话

情景对话精选

㊀
A：May I speak to Mr. John Schmidt?
B：Speaking.
甲：我找约翰·史密先生听电话。
乙：我就是。

㊁
A：May I speak to Dr. Smith?
B：Who's speaking, please?
甲：我找史密斯博士听电话。
乙：请问你是……?

㊂
A：May I speak to Dr. Jones?
B：Who's speaking, please?
甲：我找琼斯博士听电话。
乙：请问你是……?

㊃
A：May I speak to Dr. Yerkey?
B：Who shall I say is calling, please?
甲：我找尤奇博士听电话。
乙：请问您是哪位?

㊄
A：May I speak to Professor Jones?
B：Just a moment, please.
甲：我找琼斯教授听电话。
乙：请稍候。

㊅
A：May I speak to Judy Lee?
B：Hold on, please.

甲：我找朱迪·李听电话。

乙：请稍候。

⑦

A：May I speak to Dr. Palmer?

B：I'm sorry. He's not available right now. May I take a message?

A：No，thank you. I'll call back later.

甲：我找巴默先生听电话。

乙：对不起。他现在很忙。有什么话要转告吗？

甲：不用了，谢谢。我等一会儿再打给他。

A：May I speak to Mr. Ford?

B：I'm sorry. He's not available right now. May I take a message?

A：Yes，please tell him Mr. Schmidt called.

⑧

B：How do you spell your last name?

A：S-C-H-M-I-D-T

B：Got it. Thank you.

A：Thank you. Good-bye.

甲：我找福特先生听电话。

乙：对不起。他现在没空。有什么话要转告吗？

甲：有的，请告诉他史密先生找他。

乙：请问贵姓？

甲：S-C-H-M-I-D-T

乙：写好了。谢谢。

甲：谢谢。再见。

（九）

A: May I speak to Mr. Johnson?

B: He's not in at this moment.

A: Will you ask him to call me collect when he's back?

B: Certainly. May I ask who's calling, please?

A: Yes. This is Mr. Lee of Fair Wind Trading Company in Shenzhen.

甲：请接约翰逊先生。

乙：他现在不在。

甲：请他回来时打电话给我，由我付费好吗？

乙：好的？请问你是哪位？

甲：我这里是深圳顺风贸易公司，我姓李。

1. "接电话"常用语句

This is the YMCA. Jim speaking. / This is～

2. "请人接电话"常用语句

Mr. Brown, you have a call. / Mr. Brown, you are wanted on the phone. / Mary wants you on the phone.

3. "要和(某人)通电话"常用语句

I'd like to speak to Tom. / May I speak to Tom, (please)? / Would you mind calling Tom to the phone?

4. 问"哪一位"常用语句

Who is calling (or speaking), please? /Who is this, please?

5. "请对方留话"常用语句

May I take a message? /Will you leave a message?

6. "通电话"其他常用语句

请等一等。❶Hold the line, please. ❷Let me put you on hold.

你的电话。It's for you.

谢谢你来电话。Thank you for calling.

占线。❶The line is busy. ❷The line is crossed.

你打错号码。You have the wrong number.

你打几号啊? What number are you calling?

你要谁接电话? Who(m) do you wish to speak to?

稍候我请他打过去。I'll have him call you later.

明早请打电话给我。Please call me up (Give me a call)

tomorrow morning.

非 常实战测验

●活学活用●

(Maria and Jane are talking over the telephone.)

Maria：Hello. May I speak to Eric Sung?

Jane： ___(1)___

Maria：I see. When do you expect him back?

Jane： ___(2)___

Maria：Yes. Just tell him Maria Moskovik called.

Jane： I'm sorry, I didn't catch your last name.

Maria： ___(3)___

Jane： OK. I'll give him the message.

1. (A)Hold on. I'll connect you.

(B)Sure. Wait a moment, please.

(C)I'm sorry. He's not come yet.

(D)I'm sorry. He's out at the moment.

2. (A)I'm not sure. May I leave a message?

(B)Any moment. Do you want to talk to him?

(C)I'm not sure. Can I take a message?

(D)I'm sorry. His line is busy.

3. (A)That's all right.

(B)Moskovik, M-O-S-K-O-V-I-K.

(C)It's an unusual name.

(D)Don't worry. Eric and I are old friends.

● 本文翻译 ●

(玛莉亚和简在通话中。)

玛莉亚：喂,请找艾力克·宋听电话。

简： _____

玛莉亚：这样哦,他什么时候会回来?

简： _____

玛莉亚：好,就告诉他玛莉亚·莫斯克维克找他。

简： 抱歉,我没听清楚你贵姓。

玛莉亚：_____

简： 好,我会转告他。

● 解题分析 ●

1.【答案】▶(D)

【译文】▶(A)稍等,我帮你转接。

(B)好的,请稍等。

(C)抱歉,他还没来。

(D)抱歉,他现在不在。

【讲解】▶①*hold on*(电话)不要挂断

②*connect*〔kə'nekt〕*v.*(将电话)接通

2.【答案】▶(C)

【译文】▶(A)我不确定,我可以留话吗?

(B)随时(都会回来),你要和他说话吗?

(C)我不确定,你要不要留话?

(D)抱歉,他的电话占线。

【讲解】▶①May I leave a message? ＝May I give you a message?＝

May you take a message?

我可以留言吗?(打电话者说)

②Can I take a message? ＝Can you leave a message?

你要不要留话?(接电话者说)

3.【答案】▶(B)

【译文】▶(A)没关系。

(B)Moskovik,M-O-S-K-O-V-I-K。

(C)这个名字很少见。

(D)别担心,艾力克和我是老朋友。

●活学活用●

4. Stella： Is Willy there,please,Mrs. Black?

Mrs. Black：No,he's not in right now. Stella.

Stella： _____.

Mrs. Black：Sure. Just a minute. I'll get a pencil and pa-

per. . . All right.

(A)Could you give him a message for me,please?

(B)Where is he now?

(C)Are you sure he's not there?

(D)Is it possible?

【答案】▶(A)

【译文】▶史特拉　　:布莱克太太,请问威利在吗?

布莱克太太:不。史特拉,他现在不在家。

史特拉:　　_____

布莱克太太:当然可以。稍候,我去拿纸和笔来……好
的。

(A)你能帮我留话给他吗?　(B)他现在在哪里?

(C)你确定他不在那里吗?　(D)那可能吗?

【讲解】▶①*give him a message for me*　帮我留话给他(帮我转告
他)

②*message* ['mesidʒ] *n.* (借着使者、电信等的)传话,捎
口信

例:Jane left a message with the office boy.

(珍托办公室勤杂工捎个信。)

●活学活用●

5. Pat：　Hello. I need to come in and take the test for my
driver's license. What hours are you open,please?

Officer：Our downtown office is open from 8：00 a.m. to
2：00 p.m. ,and you can take the test anytime
between 8：00 a.m. and 2：00 p.m.

Pat：　And it isn't possible to do it on the weekends,is it?

Officer：_____

(A)Yes,I'm sorry.　(B)No,I'm sorry.

(C)Yes,I would.　(D)No, I don't.

【答案】▶(B)

【译文】▶帕特:喂,我必须过去考驾照。请问你们上班时间是几点?

长官:我们市中心的大楼上班时间为早上八点至下午两
点。您可以在这段时间内过来考试。

帕特:那么周末是不可能去考试的,对吗?

长官:_____

（A）是的，抱歉。　　（B）是的，抱歉。

（C）是的，我愿意。　　（D）不，我不要。

【讲解】▶①*driver's license*　*n.* 驾驶执照

②"And it isn't possible to do it on the weekends, is it?"

为否定问句，回答应用 No，不可用 Yes。故（A）、（C）均

不可选；（D）不合语意。

●活学活用●

6. Secretary：Dr. Johnson's office. May I help you?

Patient：　Yes, it's Mrs. Simpson here. I'd like to see the doctor as soon as possible. I'm having trouble with my back again.

Secretary：_____

（A）Oh! It's wonderful. See you later.

（B）Oh! You'd better not come. The doctor will be angry with you.

（C）Oh! I'm sorry to hear that. Let me see if I can get you in this afternoon.

（D）Oh! I guess the doctor can't do anything about you.

【答案】▶（C）

【译文】▶秘书：约翰逊医生诊所。我能为您效劳吗？

病人：是的。我是辛普森太太。我想尽快看医生。我的背又有问题了。

秘书：_____

（A）哦！太好了，待会儿见。

（B）哦！你最好不要来。医生会生你的气的。

（C）哦！听到这事我很难过。我看看今天下午是否可以安排你过来看病。

（D）哦！我想医生对你没有办法。

【讲解】▶①*office*　意为办公室，在此为小诊所之意。

②*have trouble with*…有问题

例：She is having trouble with her legs.

（她的腿有问题。）

③*be angry with someone*   生某人的气

④*can't do anything about you*   对你毫无办法

● 活学活用 ●

7. Secretary：Good morning. Johnson Enterprise. May I help
you?

David：   Hello. This is David Wang. May I speak with
Mr. Johnson?

Secretary：He is not here right now. _____

(A) May I leave a message?

(B) What's the matter?

(C) Wait for a little while.

(D) May I take a message?

【答案】▶(D)

【译文】▶秘书：您早。（这里是）约翰逊公司。有什么可以效劳的
吗？

大卫：喂，我是王大卫。可以跟约翰逊先生说个话吗？

秘书：他目前不在这里。_____

(A)我可以留个口信儿吗？

(B)怎么回事？

(C)等一下。

(D)要留个口信吗？

【讲解】▶①*May I take a message*？

＝Would you leave a message? 要不要留个话（口信）。

②*enterprise*   企业

● 活学活用 ●

8. A：Extension 312，please.

　B：Engaged. Will you hold on?

　A：No ，I'll call back.

　B：Oh，it's free. _____

　　(A)I'll tell him you called.

　　(B)I didn't recognize your voice.

　　(C)You have the wrong number.

　　(D)I'll put you through.

【答案】▶(D)

【译文】▶A：请接 312 号分机。

　　　　B：占线。你要稍候吗?

　　　　A：不，我会再打过来。

　　　　B：噢，线路空出了。_____

　　　　　(A)我会告诉他你来过电话。

　　　　　(B)我认不出你的声音。

　　　　　(C)你打错了。

　　　　　(D)我帮你接过去。

【讲解】▶①B 说电话已通，可知(A)(B)(C)答非所问。

　　　　②*extension* [iks'tenʃən] *n*. 分机，内线

　　　　③*engaged* [in'geidʒd] *adj*. 占线的，通话中的

　　　　④*hold on*　暂时不挂电话

　　　　⑤*put sb. through*(*to sb.*)〈电话〉帮某人接通(给另一人)

现场会话 实战复习测验●

Part A：

1. A：Hello! May I talk to Mr. Walters?

　B：Sorry，he is not in right now. _____

A：That's all right. Do you know when he'll be back?

B：He should be back by five.

A：Then, I'll try again later.

    (A) May I have his telephone number?

    (B) How can I get in touch with you?

    (C) Can I take a message?

    (D) May I call back later?

2. A：Hello. Is this 700-0787?

  B：Yes, it is.

  A：Please connect me with Mr. Huang.

  B：_____, please?

  A：This is Mr. John Park.

    (A) Who are you

    (B) Who is this

    (C) Who is calling

    (D) What is your name

3. X：I want to make a long-distance phone call.

  Y：_____

    (A) What is a long-distance phone call made of?

    (B) Where is the telephone?

    (C) I can give you a few dimes if that'll help.

    (D) I couldn't do better myself.

4. Lucy：Who's speaking, please?

  John：_____

    (A) Could I speak to Mr. Zhang, please?

    (B) One moment, please.

    (C) I'd like to leave a message.

    (D) This is John Wang speaking.

5. *On the telephone*

  Man：   I'd like to make an appointment with Professor Smith. Would 9：00 a. m. tomorrow be all right?

  Secretary： _____ He doesn't have any openings in the

morning.

Man：　　How about 12：45 p. m. ?

Secretary：That will be all right.

(A)I suppose so.

(B)Out of the question.

(C)Business is closed.

(D)I'm afraid not.

Part B：

on the telephone

X：Hello.　①　I speak to John，please.

Y：Who's calling，please?

X：This is Bob.

Y：One moment，please.... He's not in now. This is Mrs. Johnson. What　②　I do for you?

X：Oh，Mrs. Johnson. Two days ago，we talked about going to the computer exhibition together today. He　③　about it. 　④　you please tell me where I can find him?

Y：I am sorry. He didn't use to　⑤　so forgetful. Maybe you can try Bill's place.

X：Thanks a lot. Goodbye.

①(A)Shall　　　　　(B)May

　(C)Will　　　　　(D)Must

②(A)can　　　　　(B)should

　(C)ought　　　　(D)will

③(A)must have forgotten　(B)must be forgetting

　(C)should forget　　(D)should have forgot

④(A)Shall　　　　　(B)Need

　(C)Would　　　　(D)Might

⑤(A)being　　　　(B)was

　(C)is　　　　　(D)be

解题关键分析

Part A：

1.【答案】▶(C)

　　【译文】▶A：喂！可以请沃尔特先生听电话吗？

　　　　　　B：抱歉，他现在不在家。_____

　　　　　　A：好的，你知道他何时回来吗？

　　　　　　B：他5点以前应该会回来。

　　　　　　A：那么我等会儿再打。

　　　　　　　　(A)可以告诉我他的电话号码吗？

　　　　　　　　(B)我怎么和他联系？

　　　　　　　　(C)要不要留话？

　　　　　　　　(D)我呆会儿再打行吗？

2.【答案】▶(C)

　　【译文】▶A：喂，是700-0787号吗？

　　　　　　B：是的。

　　　　　　A：请帮我接黄先生。

　　　　　　B：请问_____

　　　　　　　　(A)你是谁？

　　　　　　　　(B)是哪一位？

　　　　　　　　(C)您是哪位？

　　　　　　　　(D)尊姓大名？

3.【答案】▶(C)

　　【译文】▶X：我要打一个长途电话。

　　　　　　Y：_____

　　　　　　　　(A)长途电话是用什么制成的？

　　　　　　　　(B)电话在哪里？

　　　　　　　　(C)如果有帮助的话，我可以给你一些一角硬币。

　　　　　　　　(D)我自己无法做得更好。

4.【答案】▶(D)

　　【译文】▶露西：请问谁在说话？（打电话时用语）

约翰:_____

　(A)请找张先生听电话。　　(B)请等一下。

　(C)我想留个言。　　　　　(D)我是王约翰。

【讲解】▶①接电话者请问对方是谁的一般说法即 *Who's speaking，please*? 对方即会回答 *This is*～(姓名，或只有名字)*speaking.*

②如果对方想留话则会说 *I'd like to leave a message.*

message ['mesidʒ] *n.* 信息

5.【答案】▶(D)

　【译文】▶(电话中)

男子:我想和史密斯教授约个时间,明天上午9：00可以吗?

秘书:_____。他早上不接见任何人。

男子:12：45可以吗?

秘书:可以。

　(A)我想可以。　　　(B)没问题。

　(C)不办公。　　　　(D)恐怕不行。

Part B：

【答案】▶①(B)　②(A)　③(A)　④(C)　⑤(D)

【译文】▶(电话中)

X:您好,请找约翰听电话。

Y:请问您是哪里?

X:我叫鲍伯。

Y:请稍候……他现在不在! 我是约翰逊太太,有什么事吗?

X:您好,约翰逊太太。他前两天说今天要和我去看电脑展。他一定是忘了。请问他在哪里?

Y:对不起,他并不是很健忘的人。他可能在比尔那里,您打去试看看。

X:谢谢您,再见。

Introductions
介　绍

　A：Mrs. Brown, may I introduce Mr. Smith?

㈠　B：How do you do?

　C：How do you do?

　甲：布朗太太，我来介绍，这是史密斯先生。

　乙：你好！

　丙：你好！

　A：Mrs. Brown, this is Mr. Smith.

㈡　B：Very pleased to meet you.

　C：Nice to meet you.

　甲：布朗太太，这位是史密斯先生。

　乙：幸会。

　丙：幸会。

　A：I have to go now. I'm very glad to have met you, Mrs. Brown.

㈢　B：It was nice to meet you, Mr. Smith.

　甲：我必须走了。布朗太太，今天很高兴能认识您。

　乙：史密斯先生，今天很高兴能认识您。

"介绍他人"和"自我介绍"常用语句

①琼斯先生，这位是史密斯先生。❶ Mr. Jones，this is Mr. Smith. ❷ I'd like to introduce～. ❸ Let me introduce～. ❹ May I introduce～? ❺ I'd like you to meet～. ❻ Have you met～?

②让我自我介绍。❶ May I introduce myself to you? ❷ Let me introduce myself.

③史密斯先生，你好！How do you do，Mr. Smith?

非常实战测验

● 活学活用 ●

1. Abe：I don't think I've met you. My name is Abe.

　Sue：＿＿＿＿＿＿＿

　　(A) I hear the weather's hot there.

　　(B) That's a mystery to many people.

　　(C) It's nice meeting you.

　　(D) Yes.

【答案】▶ (C)

【译文】▶ 艾伯：我想我们未曾谋面吧！我的名字叫艾伯。

　　　　苏：＿＿＿＿＿＿＿

　　　　　　(A) 听说那里的天气炎热。

　　　　　　(B) 对许多人来说，那是个谜。

　　　　　　(C) 很高兴见到您。

　　　　　　(D) 是的。

【讲解】▶ ①因为是初次见面，所以选(C)。

初次见面时可以说 *How do you do*？/ *It's nice meeting you*. 幸会（= *It's nice to meet you*.）

②(B) *mystery* ['misteri] *n.* 神秘；谜

③动词 *think* 后面所接的 *that* 从句若是否定，则否定词不放在 that 从句中，而移到 think 前。

例：❶I think(that)it is not good. (×)

❷I don't think(that)it is good. (√)

现场会话 实战复习测验●

1. Mr. Li： Allow me to introduce myself. My name is John Li.

 Miss Wu： My name is Susan Wu. Are you a freshman?

 Mr. Li： Yes，I am. And you?

 Miss Wu： _____

 (A) Yes，I'm a junior.

 (B) No，I don't think so.

 (C) Not at all. I'm in no rush.

 (D) So am I.

2. Interviewer：Tell me a little more about yourself.

 Interviewee：Hmm. _____What do you want to know?

 Interviewer：Well，where are you from?

 (A) Can I offer a suggestion?

 (B) I'm sorry，but I'm not in the mood.

 (C) I don't know where to begin.

 (D) Everybody does once in a while.

3. Tom：It's been many years since I saw you last.

 John：_____

 Tom：I wouldn't have recognized you either if someone had not mentioned your name.

 (A) You haven't changed very much.

 (B) I recognized you at first sight.

(C)I hardly thought I would miss you so much.

(D)I didn't recognize you at first.

4. A：He is from Henan Province.

   B：_____

   A：About ten years.

   (A)Oh，really? When did he move to Shanghai?

   (B)I didn't know that. How long has he lived here?

   (C)When did he live in Henan Province?

   (D)How old was he then?

   (E)What did he do there?

5. Alan Wilson：_____

   Henry Taylor：How do you do.

   (A)Mr. Taylor，I like to introduce you to Mr. Thompson.

   (B)Mr. Taylor，I'll introduce you to Mr. Thompson.

   (C)Mr. Taylor，I'm introducing you to Mr. Thompson.

   (D)Mr. Taylor，please let me introduce you to Mr. Thompson.

6. X：Glad to know you.

   Y：_____

   (A)He mentioned you several times.

   (B)I'm glad to have had the chance to know you，too.

   (C)I've been expecting to know you.

   (D)It's an honor to meet you.

解题关键分析

1.【答案】▶ (D)

   【译文】▶ 李先生：容我自我介绍。我叫李约翰。

   　　　　　吴小姐：我叫吴苏珊。你是新生吗？

   　　　　　李先生：是的。你呢？

   　　　　　吴小姐：_____

   　　　　　(A)是的，我大三了。

　　　　(B)不，我不这么想。

　　　　(C)不心客气。我不急。

　　　　(D)我也是。

　　【讲解】▶*junior* [ˈdʒuːnjə] *n.*（四年制大学）三年级学生

2.【答案】▶(C)

　　【译文】▶面谈者　　：多告诉我一点关于你的事。

　　　　　　被面谈者：嗯，_____你想知道些什么？

　　　　　　面谈者　　：呃，你是哪里人？

　　　　　　(A)我可以提个建议吗？

　　　　　　(B)很抱歉，我没这个心情。

　　　　　　(C)我不知道从何说起。

　　　　　　(D)每个人偶尔都会这样。

3.【答案】▶(D)

　　【译文】▶汤姆：自从上次见你到现在已有很多年了。

　　　　　　约翰：_____

　　　　　　汤姆：如果没有人提起你的名字，我也认不出来。

　　　　　　(A)你没有改变很多嘛。

　　　　　　(B)我第一眼就认出你来。

　　　　　　(C)我本来不认为我会这么想念你。

　　　　　　(D)起初我认不出你来。

　　【讲解】▶*at first sight*　初见

4.【答案】▶(B)

　　【译文】▶A：他来自河南。

　　　　　　B：_____

　　　　　　A：大约十年了。

　　　　　　(A)喔，真的？他何时搬到上海的？

　　　　　　(B)这我不知道。他住在这里多久了？

　　　　　　(C)他何时住在河南？

　　　　　　(D)那时他几岁？

　　　　　　(E)他在那儿做些什么？

5.【答案】▶(D)

　　【译文】▶艾伦·威尔逊：_____

亨利·泰勒:幸会、幸会。

(A)泰勒先生,我喜欢把你介绍给汤普森先生。

(B)泰勒先生,我把你介绍给汤普森先生。

(C)泰勒先生,我正在把你介绍给汤普森先生。

(D)泰勒先生,请容许我把你介绍给汤普森先生。

6.【答案】▶(B)

【译文】▶X:很高兴认识你。

Y:_____

(A)他提到你好多次。

(B)我也很高兴有这个机会来认识你。

(C)我一直期望认识你。(这句话和对方说的 Glad to know you. 之间没有直接的应对关系,应该在句尾加上 too,故不选。)

(D)能见到你是我的荣幸。(初次与对方见面时所说的话)。

Invitations
邀　请

（一）

A：If you're not doing anything tonight, how about having dinner together?

B：Fine with me.

A：When is the most convenient time for you?

B：Anytime after five will be fine.

A：OK. I'll pick you up at half past five. Bye.

B：Bye.

甲：你今晚要是没事，一起吃晚饭如何？

乙：好啊。

甲：你什么时候最方便？

乙：五点之后都可以。

甲：好的，我五点半去接你，再见。

乙：再见。

（二）

A：Would you like to have lunch with me one day next week?

B：Yes, I would.

A：Can you make it Saturday?

B：Yes. I think I can get away for an hour or two on Saturday.

A：What time is convenient for you?

B：How about noon?

甲：下礼拜找一天一起吃顿午饭如何？

乙：好啊。

甲：星期六怎么样？

乙：好，我想星期六我可以腾出一两个钟头的时间。

甲：你什么时间最方便？

乙：中午如何？

A：May I see you this afternoon?

B：I'm awfully sorry, but I'm afraid not.

A：Then how about tomorrow at 12 o'clock?

B：That would suit me fine.

A：Then I'll see you tomorrow at 12 o'clock.

B：Yes, I'll be expecting you at that time.

甲：我今天下午可以见到你吗？

乙：很抱歉，恐怕没办法。

甲：那么明天十二点如何？

乙：对我来说那会方便一点。

甲：那么我们明天十二点再见。

乙：是的，到时我会等你来。

表示"邀请"及"询问对方是否方便"和答复的常用语句

①明晚你有空吗? Are you free tomorrow evening?

我想邀你参加我的生日宴会。I'd like to invite you to my birthday party.

请一定来。Please come by all means.

你何时方便? 明日可以。When is convenient for you? Tomorrow will be all right.

你周末有没有要做什么? 没有,我没什么特别的事要做。

Do you have any plans for the weekend? No, none in particular.

②我乐意接受你的邀请。I accept your invitation with pleasure.

③谢谢你邀请我,但是,很抱歉我没办法去。It's very kind of you to invite me, but I'm sorry I can't come.

我已有约会。I have a previous engagement.

真抱歉,但下次我一定来。I'm very sorry. I'd like to come another time, though.

④谢谢你的美好晚餐。Thank you for the wonderful dinner.

我真喜欢你的茶会。I really enjoyed your tea party.

我们明天接你。We'll pick you up tomorrow.

非常实战测验

● 活学活用 ●

1. Irene: Well, if he doesn't call you, why don't you just call him?

Jessica: I can't do that! I don't know if he even likes me!

Irene: Come on, be brave.

> (A)I guess you should just forget it.
> (B)I suppose you're right.
> (C)Of course you like him.
> (D)You will never know unless you try.

【答案】▶(D)

【译文】▶艾琳：　嗯,如果他不打电话给你,你何不就打电话给他?

杰茜卡:我不能那么做! 我甚至不知道他是否喜欢我!

艾琳：　拜托! 勇敢点。_____

(A)我想你应当忘了此事。

(B)我认为你是对的。

(C)当然你喜欢他。

(D)除非你试了,否则你永远不会知道。

●活学活用●

2.John:We are planning an outing. _____

Mary:Sure.

(A)Where are you going?

(B)When will you leave?

(C)How is everything?

(D)Do you want to join us?

【答案】▶(D)

【译文】▶约翰:我们正在计划一次出游。_____

玛丽:当然。(好哇!)

(A)你要去哪里?

(B)你何时要离开?

(C)近况还好吗?

(D)你要不要加入我们?

【讲解】▶*outing* ['autiŋ] *n.* 小游;散步;远足

●活学活用●

3. John：We're going hiking this weekend. _____

   Jane：Sure. Where are you going?

   John：Mt. Tai.

     (A)What's your plan?

     (B)Do you want to come along?

     (C)I hope you could have joined us.

     (D)How about you?

【答案】▶(B)

【译文】▶约翰：这个周末我们去远足。_____

     简： 好啊！去哪里？

     约翰：去泰山。

     (A)你有什么计划？

     (B)要不要一块儿去？

     (C)真希望你已加入我们的行列了。

     (D)你呢？怎么样？

【讲解】▶①*go hiking*   徒步旅行

     ②*come along*   一道去

     ③*How about you*？你呢？你的看法如何？你的情况如

     何？

     ④(C)时态不对，指"过去"之事。

●活学活用●

4. Peter：Let's go to the movies tonight.

   John：But I have to prepare for tomorrow's math exam.

   Peter：_____，let's go! You won't flunk it!

     (A)Great   (B)Oh，no

     (C)Of course   (D)Come on

【答案】▶(D)

【译文】▶彼得：今天晚上我们去看电影吧。

约翰:但是我得准备明天的数学考试。

彼得:_____,走吧!你不会不及格的!

　　(A)太棒了　　　　　　　　(B)哦,不

　　(C)当然　　　　　　　　　(D)好啦

【讲解】▶①*flunk* [flʌŋk] (美口)*vi.* (考试等)失败;*vt.* 使(考试等)失败,使不及格。

　　　②*come on* 〔on 为副词〕,(作怂恿语)好啦,请啦(please),来吧!

<hr>

●活学活用●

5. Tom:I was wondering if you'd like to come over tonight.

　Jane:_____

　　(A)Yes,last night.

　　(B)Yes,over there.

　　(C)Sure. I'd love to.

　　(D)Yeah,I liked it too.

<hr>

【答案】▶(C)

【译文】▶汤姆:不知你今晚是否想过来。

　　　　简:　_____

　　　　　　(A)是的,昨晚。　　　　(B)是的,在那边。

　　　　　　(C)当然,我很想去。　　(D)是的,我也喜欢。

非常实战测验

1. A:I'm going to have my lunch. Do you want to join me?

　B:That's very kind. I'd like to.

　A:_____

　B:Anything will do.

　　(A)What do you fancy?

　　(B)What restaurant shall we go?

    (C) What do you eat?

    (D) Let's go to a Chinese restaurant.

2. Ted: Let's go for a drive. What do you say?

  Bill: _____

    (A) I say I'll go for a drive.   (B) It drives me mad.

    (C) All right. Let's go.   (D) I don't say anything.

3. Diana: Amy, you know the Spanish Club is having a dance next Friday night, don't you? Well, I am wondering if you'd like to go with me.

  Amy: _____ but I can't. I'm going out of town for the weekend.

    (A) Fortunately,   (B) I hate to go,

    (C) I'll be ready,   (D) I'd really like to,

4. Tom: Thanks for inviting me, John, but I've already made other plans.

  John: _____ Maybe another time.

    (A) I hope you enjoy it.

    (B) That's too bad.

    (C) Oh! I'm sorry to hear that. We certainly will wait for you.

    (D) Great! I really had a good time.

5. Tom: Shall we go out after work tonight? I know a good café.

  Jane: That sounds great. _____

  Tom: How about six-thirty?

  Jane: OK.

    (A) Shall we go by car?

    (B) Do you have the time?

    (C) What time shall we make it?

    (D) But I'll be busy studying this evening.

6. Mr. Kay: How would you like to hear a concert this evening?

  Mr. Lee: _____

    (A) OK. Let's go.

(B) I'd like to very much.

(C) But I had something else to do.

(D) Not bad.

7. X: Would you like to join us for Sunday dinner?

　Y: _____

　　(A) It's nice of you to invite me.

　　(B) The food is all ready.

　　(C) The best dish I had was onion soup.

　　(D) I've never been there, and I'm sorry I missed the fun last
　　　　time.

解题关键分析

1.【答案】▶ (A)

　【译文】▶ A: 我要去吃午餐,你想加入吗?

　　　　　B: 太好了,我想去。

　　　　　A: _____?

　　　　　B: 都可以。

　　(A) 你喜欢什么?　　　(B) 我们去哪家餐馆?

　　(C) 你吃什么?　　　　(D) 我们去中国餐馆吧!

　【讲解】▶ (A) 你喜欢什么?

2.【答案】▶ (C)

　【译文】▶ 泰德: 让我们去兜风,你认为怎样?

　　　　　比尔: _____

　【讲解】▶ (C) 好呀! 走吧!

　　(A) 我说我想去兜风。　　(B) 这让我发疯。

　　(C) 好呀! 走吧!　　　　(D) 我什么也没说。

3.【答案】▶ (D)

　【译文】▶ 黛安娜: 艾米,你知道下个礼拜五晚上西班牙俱乐部有
　　　　　　　一场舞会,对不对? 不知道你要不要跟我去?

　　　　　艾米: _____但是我不能。我周末要出城。

　　(A) 很幸运,　　　　　(B) 我讨厌去,

(C)我会准备好，　　　　　(D)我真的很想去，

4.【答案】▶(B)

【译文】▶汤姆:约翰,谢谢你邀请我,但我已做了其他的计划。

约翰:_____或许下一次。

【讲解】▶(A)希望你玩得尽兴。

(B)真是太可惜了。

(C)噢! 真遗憾。我们一定会等你的。

(D)那太好了! 我玩得很尽兴。

5.【答案】▶(C)

【译文】▶汤姆:今晚工作结束后要出去吗? 我知道一家不错的

咖啡店。

简: 听起来很棒。_____

汤姆:六点半如何?

简: 好的。

(A)我们开车去吗?　　　(B)你有时间吗?

(C)我们几点去?　　　　(D)但我今晚要学习。

6.【答案】▶(B)

【译文】▶凯先生:今天晚上想不想去听音乐会?

李先生:_____

(A)好啊! 我们走吧!

(B)我非常想去。

(C)但我还有其他事情要做。

(D)不坏。

7.【答案】▶(A)

【译文】▶X:星期天的晚餐你想加入我们吗?

Y:_____

(A)你真好,来邀请我。

(B)食物都准备好了。

(C)我吃过最好的菜肴是洋葱汤。

(D)我从未去过那里,而且我很遗憾,错过了上回的

趣事。

Apologizing; Getting Information 道歉;询问

第**5**篇

情景对话精选

一➡道歉：

㈠
A:Sorry I stood you up.
B:That's all right.

甲:抱歉,让你久等了。
乙:没关系。

㈡
A:I have to apologize for what I did to you last night.
B:Forget it!

甲:我必须为我昨晚的不礼貌行为向你道歉。
乙:算了。

二➡询问时间：

㈢
A:What time is it now?
B:It's ten o'clock sharp.

甲:现在几点了?
乙:正好十点。

㈣
A:What time do you have?
B:Nine thirty.

甲:你的表几点了?
乙:九点半。

㈤
A:Do you have the time?
B:Yes. It's eleven fifty-five.

甲：你带表了吗？

乙：带了。现在是 11 点 55 分。

（六）

A：What time is it by your watch?

B：It's five minutes before noon.

甲：你的表几点了？

乙：差五分就中午 12 点了。

三 ➡ 听不清楚请对方再说一遍：

（七）

A：Do you have the time?

B：Excuse me?

甲：你带表了吗？

乙：对不起，请你再说一遍。

（八）

A：Do you have the time?

B：What do you mean?

A：I mean "Can you tell me what time it is?"

B：Oh, I see. Yes, it's ten fifteen.

甲：你带表了吗？

乙：你什么意思？

甲：我的意思是，能不能请你告诉我现在几点了。

乙：噢，我明白了。好，现在是 10 点 15 分。

（九）

A：What time do you have?

B：I beg your pardon?

A：What time is it by your watch?

B：It's twelve noon.

┌─甲：你的表几点了？

├─乙：对不起，请再说一遍。

├─甲：你的表几点了？

└─乙：中午 12 点。

　┌─A：Can we make it in time?

⊕ 　B：I'm sorry. I don't quite follow you.

　└　Would you mind saying that once more?

┌甲：我们能及时到达吗？

└乙：对不起，我不太懂你的意思，请再说一遍好吗？

1. ➡"道歉"及其回答常用语句

①表"对不起"常用语句❶Excuse me. ❷Pardon me. ❸I beg your pardon. ❹I'm(very, awfully, terribly)sorry. ❺Please forgive me.

②表"迟到"及"麻烦他人"常用语句❶I'm sorry to be late. ❷I'm sorry I have troubled you. ❸I'm sorry to have kept you waiting so long. ❹I'm sorry I stepped on your toe. ❺It's my fault.

③表"没关系"常用语句❶That's(quite)all right. ❷Don't worry(about it). ❸It's nothing(at all). ❹Never mind. ❺It doesn't matter. ❻Just forget it.

2. ➡"请再说一遍"及"你是什么意思"常用语句

①Pardon? /Beg your pardon? /I beg your pardon?

②Please repeat what you said. /Will you say it again,please?
　Will you speak more slowly?

③What do you mean by that? /What does it mean?

3. ➡"询问时间、日期"常用语句

①What time is it now (by your watch)? It's five-thirty.

②What day of the week is it today? It's Monday. /What day
　of the month is it today? It's May 2nd.

③你的表准吗? Does your watch keep good time?
　是的,它准。 Yes, it keeps good time.
　没有,我的表快五分钟。 No, my watch is five minutes
　fast.
　不,我的表慢了五分钟。 No, my watch is five minutes
　slow.

④我的表坏了。 My watch is out of order.

⑤我已把我的表和火车站的表对过了。 I've set my watch by
　the station clock.

⑥我的表停了。你能告诉我准确时间吗? My watch has
　stopped. Could you tell me the correct time?

⑦我猜大约四点半。 I guess it's around four-thirty.

⑧现在是十二点半整。 It's twelve-thirty sharp.

4. ➡"请求协助、问东西的种类"等常用语句

①"请人协助"常用语句:
　❶May I ask a favor of you?
　❷I've got a favor to ask of you.

❸Will(Would)you do me a favor?

②"问东西的种类"常用语句：

❶What is it?

❷What kind of?

③"请人开门或做事"常用语句：

❶May I trouble you for the paper? Yes,certainly.

❷Would you mind opening the window? No,certainly not. (or No,of course not.)Would you mind closing the door?

❸Would you kindly bring me a cup of tea?

❹Will you please show me your picture?

❺May I borrow your book?

非常实战测验

●活学活用●

1. Jane：Sorry to have kept you waiting.

Sue：_____.

Jane：In the library. I was trying to finish my homework and just forgot the time.

(A)That's OK.

(B)What are you doing?

(C)What's wrong with you?

(D)Where have you been?

【答案】▶(D)

【译文】▶简：抱歉，让您久等了。

苏：_____

简：我去图书馆了。我想着要做完功课，就忘了时间了。

(A)没关系。　　　　(B)你在干什么?

(C)你怎么啦?　　　(D)你去哪儿啦?

●活学活用●

2. Guest 1：Are you the manager of this hotel? I've got some complaints about your service.

Guest 2：_____ I'm also looking for the manager. I've got some complaints，too.

(A)It is very nice of you.

(B)I'm afraid you must be mistaken.

(C)I'm glad the manager is here.

(D)I really appreciate your advice.

【答案】▶(B)

【译文】▶客人一:你是这家饭店的经理吗? 我对于你们的服务有些不满。

客人二:_____我也在找经理。我也有些不满的地方。

(A)你真好。

(B)恐怕你弄错了。

(C)我很高兴经理在这里。

(D)我真的很感激你的劝告。

【讲解】▶*complaint* [kəm'pleint] *n.* 抱怨；不满

mistaken [mis'teikən] *adj.*

mistake [mis'teik] *n.* ；*v.*　　故用 *be*＋*mistaken*

●活学活用●

3. Man A：_____．

Man B：Sure. I asked if Mr. Brown would be here tonight.

(A)Could you find Mr. Brown for me?

(B)Can you tell me how to fill in this form?

(C)Could you repeat that question?

(D)Did you notice the way he talked?

【答案】▶(C)

【译文】▶ A：_____

B：好的。我是问布朗先生今晚是否会在这里。

(A)你能否帮我找布朗先生？

(B)你能不能告诉我如何填写这张表格？

(C)你能重复一下那个问题吗？

(D)你有没有注意到他讲话的样子(方式)？

【讲解】▶ ① *fill in*　填写

② *form*　*n.* 表格

例：┌─ an application form　　申请书

　　├─ a telegraph form　　电报纸

　　└─ a tax form　　税额申报书

③ *repeat* [ri'pi:t] *v.* 重复

④(A)问非所答，(B)(D)均未针对问题，故选(C)。

━━━━━ ●活学活用● ━━━━━

4. Mary：I need to go to the library today. Do you know what time it closes?

Linda：_____.

(A)No，thanks.

(B)I'm very busy now.

(C)At about 5：30.

(D)I don't need to go there.

【答案】▶ (C)

【译文】▶ 玛丽：我今天要去图书馆。你知道它几点关门吗？

琳达：_____

(A)不，谢谢。

(B)我现在很忙。

(C)大约是五点半。

(D)我不必去那里。

【讲解】▶ *library* ['laibrəri] *n.* 图书馆

● 活学活用 ●

5. Jane：Is Julie's husband wearing a suit?

Sally：_____.

(A) He has just come back from the office.

(B) Yes, he is.

(C) Yes, he wears.

(D) He went swimming yesterday.

【答案】▶ (B)

【译文】▶ 简： 朱莉的丈夫穿着西装吗？

萨莉：_____

(A)他刚从办公室回来。 (B)是的，他穿着。

(C)是的，他穿着。 (D)他昨天去游泳。

● 活学活用 ●

6. Wife： Why didn't you tell me?

Husband：_____

(A) I guess I forgot.

(B) I'm sorry you have to wait.

(C) I thought I'd come by to say hello.

(D) I'd love to, but I have to work until six.

【答案】▶ (A)

【译文】▶ 妻子：你为何不告诉我？

丈夫：_____

(A)我想我忘了。

(B)抱歉你必须等。

(C)我想我该过来打招呼的。

(D)我愿意，但我必须工作到六点。

【讲解】▶ ①**I'd** ＝I would

②**come by**＝come over 过来

● 活学活用 ●

7. Bob：Did you say you liked this novel?

　　Jim：_____ I said it's not bad.

　　　(A) Not exactly.　　(B) I don't see why.

　　　(C) You're great.　　(D) That's quite all right.

【答案】▶ (A)

【译文】▶ 鲍勃：你说过喜欢这部小说吗？

　　　　吉姆：_____ 我说过它不错。

　　　　　(A) 未必尽然。　　(B) 我不知道为什么。

　　　　　(C) 你真好。　　　(D) 那没关系。

【讲解】▶ ①**Not exactly.** 未必是；不见得。　②**see** 知道

　　　　③**You are great.** 你真好。　　　④**all right** 没关系

● 活学活用 ●

8. Man：　I wonder if you could help me. I'm looking for Tandoor Restaurant.

　　Woman：_____

　　Man：　Tandoor. It's an Indian restaurant. It's supposed to be around here somewhere.

　　　(A) Of course. You've asked the right person.

　　　(B) No. I'm looking for my boyfriend.

　　　(C) I'm sorry. I don't work here.

　　　(D) Sure. What's the name again?

【答案】▶ (D)

【译文】▶ 男人：不知道你能不能帮个忙，我正在找丹门餐厅。

　　　　女人：_____

　　　　男人：丹门餐厅，是一个印度餐馆。好像就在这周围什么地方。

　　　　　(A) 当然，你问对了人。

　　　　　(B) 不，我正在找我的男朋友。

(C)抱歉,我不是在此工作的。

(D)当然,什么店名,请再讲一次。

●活学活用●

9. John：Mom, have you seen the blue jacket I was wearing earlier?

Mom：Yes, I put it in the washer.

John：_____ My glasses are in one of the pockets.

(A)My goodness!　　　(B)No wonder!

(C)Certainly not!　　　(D)Never mind!

【答案】▶(A)

【译文】▶约翰:妈,你有没有看到我前几天穿的那件蓝色夹克?

母亲:是的,我放在洗衣机里了。

约翰:_____ 我的眼镜在口袋里。

(A)天啊!　　　(B)难怪。

(C)当然不。　　　(D)别介意。

【讲解】▶①*earlier* 稍早　　②*washer* 洗衣机

③*My goodness.* 天啊!　　④*No wonder.* 难怪。

⑤*Certainly not.* 当然不会。　⑥*Never mind.* 不要介意。

●活学活用●

10. Jim：Wow! Why are you wearing that nice dress?

Lucy：I'm going to a job interview. _____

(A)I just like nice dresses.

(B)I intend to work hard.

(C)I want to make a good impression.

(D)I'll let you know next week.

【答案】▶(C)

【译文】▶吉姆:哇! 你为什么穿得那么漂亮(穿那么好的衣服)?

露西:我要参加求职的面谈。_____

(A)我只是喜欢好衣服。　(B)我会努力工作。

(C)我要使人有好的印象。 (D)下周我会让你知道。

【讲解】▶ ①*make a good impression*　使人有好印象

②*a job interview*　求职面谈

━━━━ ●活学活用● ━━━━

11. David：Could you give me a helping hand?

Mark：_____

David：I want to clean my garage.

(A)How's that?　　　　(B)What for?

(C)How so?　　　　　(D)Which one?

【答案】▶ (B)

【译文】▶ 大卫：能帮个忙吗？

马克：_____

大卫：我想清扫车库。

(A)那是怎么回事？/为什么会那样？

(B)要做什么？

(C)怎么会这样？

(D)哪一个？

━━━━ ●活学活用● ━━━━

12. Joe：This is heavy! What's in it?

Sue：_____

(A)Thanks. I think I can manage by myself.

(B)My new stereo equipment. I just bought it.

(C)I sure could. I'm glad you're here.

(D)Are you really interested in it?

【答案】▶ (B)

【译文】▶ 乔：这东西真重！里面装了什么？

苏：_____

(A)谢谢。我想我自己能应付。

(B)我的新立体音响设备。我刚买的。

(C)我当然可以。很高兴你在这儿。

(D)你真的感兴趣吗？（没有直接回答问题）

【讲解】▶①*stereo*　*n.* 立体音响

②*manage*　*v.* 处理，应付

● 活学活用 ●

13. Lin：Do you mind if I ask you how much you weigh?

May：_____

(A)In fact, I've been on a diet for quite a long time.

(B)Frankly, I've been trying my best to lose weight.

(C)Oh, no. Most people do care about the matter.

(D)Ha, ha. Gee, Americans don't really like to be asked such a question.

【答案】▶(D)

【译文】▶琳：你介意我问你的体重吗？

梅：_____

(A)事实上，我已经节食很久了。

(B)老实说，我已经尽全力去减肥了。

(C)噢，不介意。大部分的人十分在乎这个问题。（答句前后矛盾）

(D)哈哈，咦！美国人不太喜欢被问到这样的问题。

【讲解】▶①*lose weight*　减肥　②*gee*　*interj.* 咦！

● 活学活用 ●

14. Nan：Have you decided when you're going to retire?

Bob：_____

(A)I haven't made up my mind yet.

(B)I'm mixed up.

(C)Did you think so, too?

(D)I'm not bothering you at all.

【答案】▶(A)

【译文】▶南：　你已决定何时退休了吗？

　　　　鲍伯：_____

　　　　　　(A)我尚未下定决心。　(B)我搞糊涂了。

　　　　　　(C)你也这么想吗？　　(D)我并不是故意要打扰你。

●活学活用●

15. Ned：You seem familiar. Don't you work at McDonald's?

　　Dan：_____

　　　(A)I'm afraid not.

　　　(B)I'll be sure to.

　　　(C)I always have to look up to you.

　　　(D)No，it never happens to me.

【答案】▶(A)

【译文】▶奈德：你好面熟。你不是在麦当劳工作吗？

　　　　丹：　_____

　　　　　(A)不是。

　　　　　(B)我一定会去(做)。

　　　　　(C)我一向必须尊敬你。

　　　　　(D)不，我从未发生过这种事。

【讲解】▶①*familiar* 　*adj.*熟悉的

　　　　②(A)*I am afraid not.* 　我想不是。(缓和语气用)

　　　　　(C)*look up to* 　尊敬；赞赏

　　　　　(D) ⎡*happen to sb.* 　发生到某人身上
　　　　　　　⎣*occur to sb.* 　使某人想起来

●活学活用●

16. John：Did you go anywhere after supper?

　　Mary：I _____，but I went to the movies instead.

　　　(A)would have studied　　(B)should have learned

　　　(C)should have studied　　(D)would have learned

【答案】▶(C)

【译文】▶约翰:晚餐后你出去过吗?

玛丽:我原本是该读书的,但我没读而去看电影了。

【讲解】▶①"*should*＋*have*＋过去分词"表"过去应该做而未做的事"。

例:I should have bought it if I had had enough money.

(如果我当时有足够的钱,我就应该把它买下来。)

②用 *would*,则仅指"与过去的事实相反的假设",而无"应该"的意思。

例:If he had been there, he would have helped you.

(假使当时他在那里,他就帮助你了。)

③(A)、(D)用 *would* 不对。(B)用 *learn* 在此不合句意,且 learn 需要宾语。

现场会话 实战复习测验 ●

1. A : Sorry I'm late, but I was caught in a traffic jam.

B : That's all right. _____

A : I'm certainly not.

(A) But I prefer strawberry jam.

(B) I'm not late for our appointment, am I?

(C) You've learned to cope with our traffic, then.

(D) You're not used to our heavy traffic, are you?

2. Tom : What's the matter with your washing machine, Pat?

Pat : _____

Tom : Well, why don't you just pull out the plug? It's a waste of electricity.

(A) I don't know. The motor doesn't run.

(B) It's broken down. So I turned it off.

(C) It won't stop. What do you think I should do?

(D) What can I do? I can't lift the machine.

3. A：What can I do for you, sir?

　B：_____

　　(A)You can do anything you like.

　　(B)Nothing at this moment, thanks.

　　(C)Yes, you can.

　　(D)I don't want to talk about it.

4. Peter：How much are the tickets, please?

　Clerk：_____

　　(A)It is ＄3.00 every.

　　(B)They are sold out.

　　(C)They are ＄3.00 each. Children can get in at half price.

　　(D)The tickets are on the desk.

5. Dick：　What on earth do you think this is for?

　Nancy：_____

　　(A)I think it'll make a nice ornament.

　　(B)I don't think much of it. And you?

　　(C)It must be made of earth. An earthen pot, to be exact.

　　(D)Our life on earth is but a passing cloud.

6. Visitor：　Do you mind my sitting in on your class?

　Professor：_____

　　(A)Certainly.　　　　　　(B)Of course not.

　　(C)Hopefully.　　　　　　(D)No, I do.

7. A：Would you mind if I opened the window?（多选）

　B：_____

　　(A)No, not at all.

　　(B)Yes, it is.

　　(C)No. certainly not.

　　(D)No. Go right ahead.

8. A：May I use your restroom?

　B：_____

　　(A)Sure. It's over there.

　　(B)Do you need a rest?

(C)You don't need it.

(D)No，I am not using it.

9. A：Ouch，you are stepping on my toes.

B：I am so sorry.（多选）

A：＿＿＿＿＿＿＿＿

(A)Don't mention it.

(B)You are welcome.

(C)That's all right.

(D)Not at all.

解题关键分析

1.【答案】▶(D)

【译文】▶A：抱歉，我迟到了，因为我遇到了交通堵塞。

B：没关系。＿＿＿＿＿＿＿＿

A：我当然不习惯。

(A)但我较喜欢草莓果酱。

(B)我们的约会我并没有迟到，是吗?

(C)那么，你已经学会如何应付我们的交通了。

(D)你不习惯我们繁忙的交通，是吗?

2.【答案】▶(C)

【译文】▶汤姆：你的洗衣机怎么了? 培特。

帕特：＿＿＿＿＿＿＿＿

汤姆：嗯，为什么不拔掉插头呢? 那样会浪费电。

(A)我不知道。马达不动了。

(B)它故障了，所以我把它关掉。

(C)它停不了。你想我该怎么办?

(D)我能怎么办? 我搬不动这台机器。

【讲解】▶①*pull out* 拔出 ②*break down* 故障

③*plug* [plʌg] *n.* 插头

3.【答案】▶(B)

【译文】▶A：先生，有什么需要服务的地方吗?

　　　　B：_____
　　　　　(A)你可以做任何你喜欢的事。
　　　　　(B)谢谢，目前没有。
　　　　　(C)是的，你可以。
　　　　　(D)我不想谈论此事。

4.【答案】▶(C)
　【译文】▶彼得：请问票价是多少？
　　　　　店员：_____
　　　　　　(A)每张 3 美元。(问句为复数，应以复数回答；every没有作为副词的用法，应改为 each)
　　　　　　(B)票已经卖完了。
　　　　　　(C)每张 3 美元。儿童半价。
　　　　　　(D)票在桌上。

5.【答案】▶(A)
　【译文】▶迪克：你认为这究竟是做什么用的？
　　　　　南西：_____
　　　　　　(A)我想它会是个很好的装饰品。
　　　　　　(B)我不重视它。你呢？
　　　　　　(C)它一定是用泥土做的。精确地说是一个陶壶。
　　　　　　(D)人生只是过往浮云。
　【讲解】▶①*on earth*　究竟；在地球上
　　　　　②*ornament* [ˈɔːnəmənt] *n.* 装饰品
　　　　　③*think much of*　重视
　　　　　④*earthen* [ˈəːθən] *adj.* 陶制的；土制的
　　　　　⑤*to be exact*　精确地说

6.【答案】▶(B)
　【译文】▶旁听生：您介意我来您班上旁听吗？
　　　　　教授：　_____
　　　　　　(A)当然介意。
　　　　　　(B)当然不介意。
　　　　　　(C)有希望。
　　　　　　(D)不，我介意。

【讲解】▶①Do you mind＋V-ing...？　您介意……吗？

②sit in on＋课：旁听某课

③单选题中以正面、合乎礼貌的答案为佳。故选(B)。

　但本题若为多选，则(A)、(B)皆可。

7.【答案】▶ (A)(C)(D)

　【译文】▶A：我打开窗户，你介意吗？

　　　　　B：＿＿＿＿＿＿

　　　　　(A)不，我不介意。

　　　　　(B)对，没错。

　　　　　(C)不，当然不介意。

　　　　　(D)不介意，你开窗吧。

8.【答案】▶ (A)

　【译文】▶A：洗手间可以借用一下吗？

　　　　　B：＿＿＿＿＿＿

　　　　　(A)好啊，在那儿。

　　　　　(B)你要不要休息？

　　　　　(C)你不需要上洗手间。

　　　　　(D)不，我不用。

9.【答案】▶ (A)(C)(D)

　【译文】▶A：哎唷！你踩到我的脚了。

　　　　　B：对不起。

　　　　　A：＿＿＿＿＿＿

　　　　　(A)(C)(D)没关系

　　　　　(B)不客气

Thanking People and Replying to Thanks 感谢及回应

情景对话精选

㈠ **A**：Thank you very much. 　　甲：多谢。
　 B：You're welcome. 　　　　乙：不客气。

㈡ **A**：Thanks a lot. 　　　　　甲：多谢。
　 B：Not at all. 　　　　　　乙：不客气。

㈢ **A**：Thank you ever so much. 　甲：感激不尽。
　 B：Don't mention it. 　　　　乙：不足挂齿。

㈣ **A**：You've been a great help. 　甲：你真帮了大忙。
　 B：Glad to be of help. 　　　乙：我很高兴能帮得上忙。

㈤ **A**：Much obliged. 　　　　　甲：多谢。
　 B：Not at all. 　　　　　　乙：不客气。

㈥ **A**：I really appreciate it. 　　甲：多谢。
　 B：You're welcome. 　　　　乙：不客气。

1. ➡表"感激"及其回话常用语句

①表"感谢"常用语句：

❶ Thank you(very much, a lot, a million).

❷ Thanks a lot.

❸ Much obliged to you.

❹ It's very kind(nice) of you.

❺ You're very nice.

②表"谢谢你的……"常用语句：

❶Thank you for coming（calling，the compliment，everything）.

❷Thanks for your...

③表"不谢"常用语句：

❶You're welcome.

❸Don't mention it.

❸Not at all.

④表"能为人服务而感到快乐"常用语句：

❶I'm glad you like it.

❷I'm glad I could help you.

❸It's my pleasure.

❹The pleasure is mind.

❺No trouble at all.

⑤表"拒绝"常用语句：

❶No，thank you.

❷Thank you anyway(just the same).

非常实战测验

●活学活用●

1. Mother： I must send out these letters today，but I don't have time.

Daughter：I'll mail them for you on my way to school.

Mother：_____

Daughter：Don't worry. I won't let you down.

(A)Thank you very much.

(B)It's a pity that I have to bother you.

(C)It's very nice of you to help me.

(D)You won't forget,will you?

【答案】▶(D)

【译文】▶母亲:今天我必须把这些信寄出去,可是我没有时间。

　　　　女儿:我会在上学途中帮你寄。

　　　　母亲:_____

　　　　女儿:别担心,我不会让你失望的。

　　　　(A)非常谢谢你。

　　　　(B)很遗憾我必须麻烦你。

　　　　(C)你真好,愿意帮我的忙。

　　　　(D)你不会忘记吧! 对吗?

● 活学活用 ●

2. Man A:Maybe I could show you the way.

　　Man B:_____

　　　　(A)Oh,thanks. I like the green one.

　　　　(B)Yes. I've lived here forty years.

　　　　(C)Thanks,but I'm not familiar with this neighborhood.

　　　　(D)No,thanks. I can get there all right.

【答案】▶(D)

【译文】▶男 A:也许我可以告诉你走哪条路。

　　　　男 B:_____

　　　　(A)哦,谢谢,我喜欢绿色的那一个。

　　　　(B)好的,我在此已住了四十年。

　　　　(C)谢谢,但我对这附近地区不熟悉。

　　　　(D)不用了,谢谢! 我可以到达那儿,不会有问题的。

3. Joe：My leg is caught！Can you help me?

　　Sue：_____

　　(A)Let me see if I can move the desk.

　　(B)You might need to get some help.

　　(C)Why do you think I'd help you?

　　(D)Sure. Just do whatever you like to.

【答案】▶(A)

【译文】▶乔：我的腿卡住了！你能帮我吗?

　　苏：_____

　　(A)我看看是否能把桌子搬开。

　　(B)也许你需要帮忙。

　　(C)为什么你认为我愿意帮你?

　　(D)当然啰。你爱做什么就做什么。

【讲解】▶①sth. is caught　东西被卡(绊)住了

　　②"if"若引导名词从句,要解释为"是否"。

　　③Sure(美式)＝Surely(英式)

　　④whatever you like to (do)＝anything which you like to (do)

4. George's mother：Please remember to mail those letters for me on your way to school. (多选)

　　George：_____

　　(A)Certainly,Mom.

　　(B)Sure,you can count on me.

　　(C)But,Mom,it's Sunday today and I'm staying home!

　　(D)Yes,please,will you?

　　(E)But Father has already taken care of them.

【答案】▶(A)(B)(C)(E)

【译文】▶乔治的母亲：请你记得在上学途中帮我寄那几封信。

乔治：_____

　　(A)好的,妈妈。

　　(B)好的,包在我身上。

　　(C)但是,妈妈,今天是星期天,我要待在家里。

　　(D)好啊,请,好吗?

　　(E)但爸爸已将那些信寄了。

【讲解】▶(A)***Sure***(美式用法)***Surely***(英式用法)＝***Certainly***＝***Yes***

　　　(B)***count on***＝***rely on***"依赖"在此意译为"没问题"。

　　　(C)文意亦可。

　　　(D)答非所问。

　　　(E)***take care of*** 可以当"照料",但用于处理事情时 take care of 可翻译为"做过某事了"。

现场会话 实战复习测验 ⦿

1. John:　　　Hey, Taxi!

　Cabman:　Please get in. _____

　John:　　　Take me to the Beijing Hotel.

　Cabman:　Yes, sir.

　　(A)What are you doing?

　　(B)Are you all right, sir?

　　(C)Where to, sir?

　　(D)I'll do my best, sir.

2. X:I'd like to ask you to type a letter for me, if you don't mind.

　Y:_____

　　(A)I am glad you invited me.

　　(B)Yes, of course. Please do.

　　(C)What a splendid idea!

　　(D)It's a great honor to be of help.

3. John:Tom, would you mind watching the house this afternoon while I go golfing?

Tom：_____

  (A)Certainly. As you wish.

  (B)I'm sorry, but I promised Mary that I would help her with math.

  (C)Sure, I have to take this afternoon off.

  (D)Never mind.

4. Nora：_____

 Ruth：Certainly. Here you are.

  (A)Where am I now?

  (B)Would you please pass the pepper?

  (C)Would you like some more pizza?

  (D)Could you kindly give me some help with the problem?

5. Alison：Will you have a look at my car, please?

 Pam：_____

  (A)What's the matter with it?

  (B)Yes, you'd better.

  (C)Well, I'm not sure.

  (D)When will it be ready?

6. Mike：Could you pass me the soy sauce, please?

 Mother：_____

 Mike：Thank you.

  (A)Oh, what a shame!

  (B)I'm sorry to hear that.

  (C)Here you are.

  (D)That sounds like a good idea.

解题关键分析

1.【答案】▶(C)

 【译文】▶约翰：嘿，计程车！

     司机：请上车，_____

     约翰：到北京饭店。

司机:好的,先生。

　　(A)你在做什么?

　　(B)先生,你还好吧?

　　(C)先生,到哪儿?

　　(D)先生,我会尽全力的。

2.【答案】▶(D)

　　【译文】▶X:如果你不介意的话,我想请你帮我打封信。

　　　　　Y:_____

　　　　　(A)我很高兴你邀请了我。

　　　　　(B)当然可以了,请做吧。

　　　　　(C)多棒的主意呀!

　　　　　(D)能够帮忙是大大的荣幸。

3.【答案】▶(B)

　　【译文】▶约翰:汤姆,你介意今天下午我去打高尔夫球时帮我看家吗?

　　　　　汤姆:_____

　　　　　(A)当然,全听你的。

　　　　　(B)很抱歉,我已答应玛丽帮她解答数学。

　　　　　(C)好的,我今天下午请假。

　　　　　(D)没关系。

4.【答案】▶(B)

　　【译文】▶诺拉:_____

　　　　　露丝:当然。拿去吧!

　　　　　(A)这里是什么地方?

　　　　　(B)请把胡椒递过来好吗?

　　　　　(C)你想再要一点比萨吗?

　　　　　(D)你能不能帮我解决这个问题?

　　【讲解】▶*Here you are.* 这就是。(将物交给对方时用,强调对方。)

5.【答案】▶(A)

　　【译文】▶艾莉森:请你检查一下我的车子,好吗?

　　　　　潘:　　_____

（A)你的车子出了什么问题？

（B)是的,你最好检查。

（C)嗯,我不确定。

（D)何时会好？

6.【答案】▶(C)

　【译文】▶麦克:请你把酱油递给我好吗？

　　　　　母亲:_____

　　　　　麦克:谢谢。

　　　（A)喔,真可惜!

　　　（B)听到那件事,我很难过。

　　　（C)拿去吧。

　　　（D)那听起来似乎是个好主意。

Greeting
问 候

（一）

A: How are you?

B:
I'm fine, thank you.
Fine, thanks.
Quite well, thanks.
Very well, thank you.

甲: 你好吗？
乙: 不错，谢谢。

（二）

A: How
are you doing?
is your day going?
have you been lately?

B: Great, thanks.

甲: 最近过得怎么样啊？
乙: 很好，谢谢。

（三）

A:
What's happening?
How is it going?
How is everything with you?
How are things with you?

B:
Nothing much.
Not too much.
So so.

甲:（最近）过得怎么样啊？
乙: 马马虎虎。普通。

（四）

A: Happy(Glad, Nice, Good, Pleased, Pleasure) to meet you.
B: The pleasure is mine.

甲：很高兴见到你。
乙：这是我的荣幸。

（五）

A：I'm under the weather.

B：
| That's too bad. |
| I'm sorry to hear that. |
| I'm sorry. That's too bad. |

甲：我觉得不舒服。
乙：那真糟。

（六）

A：
| What's wrong(with you)? |
| What's the matter(with you)? |
| What happened(to you)? |

甲：你怎么啦？
乙：我感冒了。

B：I've caught a cold.

（七）

A：What's wrong?

B：I think I
| have a cold. |
| caught(a)cold. |

甲：怎么啦？
乙：我想我感冒了。

（八）

A：
| I don't feel well. |
| I feel under the weather. |

甲：我觉得不舒服。
乙：你需要看医生。

B：You need to see a doctor.

（九）

A：You're looking
| very well. |
| in great shape. |

B：Thanks. I try to keep in shape.

甲：你看起来很健康。
乙：谢谢，我试着保持身材。

■━━━━━━ ●活学活用● ━━━━━━

1. Julia：You look worried, Sam. What's the matter?

  Sam：My computer's broken down. I've no idea what's wrong with it.

  Julia：_____

  Sam：Of course, eventually. But I have a paper due tomorrow.

  (A)Can I help you?

  (B)Can I fix it for you now?

  (C)Can't you get it fixed?

  (D)What are you going to do?

【答案】▶(C)

【译文】▶朱莉娅：你看起来很烦恼，山姆。怎么回事？

  山姆： 我的电脑出故障了，我不知道毛病出在哪里。

  朱莉娅：_____

  山姆：当然，电脑终究是要修的。但是我明天就要交报告了。

  (A)我能帮你吗？

  (B)我可以帮你修理吗？

  (C)你不能送去修理吗？

  (D)你打算怎么办？

【讲解】▶①*break down* 故障

  ②*eventually* [i'ventjuəli] *adv.* 最后；终于

  ③*due* [dju:] *adv.* 预定的；到期的

  ④*get*＋宾语＋$\begin{cases} \textbf{\textit{P. P.}} \to 表示被动 \\ \textbf{\textit{V}}-\textbf{\textit{ing}} \to 表示主动 \end{cases}$

  而 it＝computer 是被修理，故用 fixed。

● 活学活用 ●

2. Sue： You look a little nervous. Is anything wrong?

David：_____

Sue： Don't worry about it. I'm sure you'll do well.

(A)My blood pressure is up.

(B)No. I'd better get going.

(C)I have a test in ten minutes.

(D)I just broke my father's vase.

【答案】▶(C)

【译文】▶苏： 你看来有点紧张。有什么不对劲吗？

大卫：_____

苏： 别担心。我相信你会考得不错。

(A)我的血压升高了。

(B)不。我最好现在就走。

(C)十分钟后，我有考试。

(D)我刚刚打碎我爸爸的花瓶。

【讲解】▶①大卫表示马上要考试，所以才显得紧张。

②*nervous* *adj.* 紧张的 ③*do well* 考得好

④*blood pressure* 血压

⑤*get going* 出发

● 活学活用 ●

3. Pat：Ow!

John：Are you OK?

Pat：_____ I hurt my ankle.

(A)Nothing serious.   (B)I'm fine.

(C)I don't know.   (D)I don't think so.

【答案】▶ (D)

【译文】▶帕特：喔！

约翰：你没事吧？

　　帕特：_____我的踝关节受伤了。
　　　　（A）没有什么严重。　　　（B）我很好。
　　　　（C）我不知道。　　　　　（D）我不认为如此。

【讲解】▶ ①帕特回话表示不认为没事，因为他伤到了脚踝。
　　　　②*ankle*　脚踝
　　　　③*Nothing serious*　没什么严重

━━━━━━━ ●活学活用● ━━━━━━━

4. A：I'm depressed. I just lost my new car.
　　B：_____
　　　（A）Guess what! You'll buy another.
　　　（B）I'm sorry to hear that.
　　　（C）I'd rather you bought a new car.
　　　（D）It is always nice to drive a new car.

【答案】▶（B）

【译文】▶ A：我好郁闷，我的新车刚刚丢了。
　　　　B：_____
　　　　　（A）你猜怎么样？你会再买一辆。
　　　　　（B）听到这件事，我真为你难过。
　　　　　（C）我宁愿你买一辆新车。
　　　　　（D）开新车总是很棒的。

━━━━━━━ ●活学活用● ━━━━━━━

5. A：Say, what do you think of your new work?
　　B：It's not bad, but the hours are long.
　　A：Oh,_____
　　　（A）that's really something!
　　　（B）how about that?
　　　（C）you'll soon get used to it.
　　　（D）you did it again.

【答案】▶（C）

【译文】▶A：嘿！你觉得你的新工作怎么样？

　　　　B：还不错，但工作时间长。

　　　　A：喔，＿＿＿＿＿＿＿

　　　　（A）那真是了不起！

　　　　（B）那怎么样啊！

　　　　（C）你很快就会习惯的。

　　　　（D）你又做到了。／你再次成功了。

【讲解】▶①B 回答他的工作不错，但抱怨工作时间长，因此 A 应用
　　　　答案（C）鼓励 B。

　　　　②*get used to...*　对……习惯

━━━━━━●*活学活用*●━━━━━━

6. Ted：You've been awfuly quiet lately. Is something wrong?

　Hal：＿＿＿＿＿＿＿

　　　（A）I hate to admit it，but you are right.

　　　（B）You're pulling my leg.

　　　（C）Let me think a while.

　　　（D）Do you know it by heart?

【答案】▶（A）

【译文】▶泰德：你最近极为沉默，有什么事不对劲吗？

　　　　海尔：＿＿＿＿＿＿＿

　　　　（A）我不想承认，但你说的没错。

　　　　（B）你在愚弄我。

　　　　（C）让我想一想。

　　　　（D）你牢记在心了吗？

【讲解】▶①*awfully　adv.*（口语）极为

　　　　Is something wrong? 出了什么问题吗？有什么不对劲
　　　　吗？

　　　　②（B）*pull one's leg*　愚弄某人

　　　　（D）*know it by heart*　牢记在心

● 活学活用 ●

7. John：What's the matter？ You really look down.

Jack：_____

John：Well，better luck next time.

(A)I always look up to you.

(B)What a strange coincidence！

(C)I failed an important test.

(D)Me？ I never look down upon you！

【答案】▶(C)

【译文】▶约翰：怎么啦？你看起来垂头丧气的。

杰克：_____

约翰：那么，祝你下回好运了。

(A)我向来都很尊敬你。

(B)多么奇怪的巧合啊！

(C)我有一次重要的考试没有及格。

(D)我？ 我从来没有看不起你啊！

【讲解】▶①*look down* 神情沮丧

②*look up to* 尊敬

③*coincidence* [kəu'insidəns] *n.* 巧合

④*fail(in)a test* 一次考试不及格

⑤*look down upon* 看轻；看不起

现场会话 实战复习测验 ●

1. Tom：Hello，Tony，I haven't seen you for a long time.

Tony：I've been ill.

Tom：_____

Tony：Yes，but I can't go back to school yet. I must have a holi-

day first.

(A) Are you better now?

(B) How are you?

(C) Sorry to hear that.

(D) I hope you get well soon.

2. A：Long time no see. How have you been?

B：I've been really well. As a matter of fact, my wife and I are expecting our first child.

A：_____

(A) Oh! Congratulations! I'm so happy for both of you.

(B) Good news! You have a wonderful time.

(C) Congratulations! Please make yourself comfortable.

(D) Don't worry, he'll be back safe and sound.

3. John：_____

Billy：Oh, I'm sorry to hear that. But cheer up! It's not the end of the world.

(A) I didn't quite catch what you said. There's a lot of noise outside.

(B) Why didn't you tell me the truth?

(C) Don't you think it'll be rainy tomorrow?

(D) I've failed my exams.

4. Mr. Smith：How's your father been?

Bob：_____

(A) He's a little under the weather.

(B) As a matter of fact, he had never been there.

(C) He has been to America.

(D) I will be out of work in a couple of days.

5. A：How's the world treating you?

B：_____

(A) Couldn't be better.

(B) It's a small world.

(C) It's a meal fit for a king.

(D) Have a nice day.

6. X：Good morning. Now what seems to be the matter?

　Y：_____

　X：I see. And have you got pains anywhere else?

　(A)I think I've got a slight fever.

　(B)This shirt is too small.

　(C)I have a terrible stomachache.

　(D)I just can't master English.

7. Sarah：Please remember me to him if you happen to see him.

　Jane：_____

　(A)That's right, I will.

　(B)As you know, I know him well enough to say hello to him.

　(C)OK, I will.

　(D)It's up to you.

解题关键分析

1.【答案】▶(A)

　【译文】▶汤姆：嗨，托尼，好久不见了。

　　　　　托尼：我病了。

　　　　　汤姆：_____

　　　　　托尼：是的，但我还无法回学校，我需要先休个假。

　　　　　(A)你现在好点了吗？

　　　　　(B)你好吗？

　　　　　(C)听到这个我很难过。

　　　　　(D)我希望你快点好起来。

2.【答案】▶(A)

　【译文】▶A：好久不见了，近来如何？

　　　　　B：我真的很好。事实上，我和我妻子正等着我们的第一个小孩出生呢。

　　　　　A：_____

　　　　　(A)喔，恭喜！我真是为你俩高兴。

(B)好消息！你有一段绝妙时光。

(C)恭喜！请让你们自己舒服自在。

(D)别担心，他会平安无恙地回来。

3.【答案】▶(D)

【译文】▶约翰：_____

比利：哦，真遗憾。不过振作起来，还没到世界末日。

(A)我不能完全听到你说的话，外面太吵了。

(B)你为什么不告诉我真相？

(C)你不认为明天会下雨吗？

(D)我考试失败了。

【讲解】▶①*fail (in) one's exam* 考试不及格

②*noise n.* 噪音

4.【答案】▶(A)

【译文】▶史密斯先生：你父亲好吗？

鲍伯：_____

(A)他有点不舒服。

(B)事实上，他从没到过那里。

(C)他去过美国。

(D)几天后，我将失业。

【讲解】▶①*under the weather*〔口〕身体不适的

②*out of work* 失业

5.【答案】▶(A)

【译文】▶A：你好吗？

B：再好不过了。

(A)再好不过了。

(B)这个世界真小。

(C)这顿饭棒极了。

(D)祝你今天过的愉快！

6.【答案】▶(C)

【译文】▶X：早安，怎么了？

Y：_____

X：原来如此。还有没有其他地方觉得疼痛？

　　　　(A)我想我有点发烧。

　　　　(B)这衬衫太小。

　　　　(C)我胃痛得很厉害。

　　　　(D)我就是无法精通英文。

7.【答案】▶(C)

　　【译文】▶莎拉:如果你有机看到他的话,帮我跟他问候一下。

　　　　　　简:　＿＿＿＿＿＿＿

　　　　(A)没错,我会的。

　　　　(B)诚如你所知,我跟他熟到可以说"哈罗"的地步。

　　　　(C)好,我会的。

　　　　(D)随便你。

Getting Directions
问　路

(一)
A：Where are we now?
B：I have no idea.

甲：这是什么地方？
乙：我不知道。

(二)
A：Excuse me. Where am I?
B：You are somewhere near the railway station.

甲：对不起，请问这是什么地方？
乙：这是火车站附近。

(三)
A：Excuse me. Can you tell me where I am?
I'm completely lost.
B：I'm sorry. I have no idea. I'm a stranger in town.
Ask the policeman over there.

甲：对不起。你能不能告诉我这是什么地方？我迷路了。
乙：抱歉，我不知道。我是外地人。问那边的警察好了。

(四)
A：Which way is to Hilton Hotel?
B：Go ahead this way and turn right at the first corner
and there it is. You can't miss it.

甲：到希尔顿饭店怎么走？
乙：从这条路向前走，在第一个街口向右转就到了。你一
定找得到。

（五）
- **A**：Excuse me. How do I get to the Palace Museum?
- **B**：You may take Trolley Bus No. 103.
- **A**：Thanks a lot.
- **B**：You're welcome.

- 甲：对不起，到故宫博物院怎么走？
- 乙：你可以搭乘 103 路无轨电车。
- 甲：多谢
- 乙：不客气。

（六）
- **A**：Where is the way out?
- **B**：Do you see a sign over there?　That's the exit.

- 甲：出口在哪儿？
- 乙：你看见那边的标示牌了吗？那就是出口。

1. ➡"问路"常用语句

①对不起，火车站怎么走啊？

Excuse me, but could（will）you tell（show, direct）me the way to the railway station?

Where is the railway station, please?

Could you tell me where the railway station is?

②你能告诉我在哪儿可以乘坐地铁吗？

Can you tell me where I can get on the subway?

③火车站离这儿有多远？

How far is it from here to the station?

④到那儿需要多长时间？

How long does it take to get there?

⑤对不起,去景山公园走这条路对吗?

Excuse me,but is this the right way to the Jingshan Park?

⑥哪条路是通往国家戏院的?

Which way is the National Theater,please?

⑦这条路通往哪里?

Where does this street go?

⑧它在哪层楼?

What floor is it on?

2. ➡"指示方向"常用语句

①沿着这条街走。Go along this street.

②在白石桥换车。Change at Baishiqiao.

③跟我走吧。Come along with me.

④请直走。Go straight on.

⑤它在左边。It's on the left.

⑥走路到火车站需要十分钟。

It's about ten minutes walk to the station.

⑦它在你左边第四间。It's the fourth room on your left.

⑧第一个红绿灯往右转。Turn right at the first traffic light.

⑨乘出租车去天津。Take a taxi for Tianjin.

⑩你不介意的话,我带你去。I'll take you there if you don't mind.

3. ➡其他

①对,没错。我要去那里,所以我可以带你去。

Yes,certainly. I'm going that way,so I'll show you.

②过那座桥,它在你右边,你不会错过。

Cross that bridge, you can't miss it on your right.

③这条路通往中关村。This street goes to Zhongguancun.

④我在这儿是外乡人。I'm a stranger here myself.

⑤我们到了。Here we are.

非常实战测验 ●────────

● 活学活用 ●

1. Carol：Sue, this is Carol. Please tell me how to get to your place.

　Sue：OK. You take bus No. 208 near your college and get off at the railway station, then take bus No. 301 heading north and get off at the Art Museum. Then you cross the street...

　Carol：Please speak slowly. ＿＿＿＿＿＿

　(A) I can't follow you.

　(B) I've no idea.

　(C) Mind your tongue.

　(D) Keep your temper.

1.【答案】▶(A)

【译文】▶凯露：苏,我是凯露。请告诉我,怎么样去你家。

　　　苏：　好的。你在你们学校那里搭乘 208 路公共汽车,然后在火车站下车,再搭乘往北的 301 路公共汽车,在美术馆下车,穿过马路……

　　　凯露：麻烦你说慢一点,＿＿＿＿＿＿

　　　(A)我跟不上。　　　(B)我不知道。

　　　(C)小心你说的话。　(D)管管你自己的脾气。

●活学活用●

2. Passenger A：Excuse me. Where can I get on the next train for Tianjin?

Passenger B：Platform 1，right here. _____ because I'm taking the same train.

(A) I hope you understand it，

(B) You'd better go early，

(C) I have no idea，

(D) There's no mistake about it，

【答案】▶(D)

【译文】▶乘客 A：对不起，到天津的下一班火车，要在哪里搭乘？

乘客 B：一号月台，就在这里。_____ 因为我是搭同一班火车。

(A) 我希望你了解，

(B) 你最好早点去，

(C) 我不知道，

(D) 不会错的，

【讲解】▶*platform* ['plætfɔ:m] *n.* 月台

There is no mistake about it. 不会错的。这是确实的。

＝There is no doubt about it. ＝I am quite certain about it.

●活学活用●

3. Man A：Maybe I could show you the way.

Man B：_____

(A) Oh，thanks. I like the green one.

(B) Yes. I've lived here for years.

(C) Thanks，but I'm not familiar with this neighborhood.

(D) No，thanks. I can get there all right.

【答案】▶(D)

【译文】▶甲：也许我可以告诉你怎么走。

　　乙：_____

　　　　(A)哦,谢谢。我喜欢那个绿的。

　　　　(B)是的。我已在这住了几年了。

　　　　(C)谢谢,但这附近我不熟悉。

　　　　(D)不用了,谢谢,我自己会走。

【讲解】▶ ①*be familiar with*　熟悉

　　　　②*neighborhood* ['neibəhud] *n*. 邻近地区

　　　　③*get there*　到达那里

　　　　④*all right*　没问题

═══════ ●活学活用● ═══════

4. Wayne：Could you tell me where Wangfujing Street is?

　　Sam：_____

　　(A)I'm going downtown with two friends.

　　(B)A pay phone is near here.

　　(C)Yes,it's three twenty-five.

　　(D) Go straight ahead for two blocks and then turn right.

【答案】▶ (D)

【译文】▶ 韦恩:能不能请你告诉我王府井步行街在哪儿?

　　　　山姆：_____

　　　　(A)我和两个朋友正要去市中心。

　　　　(B)这附近有公用电话。

　　　　(C)是的。现在是 3 点 25 分。

　　　　(D)往前直走两个街口然后右转。

【讲解】▶ ①*pay phone* ＝public phone　公用电话

　　　　②*go straight ahead*　往前直走

　　　　③*block* [blɔk] *n*.市街的一区

　　　　④(A)(B)(C)答非所问,只有(D)符合文意。

●活学活用●

5. Paul： How can I get to the Palace Museum from here?

　　David：You can take No. 103 bus in front of our school.

　　Paul： How often does the bus leave for the museum?

　　David：_____

　　　(A)Early in the morning.

　　　(B)In an hour.

　　　(C)Ten minutes later.

　　　(D)Every half an hour.

【答案】▶(D)

【译文】▶保罗：由这里到故宫博物院怎么走？

　　　　大卫：你可以在我学校门口搭乘 103 路无轨电车。

　　　　保罗：多久开往博物院一班？

　　　　大卫：_____

　　　　　(A)清晨。　　　　　　　(B)一小时之内。

　　　　　(C)十分钟以后。　　　　(D)每半小时。

【讲解】▶①*How can I get to*　我要用什么方式去……

　　　　②*Palace Museum*　故宫博物院

　　　　③*in front of*　在……的前面

　　　　④*How often*　多久；多频繁

●活学活用●

6. Mel：Excuse me. I'm a little bit lost. Can you help me?

　　Lan：_____

　　　(A)Don't mention it.

　　　(B)I expect you can tell me what to do next.

　　　(C)Where are you trying to get to?

　　　(D)I don't see why you can't.

【答案】▶(C)

【译文】▶梅尔：对不起，我有点迷路了，你能帮个忙吗？

兰：　_____

(A)别客气。

(B)希望你能告诉我接着要做什么。

(C)你要到哪里去？

(D)我不了解为什么你不能。

【讲解】▶ ①*be lost*　迷路

②*a little bit*　一点点

③(A)*Don't mention it.* = Not at all. = You are welcome. = Not a bit. 别客气。(C)*get to*　到达

现场会话　实战复习测验 ●

1. Stranger：　Excuse me. How can I get to Kraft Street?

Policeman：　_____ You can't miss it.

(A)No, this doesn't look right.

(B)I hope not.

(C)Go straight and turn at the light.

(D)You are on the wrong way.

2. A：Excuse me. Could you tell me how to get to the Confucian Temple?

B：Of course. Turn left, walk one block and turn right again. Then _____

A：I see. Thank you.

(A)you can't omit it.

(B)you can't fail it.

(C)you can't lose it.

(D)you can't miss it.

3. Mort：　Excuse me, officer, can you tell us how we get to the post office?

Officer：Go straight ahead three blocks, turn right, walk...

Sid：　　Not so fast, please, officer. _____

(A) We don't speak English.

(B) We haven't been there.

(C) We're strangers here.

(D) We walk slowly.

4. Mary: Excuse me, could you tell me the way to the nearest post office?

John: I'm a stranger here myself. That gentleman over there might be able to help you.

Mary: _____

(A) That's a shame.

(B) Never mind.

(C) Thank you very much indeed.

(D) Thank you all the same.

5. Mary: Let me show you the way to the hall.

John: _____

(A) You are welcome.

(B) Yes, let's.

(C) That's right.

(D) That's very nice of you.

6. Sid: Let's face it. We're lost.

Mort: _____ Sid. All we have to do is to ask.

(A) Don't be silly,

(B) What should we do?

(C) Anything you say.

(D) You are in bad luck.

7. Officer: Sorry. Walk to the first traffic light, then turn left.

_____

(A) You can't miss it.　　　(B) You can't lose it.

(C) Here it is.　　　(D) Here you are.

8. Old man: Excuse me. I'm going to Haidian. Which bus should I take?

Girl: _____

Old man：Yes，but I forget to take my glasses with me.

Girl：　Then the only thing that I can do is to take you to the bus because there are so many buses. Follow me，please.

Old man：Thanks. You're such a nice girl.

(A)Ask the policeman on your left side.

(B)Sorry，I don't know.

(C)Can you read?

(D)You're not a stranger，I suppose.

解题关键分析

1.【答案】▶(C)

【译文】▶陌生人：请问一下，卡福特街怎么走？

　　　警察：_____ 你就会找到。

　　　(A)不，这看起来不对。

　　　(B)我不希望这样。

　　　(C)一直走到红绿灯再转弯。

　　　(D)你走错了。

2.【答案】▶(D)

【译文】▶A：对不起，你能不能告诉我孔庙怎么走？

　　　B：当然可以。向左转，走过一个街区，再向右转。这样，_____

　　　A：我知道了，谢谢。

　　　(A)你不会把它错过的。

　　　(B)你不会做不到的。

　　　(C)你不会把它丢掉的。

　　　(D)你不会找不到的。

【讲解】▶**Confucian** [kən'fjuːʃn] *adj.* 孔子的

3.【答案】▶(C)

【译文】▶莫特：打扰一下，长官，你可不可以告诉我们如何到达邮局？

警官:往前直走三个街口,右转,再走……

思德:警官,拜托不要讲这么快。_____。

(A)我们不会讲英语。

(B)我们没来过这儿。

(C)我们是外地来的。

(D)我们走得慢。

4.【答案】▶(D)

【译文】▶玛丽:对不起,你能告诉我最近的邮局怎么走吗?

约翰:我对这里也很陌生。那边那位男士或许可以帮你。

玛丽:_____

(A)真可耻。　　　　(B)没关系。

(C)真是非常谢谢你。　(D)还是要谢谢你。

5.【答案】▶(D)

【译文】▶玛丽:我来告诉你去大厅的路。

约翰:_____

(A)不客气。　　(B)是的,我们就这么做吧。

(C)对了。　　　(D)你真好。

6.【答案】▶(A)

【译文】▶思德:让我们面对事实吧! 我们迷路了。

莫特:_____,思德。我们必须做的只是问而已。

(A)别傻了。

(B)我们该怎么办?

(C)都是你说的。

(D)你运气真坏。

7.【答案】▶(A)

【译文】▶警官:抱歉。走到第一个交通信号灯,然后左转,_____。

(A)你就不会走错了。

(B)你不会迷路。

(C)就到了。

(D)你就到了。

8.【答案】▶(C)

　　【译文】▶老人:对不起,我要去海淀,该乘哪一路公共汽车?

　　　　　　女孩:＿＿＿＿＿＿＿＿

　　　　　　老人:是的,可是我忘记带眼镜了。

　　　　　　女孩:那么,我唯一能做的,就是带你去坐公共汽车,因
　　　　　　　　　为这儿的公共汽车太多了。请跟我来。

　　　　　　老人:谢谢。你真是个好女孩。

　　　　　　(A)问问你左手边那个警察。

　　　　　　(B)抱歉,我不知道。

　　　　　　(C)你识字吗?

　　　　　　(D)我想你不是个陌生人吧!

Admiring and Congratulating
赞美与祝贺

第**9**篇

情景对话精选

(一)
A：That's a pretty sweater you are on.
B：Thanks a lot.

甲：你穿的毛衣很漂亮。
乙：多谢。

(二)
A：I just passed the exam.
B：Congratulations.

甲：我刚刚通过考试。
乙：恭喜你。

(三)
A：Merry Christmas.
B：The same to you.

甲：圣诞快乐。
乙：你也一样。

(四)
A：What a handsome boy you are!
B：I am flattered.

甲：你好帅喔！
乙：我受宠若惊。

(五)
A：You are a good husband.
B：Thank you.

甲：你是好丈夫。
乙：谢谢。

(六)
A：Happy Birthday, Mary.
B：Thank you, you are so sweet.

甲：玛丽，生日快乐。
乙：谢谢你，你人真好。

● 活学活用 ●

1. Paul：I've just passed my college entrance exam.

　　David：_____

　　Paul：I feel so relieved now.

　　(A) Well done!　　　(B) What a pity!

　　(C) How awful!　　　(D) Cheer up!

【答案】▶ (A)

【译文】▶ 保罗：我刚刚通过大学入学考试。

　　　　大卫：_____

　　　　保罗：我现在感觉很轻松。

　　　　(A) 做得好!　　　　(B) 真可惜!

　　　　(C) 真可怕!　　　　(D) 振作起来!

【讲解】▶ ①*relieve* [ri'li:v] *v.*　松一口气;使放心

　　　　②*Well done.*　做得好!（用于对别人成功或完成任务、工作时的赞叹。）

　　　　　　= Good job. = Good work. = Good show. = You did very well.

　　　　③*well-done*　*adj.*　完全煮熟的;做得好的;效果好的

● 活学活用 ●

2. Sue：Frank and I are going to get married.

　　Jane：That's wonderful!　_____

　　Sue：I am so excited.

　　(A) Congratulations!

　　(B) How's it going?

　　(C) How do you feel now?

　　(D) You have just known Frank for a month.

【答案】▶(A)

【译文】▶苏:弗兰克和我要结婚了。

简:太好了!_____

苏:我很兴奋。

(A)恭喜!

(B)(事情)进行的怎么样?

(C)你现在觉得如何?

(D)你认识弗兰克才一个月。

【讲解】▶①*Congratulations* 恭喜!

②*How is it going*?事情进行的如何?

③*How do you feel now*?你觉得如何(通常用来指健康状况)

● 活学活用 ●

3. Hal:Those Smith children certainly raised a few eyebrows at the dinner party last night.

Alf:_____

(A)Quite so.

(B)We don't often meet such well-behaved children these days.

(C)Television has damaged their eyes.

(D)They've been taught to keep their eye on the ball.

【答案】▶(A)

【译文】▶哈尔:史密斯家的孩子们在昨天晚上的宴会中,还真令人吃惊呢!

阿尔夫:_____

(A)的确如此。

(B)近来我们很少看见那么乖的孩子了。

(C)电视伤害了他们的眼睛。

(D)人家教他们要盯着那个球看。

【讲解】▶①*eyebrow* [ˈaibrau]*n.* 眉毛　*raise eyebrows* 使他人吃

惊

②*quite*(*so*)　的确如此

③*well-behaved* [welbi'heiv] *adj.* 循规蹈矩的

===== ●活学活用● =====

4. Mary：He's such a great acrobat！

　　John：Never _____ that I know done anything like that.

　　(A)can someone　　　(B)will someone

　　(C)has anyone　　　(D)will anyone

【答案】▶(C)

【译文】▶玛丽：他是个多么了不起的特技表演者啊！

　　　　约翰：我所认识的人中，从来没有一个人做过那样的事。

【讲解】▶①本题考的句型是"否定副词＋倒装句"，表示强调。

　　例：❶Never have I met such a strange person.

　　　　（我从来没遇见过这么奇怪的人。）

　　　　❷Hardly had he reached there, when it began to snow.

　　　　（他刚一到达那里，就下雪了。）

　　②本题选(C)*has anyone* 是因为说话者当时所说的是目前的经验，所以要用现在完成时 has done。

　　③*acrobat* ['ækrəbæt] *n.* 高空特技表演者；走绳索者

现场会话　实战复习测验 ●

1. Jack：　Happy birthday！

　Maria：Thanks. This is a wonderful surprise.

　Jack：　Were you really surprised？

　Maria：Don't I look at it？

　Jack：　Yeah, you do. I wish I had my camera so I could take your picture.

Maria：Like this? _____

(A)Give me a break.

(B)Mind your own business,will you?

(C)It depends.

(D)After you.

2.Jane：Do I look all right?

Gurt：_____you always do to me.

(A)You are like a fashion model；

(B)You are beautiful；

(C)Your beauty is beyond description；

(D)More than all right；

3.Mr. Wang：You look handsome in that shirt,Mr. Lee.（多选）

Mr. Lee： _____

(A)Am I?

(B)Nothing doing.

(C)Thanks for the compliment.

(D)It's very kind of you to say so.

(E)Where,where.

4.J：How marvelous you look in that blouse,Mary!

M：_____

(A)Am I?

(B)Why not look in the mirror yourself?

(C)Thanks for the compliment.

(D)Oh,it's nothing.

5.A：You don't look your age.

B：_____

(A)Whatever you say.

(B)I feel flattered.

(C)It's unfair.

(D)It's hard to say.

6.Mr. Wang：My wife has just given birth to a baby son.

Mr. Lin：_____

(A)Happy birthday to here and many happy returns.

(B)Congratulations. When will you leave?

(C)You look all right.

(D)Congratulations to you.

7. Alex：Happy New Year!

　Barbara：_____

(A)Same here!

(B)The same to you!

(C)All the same!

(D)It's the same with you!

8. Mary：My father quit smoking a few months ago.

　Jane：_____ I wish my dad could do that，too.

(A)Good for him.　　　　(B)Don't worry.

(C)I'm very grateful.　　(D)Never mind.

解题关键分析

1.【答案】▶(A)

　【译文】▶杰克：生日快乐!

　　　　　玛丽亚：谢谢。真是太意外了。

　　　　　杰克：　你真的感到意外吗?

　　　　　玛丽亚：我看起来不是吗?

　　　　　杰克：　是呀,你看起来是。真希望有照相机,那我就

　　　　　　　　　可以为你照张相。

　　　　　玛丽亚：像这样?　_____

　　　　　　(A)饶了我吧。(口语)

　　　　　　(B)别管闲事。

　　　　　　(C)要看情况了。

　　　　　　(D)随便你。

2.【答案】▶(D)

　【译文】▶简：　我看起来还好吧?

　　　　　格特：_____对我来说,你总是如此。

(A)你就像个时装模特儿；

(B)你很漂亮；

(C)你美丽得难以形容；

(D)再好不过了；

【讲解】▶You always do to me. 由 You always look more than all right to me. 简化而来。

3.【答案】▶(C)(D)

【译文】▶王先生:李先生,你穿那件衬衫真好看。

李先生:_____

(A)是吗?（应改为 Do I?)

(B)糟了!

(C)谢谢你的赞美。

(D)谢谢你这么说。

(E)哪里,哪里。（无此说法）

【讲解】▶*nothing doing*〔口〕糟了;不行

compliment ['kɔmplimənt] *n.* 称赞

4.【答案】▶(C)

【译文】▶J: 玛丽,你穿那件衬衫真好看!

M: _____。

(A)是吗?

(B)为什么你不照照镜子?

(C)谢谢恭维。

(D)噢,没什么。

5.【答案】▶(B)

【译文】▶A:你看起来年轻多了。

B:_____。

(A)你说的对。

(B)我受宠若惊。

(C)这不公平。

(D)很难说。

6.【答案】▶(D)

【译文】▶王先生:我太太刚生了一个男婴。

　　　　　林先生：_____。

　　　　　　　(A)生日快乐,一切都快乐。

　　　　　　　(B)恭喜。你什么时候走?

　　　　　　　(C)你看起来不错。

　　　　　　　(D)恭喜你。

7.【答案】▶(B)

　【译文】▶亚历克斯:新年快乐!

　　　　　芭芭拉:_____。

　　　　　　　(A)我也一样。

　　　　　　　(B)你也一样。

　　　　　　　(C)都一样。

　　　　　　　(D)和你一样。

8.【答案】▶(A)

　【译文】▶玛丽:我爸爸几个月前戒烟了。

　　　　　简: _____。我希望我爸也能戒烟。

　　　　　　　(A)真好。

　　　　　　　(B)别担心。

　　　　　　　(C)我非常感激。

　　　　　　　(D)没关系。

At the Restaurant
在餐厅中

㊀

A：May I take your order, sir?

B：Two coffees, please.

A：How would you like your coffee?

B：I'd like it ice cold.

C：Same here.

甲：先生，请问点什么？

乙：两杯咖啡。

甲：您要怎样的咖啡？

乙：我要冰咖啡。

丙：我也一样。

㊁

A：How would you like your coffee?

B：Black, please.

C：With cream but no sugar, please.

甲：您要怎样的咖啡？

乙：纯咖啡。

丙：加奶但不加糖。

㈢
A：What would you like to have?

B：I'd like to have steak.

A：How would you like your steak?

B：Well done，please.

C：Rare，please.

甲：你要吃什么？

乙：我要吃牛排。

甲：您的牛排要几分熟的？

乙：全熟的。

丙：五分熟的。

㈣
A：How would you like your egg?

B：Scrambled，please.

C：Hard-boiled，please.

D：Soft-boiled，please.

甲：您要吃怎样的蛋？

乙：炒的。

丙：煮全熟的。

丁：煮半熟的。

㈤
A：I'd like to see the menu，please.

B：Here you are，sir.

甲：请拿菜单给我看。

乙：先生，菜单在这儿。

㈥
A：Say when?

B：That's enough. Thank you.

甲：够了时请说一声。（服务生倒饮料时）
乙：够了。谢谢。

（七）
A：Can I order takeout here?
B：Yes，sir.

甲：我可以在这里订购外卖的食物吗？
乙：可以的，先生。

（八）
A：Check，please. /May I see(meet)my check?
B：Here you are，sir.

甲：请帮我结账。
乙：先生，您的账单在这儿。

"在饭馆中"常用语句

①你要吃什么？May I take(have)your order?
你要喝什么？What would you like to have(drink)?
你要吃什么甜点？What would you like for dessert?
对不起，我们没卖通心粉。I'm sorry we don't have spaghetti.
请先买餐券。Please buy your meal tickets first.
②菜单给我好吗？May I have a menu，please? /Let me have the menu，please? /Will you show me the menu，please?
请给我牛排。I'll have a steak. /Please bring me some steak.
你的牛排要怎样吃？How would you like your steak? / How do you want your steak?
半生熟，（全熟）。
Rare(Well-done)，please.

你的咖啡要怎么喝？ How would you like your coffee?

我要不加糖和奶的。 I like my coffee black.

③请在出纳那儿付账。 Please pay at the cashier's desk.

账单给我。 Bill(Check), please.

你可以给我三人坐的坐位吗？ Do you have a table for three?

我可以和你坐吗？ Would you mind sharing a table?

请将盐给我？ Will you pass me the salt, please?

非常实战测验

●活学活用●

1. Waiter：Are you ready to order?

　Jim：＿＿＿＿＿

　　(A) Yes. Everything's fine.

　　(B) Yes. Could I have the check please?

　　(C) Come back in a few minutes.

　　(D) I haven't decided yet.

【答案】▶ (D)

【译文】▶ 侍者：您准备好点菜了吗？

　　　　吉姆：＿＿＿＿＿

　　　　　　(A)是的。一切顺利。　(B)是的。请给我账单好吗？

　　　　　　(C)几分钟后回来。　　(D)我还没决定。

【讲解】▶ ①*ready to order*　准备点菜

　　　　②*Everything is fine.*　一切顺利。

　　　　③*have the check*　拿账单

● 活学活用 ●

2. Attendant：Yes，madam？

Customer：I want a hamburger and a cup of Coke.

Attendant：_____

Customer：Yes.

(A)Will that be all?   (B)Do you like it?

(C)What's next?   (D)What do you think of it?

【答案】▶(A)

【译文】▶侍者：什么事，女士？

顾客：我要一个汉堡和一杯可乐。

侍者：_____

顾客：是的。

(A)就这些吗？   (B)你喜欢它吗？

(C)再来呢？   (D)你认为它如何？

● 活学活用 ●

3. Judy：Jane，would you like some more salad？

Jane：_____

Judy：Here you are.

(A)Yes，please. It looks very delicious.

(B)Thank you. I've had plenty of it.

(C)Yes，please. It's really delicious.

(D)Thanks. But I really can't.

【答案】▶(C)

【译文】▶朱蒂：简，要再来点沙拉吗？

简：_____

朱蒂：来吧，给你。

(A)好的，请(拿给我)，看起来很好吃。

(B)谢谢你，我已经吃很多了。

(C)好的，请(拿给我)，真的很好吃。

(D)谢谢你,我真的吃不下了。

【讲解】▶①根据第三句(Judy 的回答)可知 Jane 还有吃沙拉的意愿,故(B)、(D)不对。

②根据第一句(some more salad)可知 Jane 已吃过沙拉,故答案(A)的"looks"应改为"tastes"才合适。

━━━━━━ ●活学活用● ━━━━━━

4. Waiter： How'd you like your steak done?

Customer：_____

　(A)Oh, great.

　(B)What a terrible meal!

　(C)Don't mention it.

　(D)Well-done.

【答案】▶(D)

【译文】▶侍者:你的牛排要几分熟?

　　　　客人:_____

　　　　　(A)哇,太棒了。　　　　(B)真糟的一餐。

　　　　　(C)不客气。　　　　　　(D)全熟。

【讲解】▶①*How would*〔*do*〕*you like*＋食物? 常用来询问他人有关食物的吃法。

②牛排的吃法如下:*well-done* 全熟,*medium* 七分熟,*rare* 或 *underdone* 半熟。

━━━━━━ ●活学活用● ━━━━━━

5. Jean： Can you pass me the potatoes?

Mother：_____

　(A)Sorry, they are too heavy for me to carry.

　(B)Sorry, they don't taste good.

　(C)Don't you think they are delicious?

　(D)Don't you think you've had enough?

【答案】▶(D)

【译文】▶ 简： 把马铃薯递给我好吗？

母亲：_____

(A)抱歉，它们太重了，我无法携带。

(B)抱歉，它们不好吃。

(C)你不觉得它们好吃吗？

(D)你不觉得你已经吃饱了吗？

现场会话 实战复习测验 ●

1. Waiter： May I take your order now?

   Customer：_____

   Waiter： OK. I'll come back in a few minutes.

   (A)No, not yet. We need more time.

   (B)Could you bring us the bill?

   (C)Yes, we would love to.

   (D)This is not what I ordered.

2. Customer：May I see the menu, please?

   Waiter：_____

   (A)Yes, what is it?

   (B)Here you are, sir.

   (C)No, you mustn't.

   (D)No, you needn't.

3. A：Susan, would you like some more rice noodles?

   B：_____

   A：Here you are.

   (A)Yes, please. They look very delicious.

   (B)Thank you. I'm stuffed to death.

   (C)Yes, please. They're really delicious.

   (D)Thanks. But I really can't.

4. Host：What would you like to have?

   Guest：_____

(A) A towel, please.

(B) Lemonade, please.

(C) Stationery, please.

(D) An order of scrambled eggs, please.

5. A: I don't feel like eating at home tonight. Let's go out for dinner.

B: OK, but I don't want to go to a fast-food place.

A: _____

B: Wonderful! Will you call up to reserve a table?

(A) Yes, thank you. I'll have some seafood.

(B) Why not go to a Chinese restaurant?

(C) Let's ask someone about the restaurant first.

(D) I'm tired of hamburger and fried chicken.

(E) American food is not really to my taste.

6. Waiter: How do you like your steak?

Jane: _____

(A) On the rocks.   (B) All right.

(C) Straight.   (D) Well-done.

7. A: Would you like some turkey?

B: No, thanks.

A: Why not? Don't you like turkey?

B: _____

(A) No, I don't. But I'm full.

(B) Yes, I do. But I'd rather have beef.

(C) Yes, I don't. And I think deer is a better choice.

(D) No, I do. And on second thoughts, I like some now.

8. A: Have some more hot-dogs, will you?

B: _____

(A) I've had plenty.

(B) Yes, thank you.

(C) No, thanks.

(D) Help yourself.

9. A：You are going to have dessert，aren't you?

   B：_____

   （A）Yes，I am full.

   （B）I'll have a sirloin steak，medium rare.

   （C）Black tea with two lumps of sugar，please.

   （D）Sure，the apple pie looks delicious.

解题关键分析

1.【答案】▶（A）

　【译文】▶侍者：您现在要点菜了吗?

　　　　　顾客：_____

　　　　　侍者：好的，我几分钟后再过来

　　　　　（A）不，还没，我们需要点时间。

　　　　　（B）你可以把账单给我们吗?

　　　　　（C）是的，我们很乐意。

　　　　　（D）这不是我点的。

2.【答案】▶（B）

　【译文】▶顾客：我可以看看菜单吗?

　　　　　侍者：_____

　　　　　（A）是的，这是什么?

　　　　　（B）先生，菜单在这里。

　　　　　（C）不，你不可以。

　　　　　（D）不，你不需要。

3.【答案】▶（C）

　【译文】▶A：苏珊，你还要再吃点米粉吗?

　　　　　B：_____

　　　　　A：喏，给你。

　　　　　（A）要，谢谢。看起来很好吃。

　　　　　（B）谢谢，我撑死了。（应改为 Thank you. I'm star-

　　　　　　　ving to death. 我饿死了。）

　　　　　（C）要，谢谢。真的很好吃。

(D)谢谢,但我真的不能。

【讲解】▶①*be stuffed to death*　吃的太饱,快撑死了

②*Would you like...*？＝Do you want...？肯定的回
答通常用 Yes,please. 否定的回答用 No,thanks。

4.【答案】▶(B)

【译文】▶主人:你想喝点什么?

客人:_____

(A)一条毛巾,请。

(B)柠檬水,请。

(C)文具,请。

(D)一份炒蛋。(order 指所点的(一份)食物。)

5.【答案】▶(B)

【译文】▶A:今晚我不想在家吃。我们到外面吃晚餐吧!

B:好,但我不想去快餐店。

A:_____

B:太棒了! 你要打电话订位子吗?

(A)是的,谢谢。我要吃点海产。

(B)为什么不去中国餐馆呢?

(C)我们先问问别人对于这家餐厅的看法吧!

(D)我吃腻了汉堡和炸鸡。

(E)美国食物不怎么合我的口味。

【讲解】▶*to one's taste*　合某人口味

6.【答案】▶(D)全熟的

【译文】▶侍者:您的牛排要几分熟的?

简:_____

(A)在石头上。

(B)好吧。

(C)直的。

(D)全熟的。

7.【答案】▶(B)

【译文】▶A:你要吃火鸡吗?

B:不用了,谢谢。

A：为什么不吃呢？难道你不喜欢火鸡肉？

B：＿＿＿＿＿

(A)对,我不喜欢火鸡肉。但是我吃饱了。

(B)不是的,我很喜欢吃火鸡。但是我更爱吃牛肉。

(C)不是的,我不喜欢火鸡肉。我认为吃鹿肉更好。

(D)对,我喜欢吃火鸡肉。而且我想了一下,我现在就要吃。

8.【答案】▶(C)

【译文】▶A：再吃一点热狗吧!

B：＿＿＿＿＿

(A)我已经吃很多了。

(B)谢谢你。

(C)不了,谢谢。

(D)(不要客气)请随便用。

9.【答案】▶(C)

【译文】▶A：你要吃点心,对不对?

B：＿＿＿＿＿

(A)对,我已经饱了。

(B)我要一份沙朗牛排,半熟的。

(C)请给我一杯纯咖啡,加两匙的糖。

(D)没错,那个苹果派看起来很好吃。

Social Gatherings
社交场合

一
┌ **A**：Hello，Eleanor，this is Sarah Allen.
└ **B**：Hello，Sarah. Did you receive the invitation?

┌ 甲：喂，埃莉诺，我是莎拉·艾伦。
└ 乙：喂，莎拉。你接到我的请帖了吗？

二
┌ **A**：Yes，that's what I'm calling about. Is it okay if John and I
│   are a little late？ John's out of town this week，but he'll be
│   getting in about at 6：00 or 6：30. Friday night. Then he'll
│   probably want to take a shower. . . .
└ **B**：Well，don't rush him. Come over when you can.

┌ 甲：接到了，我打电话就是为了这件事。我和约翰迟到
│   一下有关系吗？ 约翰到外地出差了，周五晚上六点
│   或六点半左右会回来。他回来后可能会冲个澡……
└ 乙：哦，不要催他，弄好了再来。

三
┌ **A**：Should we dress up？
└ **B**：No，just dress casually. In fact，why don't you plan to
│   stay for supper？

┌ 甲：我们该穿正式的服装吗？
└ 乙：不必了。穿便服就可以了。说实在的，你们晚上干
│   脆留在我家吃晚饭好了。

（四）
A：Ken，would you do me a favor?
B：Sure. What?

甲：肯，请你帮个忙好吗？
乙：好啊。帮什么忙？

（五）
A：My zipper is tuck....
B：Oh! Somebody's here already. I just heard doorbell.

甲：我的拉链卡住了……
乙：噢！有人来了。我刚听到门铃的声音。

（六）
A：Go and let them in. I'll be down in a minute.

B：Hello，Virginia and Frank!Won't you come in，please，Eleanor will be down in a minute.

C：Oh，we're the first ones here. Is there anything I can do to help?

B：Yes，Virginia. You can help Eleanor. The zipper on her dress is stuck....

A：How are things going，Frank?

D：Things have settled down a lot since our daughter's marriage.

甲：去开门让他们进来。我一会儿就下来。

乙：嗨，弗吉尼亚和弗兰克!请进!埃莉诺马上下来。

丙：噢，我们是最先到的。有什么事需要我帮忙吗？

乙：有的，弗吉尼亚。你可以帮埃莉诺。她衣服上的拉链卡住了……

甲：弗兰克，最近好吗？

丁：自从忙完我女儿的婚礼，就没有什么事了。

（七）
A：How are things at work?

B：Some of the employees were laid off last week.

A：Oh，I'm sorry to hear that.

甲：最近你工作做的怎么样？

乙：上周有几个员工被解雇了。

甲：噢！真不幸。

A：Come on in, Sarah and John. It's nice to see you again.

B：You're looking well, Ken. How are things going?

A：Fine, and you? May I get you a drink? What would you like? Orange juice, 7-up, wine. . . .

C：I'd love an orange juice.

A：With or without ice cubes?

C：With, please.

甲：萨拉和约翰，进来啊！见到你们真高兴。

乙：肯，你气色很好。一切好吗？

甲：很好，你呢？我帮你弄杯饮料。你要喝什么？橘子汁、七喜、甜酒……

丙：我要橘子汁。

甲：要不要加冰块？

丙：要，谢谢你。

A：How have you been, John? I heard you were out of Nanjing this week.

B：Yes, I just got in from Wuhan. It's really hot at this time of year. It makes me thirsty just thinking about it. I'd like whisky on rocks.

甲：约翰，最近好吗？听说这星期你出差，不在南京。

乙：是啊。我刚从武汉回来。这时候那边真热。一想起来就口渴。我要威士忌加冰。

"友人来访"常用的语句

①请进。Do come in!

请走这边。Come this way, please.

请穿上拖鞋。Please put on these slippers.

请把外套给我。May I have your coat?

请脱鞋。Please take off your shoes.

②请不要拘束。

Please make yourself at home/comfortable.

请坐。Please be seated.

③邀请客人吃(喝)常用语句:

❶Please help yourself.

❷Would you like to have some tea?

❸Would you like a cup of coffee?

❹Will you have something to drink?

❺Won't you have some more tea? Yes, thank you.

(No, thank you.)

④我不知道天色那么晚了。

I didn't know it was getting this late.

恐怕占用你太多时间。

I'm afraid I've taken too much of your time.

我玩得很高兴。

I've had a very good time.

谢谢你让我度过那么美好的夜晚。

Thank you very much for the pleasant evening.

你不能多坐一会吗?

❶Can't you stay a little longer? It's nice of you to come.

❷It was nice to have you this evening; come on! At least

have on for the road!

⑤问候他人常用语句：

❶代我向你的家人问好。

Please remember me to your family.

❷代我向你的妻子表示最真挚的祝福。

Please give my best wishes (compliments) (regards) to your wife.

❸你家人都好吗？ How is your family?

⑥布朗先生在家吗？ Is Mr. Brown at home?

他出去了。He's out.

⑦"问洗手间"常用语句：

❶Excuse me, but where can I wash my hands?

❷Excause me, but where's the lavatory?

⑧我和汤姆有约。I have an appointment with Tom.

我待会儿再打电话。I'll call again later.

非 常实战测验

● 活学活用 ●

1. Passenger 1：Would you please stop smoking? This is a nonsmoking area.

Passenger 2：I'm sorry. _____

(A) I didn't notice it.

(B) You're being rather rude.

(C) Do you mean it?

(D) Don't you think so?

【答案】▶ (A)

【译文】▶ 旅客一：你能不吸烟吗？ 这里是禁烟区。

旅客二:抱歉。_____

    (A)我没注意到。   (B)你实在相当粗鲁。

    (C)你当真吗?   (D)你不这样认为吗?

【讲解】▶答案(B)说明人的某种品格时,常用进行时。如:You're being to kind.

● 活学活用 ●

2. A:Would you like some more chicken?

   B:Yes,please. It's really delicious.

   A:Well,I'm glad you like it. How about some more rice?

   B:_____

    (A)How nice! I'd like some more dessert.

    (B)Thanks for the compliment.

    (C)No,thanks. I'm already too full.

    (D)Many thanks. I can't eat any more rice.

【答案】▶(C)

【译文】▶A:你要再来一些鸡肉吗?

     B:好的,麻烦你。真的很好吃。

     A:哦,真高兴你喜欢。再来点米饭如何?

     B:_____

      (A)真棒! 我想要再来些甜点。

      (B)谢谢你的赞美。

      (C)不,谢谢。我已经太饱了。

      (D)多谢。我吃不下了。

【讲解】▶①B表示已经太饱,婉拒 A 的邀请,要用 No,thanks. 的说法。

     ②答案(D)的 Many thanks 后要接肯定的回答。

     ③*delicious* [di'liʃəs] *adj*. 美味可口的

     ④*dessert* [di'zə:t] *n*. (餐后的)甜点

     ⑤*compliment* ['kɔmplimənt] *n*. 恭维

●活学活用●

3. May：Excuse me,but I couldn't help noticing your earrings.

Sue：_____

(A)Oh,they were presents from my parents.

(B)They are very,very beautiful.

(C)Oh,I'm sorry. I've never noticed them myself.

(D)Thank you. You can have them.

【答案】▶(A)

【译文】▶梅：对不起,我没办法不注意到你的耳环。

苏：_____

(A)噢,这是我父母送的礼物。

(B)它们非常非常漂亮。

(C)哦,抱歉,我自己从未注意过它们。

(D)谢谢你! 你可以拿去。

【讲解】▶①*cannot help*＋*V-ing*＝*cannot help but*＋*V* 不得不……

②*earring* [ˈiəriŋ] *n.* 耳环

③注意此题和时态有关：couldn't,were。故(B)不如(A)好。

现场会话 实战复习测验●

1. Mr. Brown： Thank you so much for inviting me,Mrs. Watkins. It's been a super evening.

Mrs. Watkins：Oh,I'm so pleased,Mr. Brown. But have you really got to leave now?

Mr. Brown：_____I've got to catch an early train to London in the morning.

(A)Yes,I did,Mrs. Watkins.

(B)Yes,I have to,I'm afraid.

(C) Yes, I understand.

(D) Oh! I'm so pleased.

2. X: Have you ever talked to Tom? He's very humorous.

   Y: _____

   (A) So is he.   (B) So he is.

   (C) So have I.   (D) So has he.

3. Woman: Press twelve, please. Thank you.

   Man: You're welcome. That's where I'm going to.

   Where did this conversation most probably take place?

   (A) In a laundry.   (B) In an elevator.

   (C) In a library.   (D) In a bakery.

4. A: Jack drove all night to get there for the meeting.

   B: He _____ exhausted by the time he arrived.

   (A) ought to be   (B) would be

   (C) must have been   (D) will have been

5. A: Did you make any social blunders?

   B: _____ When I sat down to dinner, I wasn't sure which

   spoon to use for the soup.

   (A) Certainly not.

   (B) I suppose I did.

   (C) What if I succeed?

   (D) I don't know anything about it.

6. (Approaching a stranger in the street.)(多选)

   Dick: _____

   Stranger: Yes, certainly.

   (A) Hi, would I speak to you for a while, OK. ?

   (B) Excuse me, but can you spare me a few moments?

   (C) Would you mind if I speak to you for a minute?

   (D) Would you please show me the way to the station?

   (E) I'm sorry, but will you be so kind as to allow me to speak to you for an instant?

7. Tony： I saw an interesting show last night.

　Susan：_____What was it about?

　Tony： It was a variety show.

　(A)So do I.　　　　　(B)So did I.

　(C)You did?　　　　 (D)Didn't you?

8. Cathy：Please make yourself at home and stay with us as long as you please.

　Wendy：_____

　(A)Thank you very much for your wonderful hospitality.

　(B)Don't make a great fuss about nothing.

　(C)I've stayed at home with my family for a very long time and now I am pleased to meet you.

　(D)We enjoy working together because we feel at home with each other.

解题关键分析

1.【答案】▶(B)

　【译文】▶布朗先生：　　非常谢谢你的邀请,沃特金斯太太。这是非常棒的一晚。

　　　　　沃特金斯太太:喔! 布朗先生我真的很高兴。但你现在真的得走吗?

　　　　　布朗先生：　　_____,我一早得搭早班火车去伦敦。

　　　　　(A)是的,沃特金斯太太。

　　　　　(B)是的,恐怕我一定要走。

　　　　　(C)是的,我明白。

　　　　　(D)噢,我太高兴了。

2.【答案】▶(B)

　【译文】▶X:你和汤姆交谈过吗? 他非常幽默。

Y：_____

(A)他也是。   (B)他的确是的。

(C)我也有。   (D)他也有。

【讲解】▶①*humorous* ['hju:mərəs] *adj.* 有幽默感的

②*So he is.* ＝Yes, he is. 是，他的确是。(*So is he.* ＝He is, too. 他也是。)

3.【答案】▶(B)

【译文】▶女士：请按十二，谢谢。

男士：不客气。我正要到那里去。

这段会话最可能发生在什么地方？

(A)在洗衣店里。   (B)在电梯里。

(C)在图书馆里。   (D)在面包店里。

4.【答案】▶(B)

【译文】▶A：杰克开了整晚的车为了去那里开会。他到达时_____筋疲力竭。

B：是的。

(A)应该是   (B)一定

(C)想必   (D)肯定

5.【答案】▶(B)

【译文】▶A：你在社交方面失误过吗？

B：_____。当我坐下来用晚餐时，我不确定喝汤要用哪支汤匙。

(A)当然没有。

(B)我想是的。

(C)成功又怎么样？

(D)我不知道。

【讲解】▶blunder ['blʌndə] *v.* 失误

6.【答案】▶(B)(D)

【译文】▶(向街上一位陌生人走过去。)

狄克：_____

陌生人:当然好啊。

 （A）嗨,我可以跟你说说话吗?（Would 应改为 Could,且 Could I speak to you...? 应是对已认识的人说的,在此不合适。）

 （B）抱歉,可以耽搁你一会儿吗?（可以对陌生人或已认识的人说。）

 （C）你介意我跟你说话吗?

 （D）请你告诉我车站怎么走好吗?

 （E）很抱歉,能不能请你容许我跟你说说话?（I'm sorry. 应改为 Excuse me.）

【讲解】▶①*approach* [ə'prəutʃ] *v.* 走近

　　　②*spare* [spɛə] *v.* 拨时间给某人

7.【答案】▶(C)

【译文】▶托尼:昨晚我看了一个有趣的表演。

 苏珊:_____? 是什么样的表演?

 托尼:是多变化的表演。

 （A）我也是。　　　（B）我也是。

 （C）真的?　　　　（D）是吗?

8.【答案】▶(A)

【译文】▶凯西:请不要客气,留久一点。

 温迪:_____

 （A）谢谢你热情的招待。

 （B）请勿庸人自扰。

 （C）我和家人在一起已经太久了,我现在很高兴能和你在一起。

 （D）我们很高兴能在一起工作,因为我们在一起觉得很自在。

Shopping
购　物

（一）
A：May I help you, sir?

B：No, thank you. I'm just looking.

A：We have a lot more upstairs.

B：Oh, you do? You certainly have a large selection.

甲：需要帮忙吗，先生？

乙：不用，谢谢。我只是随便看看。

甲：楼上还有很多。

乙：真的？你们的货真多。

（二）
A：What price range do you have in mind?

B：I want to stay under 80.

甲：你的预算有多少？

乙：80 元以下。

（三）
A：What price range do you have in mind?

B：Eighty dollars is my ceiling.

甲：你的预算有多少？

乙：最多 80 元。

（四）
A：Can you give me a discount on this?

B：Oh, no, sir. It's a real bargain.

甲：这个东西能不能打折？
乙：不行，先生。这是特价品。

(五)
A：Can you make it a little cheaper?
B：No, sir. It's a good buy.

甲：你能算便宜一点吗？
乙：不行，先生。这个价钱已经很划算了。

(六)
A：Can you come down a little?
B：I'm sorry. We can't.

甲：你能算便宜一点吗？
乙：很抱歉。不行。

(七)
A：Can I get it tax-free?
B：Sure, if you show me your passport.

甲：我买这个东西的话，能免税吗？
乙：只要你有护照就可以。

(八)
A：Will you gift-wrap this, please?
B：Certainly.

甲：请你把这个包装成礼物好吗？
乙：好的。

(九)
A：Cash or charge?
B：Charge, please.

甲：您要付现金还是记账？
乙：请记账。

(十)
A：Can I pay by check?
B：I'm afraid you can't. We only accept traveler's checks and credit cards.

甲：我可以用支票付账吗？
乙：恐怕不行。我们只接受旅行支票和信用卡。

（十一）
A：I'm afraid I was short-changed.
B：Oh，really？ Let me look into it.

甲：你好像少找我钱了。
乙：真的吗？ 我来看一下。

（十二）
A：Could I have a refund on this?
B：Of course. Take it to the counter over there，please.

甲：这个东西能退货吗？
乙：当然可以。请到那边的柜台。

（十三）
A：Could you show me another one，please.
B：Certainly.

甲：请拿另外一件让我看看。
乙：好的。

（十四）
A：Could you give me something to write on，please?
B：Will this do?
A：Yes，That will do. Thank you.

甲：请给我一张纸写字。
乙：这样可以吗？
甲：可以的，谢谢您。

（十五）
A：Can you come down a little?
B：Sorry. We can't. It's a bargain.

甲：能不能算便宜一点？
乙：抱歉，不行。这是特价品。

（十六）
A：Can you make it cheaper?
B：All right. I'll take 10％ off.

甲：能不能算便宜一点？
乙：好吧。算你九折。

⑭
A：I'll give you a 10％ discount.
B：That's more like it.

甲：我算你九折。
乙：这还差不多。

⑮
A：Can I have a refund?
B：Sorry. No refund.

甲：能不能退货？
乙：抱歉，恕不退货。

⑯
A：I was overcharged.
B：No. It was a square deal.

甲：你们敲我竹杠。
乙：不，这是公平交易。

⑰
A：This is robbery!
B：Exchange is no robbery.

甲：这简直是抢劫嘛！
乙：交易不算抢劫。

⑱
A：You took me in!
B：We didn't.

甲：你们欺骗我。
乙：我们没有欺骗你。

在"商店"常用的语句

①我能为你效劳吗？

Can I help you?

What can I do for you?

Can I do anything for you?

Is there anything I can do for you?

②让我看一看洋娃娃。

Let me see dolls. /I'd like to see dolls.

我想买一双鞋。I want to get(to buy)a pair of shoes.

我只是看看，谢谢。I'm just looking(around)，thank you.

③这顶帽子怎样？ How do you like this hat?

你对这些有兴趣吗？ Would you be interested in these?

你戴（穿）什么尺寸？ What size do you wear?

这货物有保证书吗？ Is this merchandise guaranteed?

这是不是最新的式样？Is this the latest style?

这可试试吗？May I try it on?

④这个多少钱？

How much is this(are they)？/How much does it cost?

你可以打折吗？Can you give me a discount?

我们不议价。

We never ask two prices. /We ask only one price.

我该付多少钱？How much do I owe you?

这很便宜。It's cheap(reasonable).

这很贵的。It's expensive(unreasonable).

⑤这是五百元钞票。Here is a five hundred dollar note.

你身边有零钱吗？Don't you have small money with you?

这是找你的零钱。Here is your change.

对不起,让你久等了。

I'm sorry to have kept you waiting so long.

要不要包起来？Shall I wrap it up? /Shall I package it?

劳驾帮我送去。Will you deliver it?

⑥还要别的东西吗？Anything else?

慢慢来。Take your time please.

恐怕我们没有卖那种东西。

I'm afraid we don't have them. /Sorry, we don't handle that
article.

对不起,那种东西都卖完了。

I'm sorry they are all sold out. /We are out of the article
now.

非常实战测验

●活学活用●

Woman A：That dress looks fantastic on you.

Woman B：I think I look fat in it. __1.__

Woman A：Oh，no. You look very nice. And the color is perfect on you.

Woman B：__2.__ I guess I'll take the sweater for now. I can always buy the dress later.

Woman A：__3.__ Let me take the sweater up to the cash register for you and write up your bill. But I'd still say the dress does look good on you.

Woman B：__4.__ Well，then，I think I'll take it anyway.

Woman A：You can't be wrong with it. __5.__ how are you going to pay?

1. (A)Are you sure?　　　　　(B)May I try it on?
　 (C)Don't you agree?　　　 (D)Do you have another one?

2. (A)You have good taste.　(B)I don't know.
　 (C)Yes，I see.　　　　　　(D)You bet.

3. (A)Fine.　　　　　　　　 (B)No，you're wrong.
　 (C)That's right.　　　　　 (D)How come?

4. (A)Excuse me.　　　　　　(B)Oh，my goodness.
　 (C)Are you sure?　　　　　(D)Excellent!

5. (A)I beg your pardon，　　(B)By the way，
　 (C)Frankly speaking，　　 (D)No kidding，

【答案】▶ 1.(C)　2.(B)　3.(A)　4.(C)　5.(B)

【译文】▶ 甲女：那件洋装穿在你身上真是美极了。

　　　　 乙女：我想我穿这衣服看起来胖胖的。＿＿＿＿＿

　　　　 甲女：哦，不！你看起来很好看。这颜色在你身上也很完

美。

乙女：_____我想我暂时先买这件毛衣好了,以后我随时都可以买这件洋装的。

甲女：_____我为你把这毛衣拿到收银机那里,并填写你的发票。但我仍然要说:那件洋装穿在你身上真是很好看。

乙女：_____嗯,那么我想我还是买下好了。

甲女：买它你是错不了的,_____你将怎么付款?

1.(A)你确定吗?　　　　(B)我可以试穿吗?

(C)你不同意吗?　　　　(D)你有另一件吗?

2.(A)你的品味真高。　　(D)我不确定。

(C)是的,我知道。　　　(D)当然。

3.(A)好。　　　　　　　(B)不,你错了。

(C)那对。　　　　　　　(D)怎么会这样呢? 为什么呢?

4.(A)抱歉!　　　　　　(B)哦,老天!

(C)你确定吗?　　　　　(D)太棒了!

5.(A)请原谅,对不起,　　(B)顺便提一下,

(C)坦白说,　　　　　　(D)没有开玩笑

●活学活用●

6. Son： Will it be expensive?

Mother：_____

(A)Oh,really?

(B)Okay. I understand.

(C)Don't worry. I'll pay.

(D)Oh,don't let me keep you.

【答案】▶(C)

【译文】▶儿子:会很贵吗?

母亲:_____

(A)哦,真的吗?

(B)好,我懂。

(C)不用担心,我会付钱。

(D)噢,不要让我害你迟到了。

══════ ●活学活用● ══════

7. Customer：Excuse me. Have you got any sugar? I looked,
　　　　　　but I couldn't find any.

　　Clerk：　　I'm sorry. ＿＿＿＿＿＿

　　(A)Come back later.

　　(B)We're out of it.

　　(C)You looked the wrong place.

　　(D)You could see it if you'd only look.

【答案】▶(B)

【译文】▶顾客:抱歉。你们有糖卖吗? 我看过,但找不到。

　　　　店员:抱歉。＿＿＿＿＿＿

　　　　　　(A)以后再来。

　　　　　　(B)糖卖完了。

　　　　　　(C)你看错了地方。

　　　　　　(D)你只要一看就可以看得到。

【讲解】▶①*out of it* （东西)没有了;卖完了

　　　　②*have got＝have* 有

　　　　③*look the wrong place* 看错地方

══════ ●活学活用● ══════

8. Clerk：　　That sweater looks good on you. What do you
　　　　　　think of it?

　　Customer：＿＿＿＿＿＿

　　(A)It feels tight.

　　(B)It's a good buy.

　　(C)How much does it cost?

　　(D)No. It's not the right style.

【答案】▶(A)

【译文】▶店员:那件运动衫在你身上看起来不错。你觉得它如何?

　　　　顾客:＿＿＿＿＿＿＿

　　　　　　(A)我觉得有点紧。　　　(B)那是件廉价品。

　　　　　　(C)它要多少钱?　　　　(D)不。它的款式不对。

【讲解】▶①*feel tight*　觉得紧一点

　　　　②*look good on sb.*　某人穿起来好看

　　　　③*What...think of...*　对……的看法如何?

　　　　④*a good buy*　廉价品

　　　　⑤*not the right style*　款式不对

●活学活用●

9. Clerk：　　　May I help you?

　Customer：　Yes, please. I bought this shirt here yester-
　　　　　　　day. Two buttons are missing. Look!

　Clerk：　　＿＿＿＿＿＿＿

　　(A)I'll bring you another suit.

　　(B)Don't worry about it. You can fix them yourself.

　　(C)What you said is very interesting.

　　(D)I'm sorry. I'll change it for you.

【答案】▶(D)

【译文】▶店员:有什么事要我效劳吗?

　　　　顾客:是的,请帮个忙。我昨天在这里买了这件衬衫。两
　　　　　　　个扣子掉了。你看!

　　　　店员:＿＿＿＿＿＿＿

　　　　　　(A)我拿另一套给你。

　　　　　　(B)不要担心。你自己可以修补。

　　　　　　(C)你说的话非常有趣。

　　　　　　(D)抱歉,我帮你换。

【讲解】▶①顾客说买了件掉了钮扣的衬衫,店员应该很客气的致歉。

　　　　②答案(A)中,*suit* n.套装,并非 shirt 之单位。

　　　　③*fix* [fiks] v.　修理;钉牢

========= ● 活学活用 ● =========

10. Lucy：I don't think we'll find a better buy than this.

　　Judy：_____

　　Lucy：Well, if you insist.

　　（A）Let's try at least on more place.

　　（B）You're right.

　　（C）It's a deal.

　　（D）We might as well order some.

【答案】▶（A）

【译文】▶露茜：我不认为我们能找到比这个更好的便宜货了。

　　　　朱迪：_____

　　　　露茜：好吧，如果你坚持的话。

　　　　（A）我们至少再试一家吧！

　　　　（B）你的话很对。

　　　　（C）那就成交了。

　　　　（D）我们不妨订购一些。

现场会话 实战复习测验 ●

1. A：Can I get three for the price of two?（选错）

　 B：_____

　　（A）Of course, but this week only.

　　（B）Nothing else, thank you.

　　（C）Yes, they are on sale.

　　（D）Yes, except for those marked otherwise.

　　（E）They've been reduced for quick sale. Yes.

2. Girl：　　Good afternoon, madam. _____

　 Woman：No. Can you help me, please?

　 Girl：　　Yes, madam. What are you looking for?

　 Woman：I'd like to buy a purse.

(A) Are you waiting for me?

(B) Would you like anything else?

(C) Have you been waited on?

(D) What can I do for you?

3. Tailor： In what fashion(style)do you like to have your suit made?

Customer： _____

(A) I prefer a more conservative style.

(B) I would like to have you make my measurement.

(C) That's all right. Wearing jeans is comfortable.

(D) I am awfully sorry. I won't wear them again.

4. Clerk： Do you want to charge it?

Customer： _____

(A) Yes, here's my credit card.

(B) In two weeks.

(C) No, that's all, thanks.

(D) I like it.

5. Woman：Someone tells me that you are buying an expensive villa.

Man： _____

(A) I'm glad you are going abroad.

(B) That's right. I'm going to move in next weekend.

(C) Yes, I do. I'll let you know when we sign the contract.

(D) Brick houses are more expensive than wooden houses.

解题关键分析

1.【答案】▶ (B)

【译文】▶ A:我能不能以两个的价钱买三个?

B: _____

(A) 当然可以,但是只限于本周。

(B) 不要其他东西了,谢谢。

(C)可以,这些是特价品。

(D)可以,除了那些标价不同的以外。

(E)为了要快点卖出去,这些东西已经降价了。可以
的。

【讲解】▶ ①*on sale*〔美〕特价中

②*otherwise* ['ʌðəwaiz] *adv.*　不同地

2.【答案】▶(C)

【译文】▶女孩:午安,夫人。_____

女士:没有。请帮帮我好吗?

女孩:好的,夫人。你在找什么东西?

女士:我想买个钱包。

(A)你在等我吗?　　　(B)你还要其他东西吗?

(C)有人为你服务了吗?　(D)我能为你效劳吗?

3.【答案】▶(A)

【译文】▶裁缝:你的西装要做成什么样式?

顾客:_____。

(A)我喜欢传统一些的样式。

(B)我想按你的尺寸做。

(C)就那样。穿工作服很舒服。

(D)太抱歉了,我不穿西装。

【讲解】▶ ①conservative　*adj.* 保守的

②measurement　*n.* 尺寸

4.【答案】▶(A)

【译文】▶店员:你要记账(charge)吗?

顾客:_____。

(A)是的,这是我的信用卡。

(B)两周之内。

(C)不,谢谢。

(D)我不喜欢记账。

5.【答案】▶(B)

【译文】▶女士:有人告诉我,你买了一栋昂贵的别墅。

男士:_____

(A)我很高兴你要出国。

(B)对。我下周末就要搬进去了。

(C)是的。我会让你知道我们什么时候签合约。

(D)砖房比木屋贵。

【讲解】▶ *villa* ['vilə] *n.* 别墅

Traffic 交通

情景对话精选

- **A**：What's the cheapest way to go there?

- **B**：By subway.

- **A**：Is there a subway station near here?

- **B**：Yes. There's one just on the other side of the building.

- **A**：Where do I get a ticket?

- **B**：On the bus.

- **甲**：到那边乘什么交通工具最便宜？

- **乙**：乘地铁。

- **甲**：这附近有地铁车站吗？

- **乙**：有啊。这栋大楼的另一边就有一个。

- **甲**：车票要到哪里买？

- **乙**：在车上买。

- **A**：A one-way（ticket）to Boston，please.
- **B**：Six dollars fifty.

- **甲**：到波士顿单程票一张。
- **乙**：六美元五十美分。

（三）
A：One round-trip to L. A. ，please.
B：Twenty dollars.

甲：洛杉矶往返票一张。
乙：二十美元。

（四）
A：One single to London，please.
B：Here you are.

甲：到伦敦单程票一张。
乙：车票在这儿。

（五）
A：Two returns to London，please.
B：Here you are.

甲：到伦敦往返票两张。
乙：车票在这儿。

（六）
A：One double to London，please.
B：Here you are.

甲：到伦敦往返票一张。
乙：车票在这儿。

（七）
A：One adult one-way and two children to New York，please.
B：Here you are.

甲：到纽约单程成人票一张，儿童票两张。
乙：车票在这儿。

（八）
A：One and two halves single to London，please.
B：How many did you say，sir？

甲：到伦敦全票一张半票两张。
乙：你说要几张票，先生？

（九）
A：What's the fare，please？
B：Twenty-five dollars.

甲：请问车票多少钱？
乙：二十五美元。

（十）
A：Is this seat taken？
B：No，it isn't.

甲：这个位子有人坐吗？

乙：没有。

(十一)　A：Is this seat empty?

B：Yes, it is.

甲：这个位子有人坐吗？

乙：是的。

A：Am I on the right train to (for) Shanghai?

B：Yes, you are. How far are you going?

(十二)

A：I'm going to Nanjing. Please let me know when I get there.

B：All right.

甲：(我坐的) 这班火车是开往上海的吗？

乙：是的。你要到哪儿？

甲：我要到南京。车子抵达时请告诉我一声。

乙：好的。

(十三)　A：I forgot to get off at my stop.

B：Did you?（You did?）

甲：我到站忘了下车。

乙：真的？

(十四)　A：I missed my stop.

B：Did you?（You did?）

甲：我坐过站了。

乙：真的？

(十五)　A：You should have gotten off at the last stop.

B：Should I?

甲：你在上一站就应该下车的。

乙：真的吗？

A：How come you are late again?

B：I was stuck in traffic jams.

甲：你为什么又迟到了？

乙：交通堵塞。

A：Pull over please.

B：All right.

A：How much do I owe you?

B：Ninety yuan.

A：Here's one hundred yuan. Keep the change. Bye.

B：Thanks，bye.

甲：请靠边停车。

乙：好的。

甲：车费是多少？

乙：90 元。

甲：这是 100 元。不用找零了。再见。

乙：谢谢。再见。

A：Want to go shopping with me?

B：Not now. It's rush hour. Traffic is pretty heavy.

甲：要和我去逛街吗？

乙：现在不要。现在是交通高峰时段，交通很拥挤。

A：There are many cars on this road.

B：Let's take another road.

甲：这条路上有许多车。

乙：我们走另一条路吧。

"在火车站"常用语句

①我在哪儿买票？

Where is the ticket office? /Where can I get a ticket?

给我一张去往伦敦的车票。One ticket for London.

给我两张到伦敦的二等票。

I want two second-class round-trip tickets to London.

二等票多少钱一张？How much is a second-class?

这张票有效期限几天？

How many days (How long) is this ticket good (valid or available)?

②我们现在在哪里？Where are we now?

由此地到南京还有几站？

How many stops is Nanjing from here?

这趟车是否每站都停？

Does this train stop at every station?

请在济南下车换车到西安。

Get off at Jinan and change to a train for Xi'an.

在路上需要换车吗？

Do I have to change trains on the way?

③出口在哪里呀？Where is the way out (exit)？

我必须从哪个大门进去？Which entry do I enter?

请下楼从第二通道上车。

Go down the steps and get on the train on Track No. 2.

④开往南京的火车何时到达？

When is the express for Nanjing due here?

火车准时吗？Is the train on time?

下一班去南京的火车什么时候开？

When is the next train for Nanjing?

火车十点整开车。The train leaves at ten sharp.

⑤我可以看看你的车票吗？May I see your ticket，please?

这已过期了。It's overdue.

先生，票还你。Here you are. /Here it is. /Here，sir.

非常实战测验

●活学活用●

1. George：The bus doesn't leave for another half hour. What should we do?

Hal： How about just buying a newspaper and waiting here?

George：Yeah，maybe that would be best. I wouldn't want to miss this bus. _____

(A) The next one won't be here for two hours.

(B) Too bad it just left.

(C) Nice talking with you.

(D) See you in an hour.

【答案】▶(A)

【译文】▶乔治：汽车半小时内不会开走。我们该做什么？

海尔：就买份报纸在这儿等如何？

乔治：好啊，也许那样最好。我可不想错过这班车。_____

(A)下班车两小时内不会来到这儿。

(B)它刚离开，真糟糕。

(C)很高兴与你聊天。

(D)几小时之后再见。

●活学活用●

2. Tom：There's been a steady increase in the number of cars on the road.

Jane：Yes, and it's high time the Government did something about it.

Jane thinks that _____

(A) the government has managed to control the increase of cars.

(B) immediate action is called for to control the growth.

(C) it takes time for the Government to reduce the number of cars.

(D) the Government should find the right time to get some of the old cars off the roads.

【答案】▶(B)

【译文】▶汤姆：马路上车辆一直不断地增加。

简： 是的,该是政府采取行动的时候了。

简认为 _____

(A)政府已设法控制车辆的增加。

(B)需要立刻采取行动来控制车辆的增加。

(C)政府减少车辆数目需要时间。

(D)政府应该找个适当的时间使一些旧车不再开上马路。

【讲解】▶①*call for* 需要

②*on the road* 作形容词定语,修饰 cars。"it's high time ＋从句(动词用虚拟语气)"为口语的用法。

③*steady* ['stedi] *adj.* 持续的;稳定的

④*increase* [in'kri:s] *n.* 增加

⑤*immediate action* 紧急行动

⑥*reduce* *vt.* 减少

现场会话 实战复习测验 ●

1. A：_____

   B：About two hours.

   A：Thank you.

   B：Not at all.

   (A)How often will you be back?

   (B)Can you tell me what time it is?

   (C)It won't be long,isn't it?

   (D)How long must I wait for the next train?

2. John：After we had hurried to the raiway station,we found that the train had just gone.

   Mary：_____

   (A)No,not at all.　　　(B)What a shame!

   (C)I cannot believe it.　(D)Don't bother.

3. John：I'm going to take a short nap. Can you wake me up when the train stops in Nanjing?

   Brian：OK.

   John：Thanks.

   Brian：John,wake up. _____

   John：Thanks.

   (A)We got out.　　　(B)We have arrived at home.

   (C)Here you go.　　　(D)We're here.

4. Tom：Is there no earlier train?

   John：_____

   (A)No,this is the earliest.

   (B)Yes,there is no earlier train.

   (C)Don't mention it!

   (D)That's too bad!

5. Brian：Traffic congestion is extremely serious in New York!

Amy：You can say that again.

Amy means that _____

(A)she agrees with Brian.

(B)she expects another traffic jam.

(C)she wants Brian to repeat what she just said.

(D)traffic congestion will be with us for a long time.

6. X：God，I hate getting stuck in traffic jams.

Y：Me，too. It's such a waste of time.

X：_____

Y：That's right. Then our parents wouldn't have to worry.

(A)Never mind.

(B)Traffic jams are terrible.

(C)Do you think we'll be late?

(D)It's too bad we don't have mobile phones.

7. Susan：I think I'll take a taxi downtown.

Helen：_____Traffic is pretty heavy at this time of the day.

Susan：Not in the direction I'm going.

Helen：Well，I still don't think you should.

(A)I wouldn't if I were you.

(B)It's better than taking the subway.

(C)That's a good idea.

(D)Why didn't you take the bus?

8. Joe：It gets more and more difficult to stroll on Taipei's side-
　　　walks.

Sue：_____There are too many street vendors blocking the
　　　way.

(A)So it is.　　　　　(B)That does it.

(C)So it does.　　　　(D)So does it.

解题关键分析

1.【答案】▶(D)

【译文】▶A：_____

B：大约两小时。(回答 How long 的问句,要用"一段时间")

A：谢谢。

B：不客气。

(A)你多长时间回来?

(B)你能告诉我几点了吗?

(C)时间不太长,是吧?

(D)下趟车我要等多久?

2.【答案】▶(B)

【译文】▶约翰：我们赶到火车站后,发现火车刚走。

玛丽：_____。

(A)不,没走。　　　(B)真可惜。

(C)我不信。　　　(D)别烦了。

3.【答案】▶(D)

【译文】▶约翰：　我要小睡片刻。火车到南京时,你可以叫醒我吗?

布雷恩：好的。

约翰：　谢谢。

布雷恩：约翰,醒醒吧。_____

约翰：　谢谢。

(A)我们出去。

(B)我们已经到家了。

(C)你去吧。

(D)我们到了。

【讲解】▶*take a short nap*　小睡片刻

4.【答案】▶(A)

【译文】▶汤姆：没有更早班的火车了吗?

约翰：＿＿＿＿＿＿

(A)没有,这班是最早的。

(B)有的,没有更早的火车了。

(C)不用客气!

(D)那太糟了!

5.【答案】▶(A)

【译文】▶布雷恩:纽约的交通堵塞真是非常严重!

艾米： 你说得对极了!

艾米的意思是＿＿＿＿＿＿

(A)她同意布雷恩。

(B)她期待另一次交通堵塞。

(C)她要布雷恩重复她刚才说的话。

(D)交通堵塞将会陪伴我们好长一段时间。

【讲解】▶①*congestion* [kən'dʒestʃən] *n*.拥挤

②*You can say that again.* 你说得对极了!

6.【答案】▶(D)

【译文】▶X:天啊! 我真痛恨塞车,动弹不得。

Y:我也是。塞车多么浪费时间啊!

X:＿＿＿＿＿＿

Y:是啊。那样的话,我们的父母就不用担心了。

(A)没关系。

(B)塞车很可怕。

(C)你认为我们会迟到吗?

(D)只可惜我们没有移动电话。

【讲解】▶①*terrible* ['terəbl] *adj*.可怕的

②*mobile* ['məubail] *adj*.可移动的

7.【答案】▶(A)

【译文】▶苏珊:我想,我要搭计程车到闹市区去。

海伦:＿＿＿＿＿＿每天这个时候,交通都很拥挤。

苏珊:我要去的那个方向不会。

海伦:嗯,我还是觉得你不该搭计程车去。

(A)如果我是你,我就不会这么做。

(B)比乘地铁好。

(C)这是个好主意。

(D)你当时为什么不乘公共汽车？

8.【答案】▶(C)

　【译文】▶乔:在台北的人行道上散步真是越来越难了。

　　　　苏:_____街上摊贩太多,把路都堵住了。

　　　　(A)是啊!(用于原句使用 be 动词时)

　　　　(B)是那件事造成的。

　　　　(C)是啊!(原句使用一般动词,故以助动词回答)

　　　　(D)它也是。

　【讲解】▶①*stroll* [strəul] *v.* 漫步

　　　　②*vendor* ['vendɔ:] *n.* 小贩(＝vender)

　　　　③*So it is.* 是啊!(＝Yes,it is.)

　　　　④*So it does.* 是啊!(＝Yes,it does.)

Taking an Airplane
乘飞机

㊀ A: Is this the right counter to check in for this flight?
B: Yes, it is.

甲: 这班飞机在这个柜台办登机手续吗？
乙: 是的。

㊁ A: Is the plane on schedule?　　　甲: 这班飞机准时吗？
B: Yes, it is.　　　　　　　　　　乙: 是的。

㊂ A: What's the time difference between Taipei and New York?
B: Eleven hours. Taipei is eleven hours ahead.

甲: 台北与纽约的时差是多少？
乙: 十一小时。台北快十一小时。

㊃ A: Are we losing or gaining a day on the way to the U. S. A.

B: We are gaining a day.

A: Does it mean we're arriving on the same day?

B: That's right.

甲: 我们到达美国的日期是要少算一天还是多加一天？

乙: 我们要多加一天。

甲: 也就是说我们将于同日抵达吗？

乙: 对。

㈤
A：What's the actual flying time from here to New York?
B：It's about twenty hours.
A：Can you tell me what time we're arriving?
B：Sure. Let me see... at 7:45 a. m. local time tomorrow.
甲：从这里到纽约要飞多久?
乙：大约是 20 小时。
甲：能告诉我我们何时会抵达吗?
乙：当然可以。我看看 …… 当地时间明天早上 7 点 45 分。

㈥
A：Would you mind trading seats with me?
B：Not at all.
A：Oh，thank you. It's very kind of you.
B：You're welcome. I prefer a window seat.
甲：我们可以换一下座位吗?
乙：好的。
甲：谢谢您。您真好。
乙：不客气。我比较喜欢靠窗的座位。

㈦
A：Excuse me.
B：Yes?
A：Could I have a blanket?
B：Certainly. Just a moment，please.
甲：对不起。
乙：有什么事吗?
甲：能给我一条毛毯吗?
乙：好的。请等一会儿。

（八）
- **A**：What would you like—chicken or beef?
- **B**：Beef, please.
- **A**：Tea or coffee?
- **B**：Coffee, please.

- 甲：您要鸡肉还是牛肉？
- 乙：牛肉。
- 甲：您要茶还是咖啡？
- 乙：咖啡。

（九）
- **A**：Do you have anything to declare?
- **B**：No, I don't. I only have personal effects.

- 甲：您有没有需要申报的东西？
- 乙：没有。我只有随身用品。

（十）
- **A**：How long are you staying?
- **B**：Four weeks.
- **A**：Are you here on business or on vacation?
- **B**：I'm here on business.
- **A**：What line of business are you in?
- **B**：I export sporting goods.

- 甲：您预备停留多久？
- 乙：四周。
- 甲：您是来办事还是来度假的？
- 乙：我是来办事的。
- 甲：您是从事哪一种行业？
- 乙：我出口运动器材。

A：I'd like to reconfirm my reservation，please.

B：What reservation are you holding?

A：SQ Flight 209 leaving tomorrow at 11:45 a.m. for L.A.

B：Your name，please.

A：John Smith.

B：Hold on，please. Yes，sir. You're booked on SQ Flight 209 for L.A. tomorrow.

A：Could you put me in the no-smoking section?

B：Certainly. Aisle or window?

A：Aisle，please.

B：All right，sir. Here you are.

甲：我想再确认一下我预订的班机。

乙：您预订的是哪一班?

甲：新加坡航空 209 班机明天早上 11 点 45 分飞往洛杉矶。

乙：请问您的姓名?

甲：约翰·史密斯。

乙：请稍候。是的，先生。您预订的班机已登记好了。

甲：请给我禁烟区的座位好吗?

乙：好的，请问要靠过道的座位还是靠窗的?

甲：请给我靠过道的座位。

乙：好的，先生。您的票在这儿。

A：I'm a transit passenger for this flight. Can you tell me where to go?

B：Let me see. Oh, you're at the wrong gate. Your plane leaves from Gate No. 9.

甲：我是这班机的过境旅客。请告诉我该怎么走好吗？

乙：我看看。您走错登机门了。您的登机门是九号。

1. ➡在"机场"常用的语句

①我订了十一点飞往旧金山的班机。

I have a reservation（seat）on the eleven o'clock flight to San Francisco.

我可以看看您的机票吗？ May I see your ticket, please?

在这里。 Here you are.

票上说起飞前两小时必须办理登机手续。

The ticket says we should check in two hours before take-off time.

②这班飞机准时吗？ Is the flight on time?

这班飞何时起飞？ What time does the airplane take off?

③您有行李吗？ Do you have any baggage?

有，我带了一个手提箱和一个小包。

Yes, I have one suitcase and a small bag.

我们会留意您的手提箱的。

We'll take care of the suitcase.

2. ➡在"邮局"常用的语句

①请给我三张五分钱的邮票。

Please give me three five-cent stamps.

我这封信要寄挂号。May I have this letter registered?

我想将明信片寄限时。

I want to send this postal card by special delivery.

②包裹里是什么东西？What's in this package?

请为我称这封信。

Will you please weigh this letter for me?

这个包裹我要寄航空到韩国。

I want to send this package to South Korea by airmail.

邮资是多少？How much is the postage?

3. ➡"询问状况"时常用的语句

①你哪里不舒服？What's troubling you?

你发烧了吗？Do you have a fever?

今天觉得怎么样？How do you feel today?

你的胃口好吗？How's your appetite?

②你怎么了？Is anything wrong with you?

我头痛（牙痛、胃痛。）

I have a headache(toothache,stomachache).

我感冒了。I've caught a cold.

我胃口不好。I have no appetite.

我咳得厉害。I cough a great deal.

我喉咙痛。I have a sore throat.

● 活学活用 ●

1. Clerk: Grand Airlines. May I help you?

Client: Yes, I'd like to book a flight from Los Angeles to Mexico City on Wednesday the 22nd, please.

Clerk: _____.

(A) All right. Let me see if it's available.

(B) All right. You may have the book.

(C) No, it's very expensive.

(D) What about taking the bus?

【答案】▶ (A)

【译文】▶ 职员：宏伟航空公司。我能为您效劳吗？

顾客：是的。我想订二十二号星期三从洛杉矶飞往墨西哥的班机。

职员：_____

(A) 好的。我来看看是否有空位。

(B) 好的。你可以拥有这本书。

(C) 不。它非常昂贵。

(D) 坐公共汽车如何？

【讲解】▶ ① *airlines*　航空公司

② *book a flight*　订班机

③ *available　adj.* 可利用的，可得到的，有效的

④ (B)(D) 不合文意，(C) 顾客并没有问价钱，故不选

●活学活用●

2. John：So you just arrived yesterday. You must be tired.
　　　　How did you come?
　Scott：_____.
　　(A)By plane.　　　　　　(B)Yesterday.
　　(C)I'm not really tired.　(D)No，you can't.

【答案】▶(A)

【译文】▶约翰：　你昨天刚到，你一定累了。你是怎么来的？
　　　　斯科特：_____
　　　　(A)乘飞机。　　　　　(B)昨天。
　　　　(C)我真的不累。　　　(D)不，你不可以。

【讲解】▶①*arrive* [ə'raiv] *v.* 到达
　　　　②*by*＋交通工具　搭乘……
　　　　　例：by bus　乘公共汽车
　　　　　　　by taxi　乘计程车
　　　　　　　by plane　乘飞机
　　　　　　　by train　乘火车

●活学活用●

3. Clerk：　1.
　Joe：　Yes，I'd like some information about flights to
　　　　Victoria. How many are there per day?
　Clerk：One. The plane leaves at 10：15 in the morning.
　Joe：　2.
　Clerk：It takes about 16 hours.
　1.(A)What do you want?
　　(B)Do you like some information?
　　(C)Can I help you?

(D) How are you today?

2. (A) How long does it take to get there?

(B) How much is it for one day?

(C) When will it depart?

(D) How can we get there?

【答案】▶ 1. (C)　2. (A)

【译文】▶ 职员:有什么要效劳的吗?

乔:　是的,我想知道飞往维多利亚班机的资料。每天有几班?

职员:一班,飞机在早上 10 点 15 分起飞。

乔:　到那里要飞多久?

职员:约十六小时。

1. (A) 你想要什么?

(B) 你想要一些资料吗?

(C) 〔店员对顾客的招呼语〕有什么要效劳的吗?

(D) 你今天好吗?

2. (A) 到那里要多久时间?　　(B) 一天多少钱?

(C) 它何时离开?　　(D) 我们要如何到达那里?

●活学活用●

4. Passenger:Where is my suitcase? I can't find it anywhere!

Clerk:　　We'll notify you as soon as we find it.

Passenger:＿＿＿＿ I need it right now.

(A) I can't wait!

(B) OK. Please do so.

(C) What can I do for you?

(D) Well, never mind.

【答案】▶ (A)

【译文】▶ 旅客:我的手提箱在哪里? 我到处找都找不到它。

站员:我们一找到就会通知你。

旅客：_____我现在就需要它。

(A)我不能等! (B)好的。请这样做。

(C)我能帮你做什么吗? (D)噢,别介意。

【讲解】▶①依旅客回答"*I need it right now*",可知旅客没有时间等待。

②*as soon as* 一······就······

现场会话 实战复习测验 ●

1. Julie：We're here! I can't believe it!

   Mike：That makes two of us! What do we do now?

   Julie：I guess we should go to _____ and pick up our bags.

   (A) the baggage claim

   (B) the customs

   (C) the snack bar

   (D) the information counter

2. Stewardess：Please get ready for take-off!

   Passenger：_____

   (A) I have already taken off my shoes.

   (B) I refuse to take off anything.

   (C) Please wait, I am not ready to take off yet.

   (D) Thank you, I am all set for take-off.

3. X：Are you ready to leave for the airport?

   Y：_____

   X：Of course not. I get to share a little bit of the trip with you.

   (A) Are you coming with me?

   (B) I've been ready and waiting for you.

   (C) Are you sure you don't mind seeing me off?

   (D) I certainly appreciate the ride.

4. A：The travel agent still hasn't sent us the tickets for our trip.

   B：_____

C：I hope he won't forget to bring them to the airport.

    (A)Jim picked them up for us.

    (B)I'm sure they will send them soon.

    (C)Jim will send them to your house.

    (D)You have to go and get them.

5. Customer：I'd like to make a reservation on a flight to Los Angeles.

   Clerk：_____

    (A)I'd like to leave on Thursday, the 14th.

    (B)Yes, sir. When will you be leaving?

    (C)What's the one-way economy fare?

    (D)Well, it stops at Tokyo.

    (E)Why does it take so long?

6. A：What's the best way to get to the airport?

   B：By subway, if you want to save time.

   A：_____

   B：That depends on the traffic.

    (A)How many stops are there on the way?

    (B)How long will it take to go by taxi?

    (C)How often do I have to change on the way?

    (D)How much does it cost from here?

解题关键分析

1.【答案】▶(A)

  【译文】▶朱莉：我们到了！我真不敢相信！

         迈克：我也一样(不敢相信)！现在我们要做什么？

         朱莉：我想我们应该去_____领取我们的提袋。

         (A)行李提领处   (B)海关

         (C)小吃店   (D)询问台

  【讲解】▶①*baggage claim* 行李提领处

       ②*snack bar* 小吃店；卖小吃的柜台

2.【答案】▶(D)

　【译文】▶空中小姐：请准备好，要起飞了！

　　　　　乘客：＿＿＿＿＿＿＿

　　　　　(A)我已经脱掉鞋子了。

　　　　　(B)我拒绝脱掉任何东西。

　　　　　(C)请等一下，我还没准备好起飞。(应是驾驶员说的)

　　　　　(D)谢谢，我准备好了。

　【讲解】▶①*stewardess* ['stjuːədis] *n.* 空中小姐

　　　　　②*take - off* [teik ɔf] *n.* (飞机)起飞(＝*take off*)

　　　　　③*set* [set] *adj.* 准备好的

3.【答案】▶(C)

　【译文】▶X：你准备前往机场了吗？

　　　　　Y：＿＿＿＿＿＿＿

　　　　　X：当然不介意。我要与你共度一小段旅程。

　　　　　(A)你要跟我一起去吗？

　　　　　(B)我早就准备好，在等你了。

　　　　　(C)你确定不介意为我送行？

　　　　　(D)真感谢你载我一程。

　【讲解】▶①*see sb. off* 为某人送行　②*ride* [raid] *n.* 乘坐

4.【答案】▶(A)

　【译文】▶A：旅行社职员还未送来我们旅行的机票。

　　　　　B：＿＿＿＿＿＿＿

　　　　　C：希望他不会忘了带机票到机场。

　　　　　(A)吉姆去给我们取。

　　　　　(B)我想他们很快就会送到。

　　　　　(C)吉姆将把票送到你家。

　　　　　(D)你必须去取票。

5.【答案】▶(B)

　【译文】▶顾客：我想预订飞往洛杉矶的机位。

　　　　　职员：＿＿＿＿＿＿＿

　　　　　(A)我想在十四日星期四离开。

　　　　　(B)好的，先生。您何时要离开？

(C)经济舱的单程票价是多少?

(D)嗯,会在东京停留。

(E)为什么要花这么久的时间?

【讲解】▶①*flight*［flait］*n.* 飞行

②*economy fare*(客机的)经济舱票价

6.【答案】▶(B)

【译文】▶A:到机场最好的方式是什么?

B:乘地铁,假如你想省时间的话。

A:＿＿＿＿＿＿

B:那得视交通状况而定。

(A)一路上有多少站?

(B)乘出租车要多久?

(C)一路上我要换多少次车?

(D)从这去要多少钱?

At the Hotel
旅馆住宿

情景对话精选

㈠ **A**：I'd like to check in, please.
   B：Do you have a reservation?

甲：我要登记住宿。
乙：请问您有预约吗？

㈡ **A**：Can you tell me how to fill out this form?
   B：Certainly. Just put your name and address here, and
   I'll take care of the rest.

甲：请告诉我表格怎么填好吗？
乙：好的，您只要在这里写上姓名和地址，其他由我来写。

㈢ **A**：What's the rate for a single room.
   B：Seventy dollars a night.

甲：单人房价格是多少？
乙：一晚七十美元。

㈣ **A**：I'd like to book a room for tonight.
   B：Single room or double?

甲：我要预订今晚的房间。
乙：单人房还是双人房？

㈤ **A**：What's the rate for a twin room?
   B：Ninety dollars.

甲：双人房价格是多少？
乙：九十美元。

A：This is the Bell Captain. May I help you?

B：Yes. This is Mr. Jones in Room 709. Please send up a boy to help me with the luggage.

A：How much luggage do you have?

B：Two big cases and two small bags.

A：Can I deposit valuables here?

B：Yes. Please put your articles in this envelope and seal it.

甲：我是服务领班。请问有什么能帮您的？

乙：我是 709 房间的琼斯先生。请派一个服务生上来帮我提行李。

甲：您有多少行李？

乙：两个大皮箱和两个小提袋。

甲：贵重的东西可以寄存在这里吗？

乙：可以。请把东西装在这个纸袋里封起来。

A：Please make the bed while I'm out.
B：Yes, sir.

甲：请在我外出时帮我整理床铺。
乙：好的，先生。

A：Would you please wake me up at seven tomorrow morning?
B：Certainly. May I have your room number, please.

甲：请你明天早上七点叫醒我好吗？
乙：好的，请问您是几号房？

A：Could you connect me to Extension 607, please?
B：Certainly, sir.

甲：请帮我接 607 号分机。
乙：好的，先生。

⑪

A：Could you give me a hand?

B：Certainly. What's up?

A：I locked myself out.

B：Please wait here. I'll send someone up with a duplicate key.

甲：请帮个忙好吗?

乙：好的。有什么事吗?

甲：我被锁在门外了。

乙：请在这儿等。我请人拿副钥匙上来。

⑫

A：Is there any message for me?

B：No，sir.

甲：有人留话给我吗?

乙：没有，先生。

"在旅馆中"常用的语句

①你能给我一间空房吗?

Can you give me (Can I have)a room(for tonight)?

I want a room，please.

您有预订吗?

Do you have a reservation?

先生，对不起，我们旅馆客满了。

I'm sorry，but we're full up，sir.

房间都被订光了。All the rooms are booked up.

你要哪种房间? What kind of room would you like?

我要一间双人套房。I want a single room with twin beds.

②请您登记好吗？

Will you fill out this form?

Will you register here?

您要何时退房付账？

What time do you have to check out?

What is your checkout time?

您打算何时退房？ When are you checking out?

③房间价格是多少钱？

What's the rate?

How much do you charge per night?

单人房价格是多少？

What is the charge for a single room?

房间价格包括所有的费用了吧？

Does the price of the room include everything?

非常实战测验

●活学活用●

1. Guest：Hi! I wonder if you have a double room for tonight.

Clerk：_____

Guest：Okay, thanks anyway.

(A) One moment, please. I'll see if there are any flights.

(B) Sure. Please fill out this form for us.

(C) Sorry. I'm afraid we have no vacancies at this time.

(D) How long are you planning to stay here, sir?

【答案】▶ (C)

【译文】▶客人：　嗨！不知道今晚你们有没有双人房。

服务员：_____

客人:好吧,不论如何,谢谢您。

(A)请等一下。我看看是否还有任何班次。

(B)没问题。请把这张表填一下。

(C)抱歉。这时候恐怕没空房了。

(D)先生,您要在这里住多久?

【讲解】▶ ①*wonder*　不知道

②*double room*　双人房

③*one moment*　等一下

④*flight*(飞机)的飞行班次

⑤*fill out* = *fill in* = *fill up* 填写

⑥*form*　表格

⑦*vacancy* 空位

━━●活学活用●━━

2. Mr. Clement：　　　　I'd like to have a room.

Hotel Receptionist：＿＿＿＿＿

(A)Certainly, there's plenty of room.

(B)Certainly, have you ordered in advance.

(C)Sorry, sir, but the room isn't ready yet.

(D)Do you have a reservation, sir?

【答案】▶ (D)

【译文】▶ 克莱门特先生:我想定间房间。

旅馆接待员：＿＿＿＿＿

(A)当然可以,还有许多空房。

(B)当然可以,您有预先订购吗?

(C)抱歉,先生,这间房尚未准备妥当。

(D)您有预先订房吗?

【讲解】▶ ①*receptionist* 接待员

②*room* 当不可数名词用作"空间"解。因此 *plenty of room* 指"许多空间",而非"许多房间"。

③*order* 订购(货物);点(菜)

现场会话 实战复习测验 ●

1. Guest： Excuse me，there's something you could help me with.

   Desk clerk： What seems to be the problem，sir?

   Guest： There isn't any hot water in my room.

   Desk clerk： _____

   (A) Well，it's nice to hear you say so.

   (B) Oh，I'm sorry. I'll have it taken care of right away.

   (C) Oh，excuse me. We ran out of water last month.

   (D) Well，don't bother me，please.

2. Woman：We don't seem to have a reservation for you，sir. I am sorry.

   Man： But my secretary said that she had made reservations for me here. I phoned her from the airport this morning just as I left home.

   Where did the conversation most probable take place?

   (A) At an office.

   (B) At an airport.

   (C) At a restaurant.

   (D) At a hotel

3. Clerk： Do you want to charge it?

   Customer： _____

   (A) Yes，here's my credit card.

   (B) In two weeks.

   (C) No，that's all，thanks.

   (D) I like it.

4. A：I'd like a single room，please.

   B：Certainly. _____

   A：No，I don't. Do you have any vacancies?

(A)Your name,please?

(B)Do you want to check out?

(C)Do you have a reservation,sir.

(D)Do you have any cash?

5. A：Do you know a good hotel in this town?

B：The Jefferson Hotel is good.

A：_____

B：It's quite close—about four blocks.

(A)What did you say?

(B)How far is it from here?

(C)How long is it from here?

(D)Why is it so good?

6. A：Which do you prefer,a Japanese-style inn or a western-style hotel?

B：_____

(A)Yes,a Japanese-style inn.

(B)A western-style hotel.

(C)Now you're talking.

(D)Let alone a western-style hotel.

解题关键分析

1.【答案】▶(B)

【译文】▶客人：　　抱歉,请你帮我一个忙。

柜台职员：哪里有问题,先生?

客人：　　我的房间里没有热水。

柜台职员：_____

(A)嗯,听到你这么说真好。

(B)喔,很抱歉。我会立刻处理。

(C)喔,抱歉。我们上个月就把水用完了。

(D)好啦,请不要烦我。

【讲解】▶①*take care of*　留心;照料

②*run out of* 用完

③*check in* 和 *check out* 通常是用在饭店或旅馆。刚到
馆店时,在柜台登记,叫 check in;离去时,到柜台结
账,叫 check out。check in 也可用在机场,表示"登
机前的登记手续"。check out 则可用于图书馆,例
如:How many books may I check out at a time? 我
一次可以借出几本书?

2.【答案】▶(D)

【译文】▶女士:我们好像没有给你预订,先生。真抱歉。

男士:但是我的秘书说她已经给我在这里预订了。今
天早上我离开家时,从机场给她打电话了。

这段对话最可能发生在什么地方?

(A)办公室。　　　(B)机场。

(C)饭馆。　　　(D)旅馆。

【讲解】▶*have a reservation for sb.*　有……的预订

make a reservation for~　为……预订

3.【答案】▶(A)

【译文】▶店员:您要记账吗?

顾客:_____

(A)是的,这是我的信用卡。　(B)过两星期。

(C)不,那就够了,谢谢。　(D)我喜欢。

4.【答案】▶(C)

【译文】▶A:我想要个单人房间。

B:当然可以。_____

A:不,没有。还有空房吗?

(A)你的姓名?

(B)你要结账吗?

(C)你预订了吗,先生?

(D)你有现金吗?

【讲解】▶*check out*(结账后)离开旅馆;*check in*(在旅馆等)登记
住宿

5.【答案】▶(B)

【译文】▶A:你知道城里有什么好旅馆吗？

B:杰斐逊旅馆不错。

A:_____

B:很近——大约四个街区。

(A)你说什么？

(B)离这里有多远？

(C)从这里去要多久？（问时间）

(D)为什么它这么好？

6.【答案】▶(B)

【译文】▶A:你比较喜欢日式的旅馆还是西式的旅馆？

B:_____

(A)日式的旅馆。

(B)西式的旅馆。

(C)目前你正谈到的。

(D)更不用说西式旅馆了。

【讲解】▶*let alone* 至于……更不用说

Expressing Opinions
表达意见

㈠ A: Tom is certainly a nice boy, isn't he?
B: You can say that again.

甲: 汤姆真是个好孩子, 不是吗?
乙: 你说得对极了。

㈡ A: Perseverance is what makes people succeed.
B: I couldn't agree with you more.

甲: 毅力是使人成功的因素。
乙: 我完全同意你的看法。

㈢ A: All things are difficult before they are easy.
B: You have a point there.

甲: 事在人为。
乙: 你说得有道理。

㈣ A: After all, the greatest talkers are the least doers.
B: I'm entirely with you.

甲: 毕竟, 最会说的人最不会做事。
乙: 我完全同意你的看法。

㈤ A: Look! What a heavy snow fall!
B: You haven't seen nothing yet.

甲: 看啊, 好大的雪啊!
乙: 更大的雪还在后头呢!

㈥ A: He'll certainly make it, won't he?
B: I doubt it.

甲:他一定会成功,不是吗?
乙:我很怀疑。

(七)
A:I believe Hart will eventually win the nomination.
B:That is open to debate.

甲:我相信哈特一定会赢得提名。
乙:那可不一定。

(八)
A:After all,it's easier said than done.
B:I don't see eye to eye with you there.

甲:毕竟,说的比做的容易。
乙:这一点我不敢苟同。

1. ➡表"一般同意说法"常用语句

①当然的。自然的。不用说。Of course.

②不错。是的。Quite.

③真的。实在的。Yes,certainly.

④是啊。我也那么想。Yes,I think so too.

⑤真的,不错。Exactly. Quite so. Just so.

⑥那是没有疑问的。There is no doubt about it.

2. ➡表"强调同意说法"常用语句

①那好极了。Good! Excellent!

②那妙极了。That's splendid.

③正是。That's it.

④可不是嘛。I quite agree with you.

⑤你说得很对。Yes,you are quite right. You can say that again.

I couldn't agree more with you.

⑥那正是我的意思。

Yes,that's just what I was going to say.

3. ➡ 表"不同意说法"常用语句

①不！我不能同意你。No,I don't agree with you.

②是,我可有点疑惑。Yes,but I rather doubt that.

③嗳！我恐怕是不能完全同意的。

Well,I'm afraid I can't quite agree.

④不,那就是我不赞成的地方。

Oh,no. That's where I disagree with you.

⑤我总有点儿怀疑。

I'm rather inclined to doubt it.

非常实战测验 ●━━━━━━━━━━

● 活学活用 ●

1. Yanglin：You must be very excited about going to France

for schooling.

Chenmei：_____ but I'm afraid I can't do well because

my French is poor.

(A)Never mind,　　　　　(B)Well,I ought to be,

(C)I don't know yet,　　　(D)Certainly not,

【答案】▶(B)

【译文】▶杨林:要去法国读书,你一定很兴奋吧!

陈梅:_____但我怕读不好,因为我的法文很差。

(A)不用介意， (B)噢,应该是,

(C)我还不知道， (D)当然不,

●活学活用●

2.Jane：I'm too fat. I want to lose weight.

Tony：_____

Jane：I know that. But I love food.

(A)You shouldn't eat so much.

(B)You should change your diet.

(C)Be careful;your health is in danger.

(D)You should do somthing about it.

【答案】▶(A)

【译文】▶简： 我太胖了。我必须减肥。

托尼：_____

简： 我知道,但我喜欢吃。

(A)你不应吃太多。

(B)你要改变你的饮食。

(C)小心,你的健康有危险。

(D)关于此事,你要做点什么。

【讲解】▶①*lose weight* 减肥 *put on*(*gain*)*weight* 增加体重

②*in danger* 有危险;在危险中

●活学活用●

3.Mike：I have been planning to buy a computer for a long time.

Bob：_____

Mike：I have to save money first.

(A)What on earth are you going to do?

(B)What is the purpose?

(C)What are you waiting for?

(D)What can I do for you?

【答案】▶(C)

【译文】▶麦克:我很长时间以来一直计划着想买一台电脑。

　　　　鲍勃:＿＿＿＿＿＿＿

　　　　麦克:我必须先存钱。

　　　　　(A)你到底想做什么?

　　　　　(B)目的是什么?

　　　　　(C)那你还等什么?

　　　　　(D)我能帮你做什么吗?

【讲解】▶①鲍勃反问麦克为何等待许久还不买电脑,故选(C)。其余答案皆不合下句文意。

　　　　②***What on earth...?*** ＝ What in the world...?　　到底;究竟

● 活学活用 ●

4. Jim: John always does what he's told to do to the letter.

　　Kim: ＿＿＿＿＿＿＿

　　(A) He's always been a good reader.

　　(B) I wish more students were like him.

　　(C) That's what happens to bookworms.

　　(D) I wish he'd be more conscientious.

【答案】▶(B)

【译文】▶吉姆:约翰一向能不折不扣地执行受托之事。

　　　　金: ＿＿＿＿＿＿＿

　　　　　(A)他一向是个好读者。

　　　　　(B)希望有更多的学生像他那样。

　　　　　(C)那就是书呆子的样子。

　　　　　(D)希望他会更尽心尽力。

【讲解】▶①对方赞美约翰忠于自己的事,所以选(B)。

　　　　②***to the letter*** 确实地;不折不扣地

　　　　③(C)***bookworms*** 书呆子

　　　　④(D)***conscientious*** [ˌkɔnʃiˈenʃəs] *adj.* 有良知的、本着良心做事的

● 活学活用 ●

5. Sam：I thought he had passed all the exams with straight A's.

Kay：_____

(A)What I don't understand is why you thought so.

(B)We are all proud of him.

(C)I can certainly understand how he did that.

(D)I hope he can help me get straight A's, too.

【答案】▶(A)

【译文】▶萨姆：我原先以为他以甲等的成绩通过了所有的考试。

凯：_____

(A)我不了解的是，为什么你会这么想。

(B)我们全都以他为荣。

(C)我当然能了解他是如何做到的。

(D)我希望他也能帮助我得到全部甲等的成绩。

【讲解】▶①事实上，他并没有以甲等的成绩通过所有的考试，故不选 B，C，D。

②*straight A's* 〔美〕(学校成绩)全部甲等

● 活学活用 ●

6. Mary：Helen is a mere washerwoman, yet she's now buying a big house.

Carol：Yes. Because she's always saved _____.

(A)what little she earns

(B)how little she earns

(C)for little she earns

(D)with little she earns

【答案】▶(A)

【译文】▶玛丽：海伦只不过是个洗衣妇，然而她现在要买一幢大房子了。

卡罗尔：是啊！因为她一向把她所赚的那么一点钱全部
　　　　存起来。

【讲解】▶①"what＋(形容词)＋名词或 what＋代名词"意为"所有
　　　的……,任何的……",其中的 what＝all the。
　　　　例：I will give you what books I possess.
　　　　　（我要把我所有的书都给你。）
　　　②(A)中的 what little＝what little money＝all the little
　　　　money 意为"仅有的一点点"。
　　　③*save* 在此当及物动词用,须接宾语,故(C)(D)不合。

━━━━━ ●活学活用● ━━━━━

7. John：I think highly of Robert as a scholar.
　 Mary：Really? To my mind he is _____ a writer.
　　　(A)not so much a scholar as
　　　(B)not nearly a scholar as
　　　(C)not more a scholar as
　　　(D)not as much a scholar than

【答案】▶(A)
【译文】▶约翰：罗伯特身为一名学者,我很推崇他。
　　　　玛丽：真的吗? 依我看,与其说他是个学者,不如说是个
　　　　　　作家。
【讲解】▶*think highly of*　尊敬;重视
　　　　例：He thinks highly of doing things at the right time.
　　　　　（他重视做事的时机。）

现场会话　实战复习测验●

1. John：How do you find the soup?
　 Mary：_____
　　　(A)It seems a bit thin.

(B)I found it in the kitchen.

(C)I got it with the help of my sister.

(D)Thanks, the same to you.

2. Mrs. Tate: I can't understand the youth of today. All they're interested in is pop music and money, and having a good time.

　　Mrs. Lee: _____ (多选)

　　(A)Yes, that's right. In my opinion they don't have any respect for their parents.

　　(B)True. I think they're spoiled rotten.

　　(C)I agree. Life is like a dream.

　　(D)Yes, I think so too.

3. John: Wasn't it a marvellous concert?

　　Mary: _____ (多选)

　　(A)I couldn't agree with you more.

　　(B)Well, not as good as I expected.

　　(C)As you wish.

　　(D)How nice of you to go out with me!

　　(E)Yes, it was terrible.

4. A: It's very embarrassing to visit my uncle. You never know what he is talking about.

　　B: _____

　　A: That's true. My aunt is about the only person who can understand him.

　　(A)If no one understands him, he must have very few friends.

　　(B)We have much to learn from speaking with him.

　　(C)On the contrary, he is a good mixer.

　　(D)We certainly need mutual understanding in this modern world.

5. X: What do you think of Britain?

　　Y: Well, as you know, I've only seen London. And, of course, not all of that.

  X：_____

  Y：I like it fine. It's very intersting. Everything is new，fresh，
and different for me.

    (A)Then how do you like living in London?

    (B)How long have you been here?

    (C)Then how do you like London's weather?

    (D)You don't say so? Do as you like this weekend.

6. A：This school is lucky to have a teacher as good as Miss Lin.

  B：She is one in a million.

  A：_____

    (A)I couldn't agree more.

    (B)Are you sure?

    (C)Don't take it so hard.

    (D)There you go again.

7. A：The streets are never deserted in the big city.

  B：_____ They are always noisy and crowded.

    (A)Who cares?

    (B)I don't know.

    (C)Yes，they are.

    (D)I agree with you.

解题关键分析

1【答案】▶(A)

【译文】▶约翰：你觉得汤怎么样？

      玛丽：_____

        (A)似乎稀了点儿。

        (B)我在厨房找到的。

        (C)我姐姐帮我找到的。

        (D)谢谢你，你也一样。

2.【答案】▶(A)(B)(D)

【译文】▶泰特太太：我无法了解今日的年轻人。他们感兴趣的
　　　　　　　　只有流行音乐、钱和玩得痛快。

　　　　　李太太：＿＿＿＿＿＿＿

　　　　　(A)是的，没错。我认为他们一点也不尊敬父母。

　　　　　(B)没错。我想他们被宠坏了。

　　　　　(C)我同意。人生就像一场梦。

　　　　　(D)是的，我也这么认为。

【讲解】▶*pop*〔pɔp〕*adj.*〔口〕流行的

3.【答案】▶(A)(B)

【译文】▶约翰：这音乐会真棒，不是吗？

　　　　　玛丽：＿＿＿＿＿＿＿

　　　　　(A)我再同意不过了。

　　　　　(B)嗯，不如我期待的那么好。

　　　　　(C)如你所愿。

　　　　　(D)谢谢你跟我出来！

　　　　　(E)是的，真烂。

【讲解】▶*marvel(l)ous*〔'mɑːviləs〕*adj.*〔口〕极佳的

4.【答案】▶(A)

【译文】▶A：拜访我舅舅是很尴尬的。你从来也不晓得他说什
　　　　　　么。

　　　　　B：＿＿＿＿＿＿＿

　　　　　A：那是真的。我舅妈是唯一了解他的人。

　　　　　(A)如果没有人懂得他，他的朋友一定很少。

　　　　　(B)同他谈话我们学到了很多东西。

　　　　　(C)正相反，他是一个会交际的人。

　　　　　(D)在现代世界中我们当然需要相互谅解。

【讲解】▶*a good mixer*　容易与人相处的人

　　　　　mutual understanding　互相了解

5.【答案】▶(A)

【译文】▶X：你认为英国怎么样？

　　　　　Y：嗯，如你所知的，我只见过伦敦。当然并非全部。

　　　　　X：＿＿＿＿＿＿＿

Y:我很喜欢。那儿非常有意思。对我来说一切都很新
　鲜,不同。

　　(A)那么你喜欢在伦敦居住吗?

　　(B)你在那儿多久了。

　　(C)你喜欢伦敦的天气吗?

　　(D)你不这么说? 这个周末你想做什么就做什
　　么。

6.【答案】▶(A)

　【译文】▶甲:学校有林小姐这样的好老师,真是三生有幸啊!

　　　　乙:她可是万中选一的好老师。

　　　　甲:＿＿＿＿＿＿

　　　　(A)我非常同意你的话。

　　　　(B)你确定吗?

　　　　(C)别太认真了。

　　　　(D)又来了。

7.【答案】▶(D)

　【译文】▶甲:大城市的街道永远静不下来。

　　　　乙:＿＿＿＿＿＿街道上总是嘈杂拥挤。

　　　　(A)管他的!

　　　　(B)我不知道。

　　　　(C)是的,它们是。

　　　　(D)我同意你的话。

Watching Television
看电视

A：Do you like to watch TV?

B：Yes. I watch TV quite often.

A：What TV program do you like best?

B：I like news programs best.

A：What time is the news?

B：The news is on at seven thirty.

A：What's on after the news?

B：There is a sports report after the news.

甲：你喜欢看电视吗？

乙：是的,我常看电视。

甲：你最喜欢什么电视节目？

乙：我最喜欢新闻节目。

甲：新闻在几点钟开始？

乙：新闻在七点半开始。

甲：新闻之后是什么节目？

乙：新闻之后有体育报导。

A: Is there a cartoon on Channel 3?

B: Yes. Let's watch the cartoon on Channel 3.

A: All right. I'll turn on the television. Hey, where is the remote controller?

B: It's under the sofa.

A: Oh, yes.

B: Shall I fix us something to drink?

A: Yes, please. I love to drink coffee while I watch TV.

甲: 第三频道有卡通节目吗?

乙: 有的,我们就看第三频道的卡通片吧!

甲: 好,我把电视打开。嘿,遥控器在哪儿?

乙: 就在沙发下面。

甲: 啊,有了。

乙: 要不要我弄点喝的东西?

甲: 好啊,你弄吧!我看电视的时候喜欢喝咖啡。

"和收音机及电视有关"常用语句

① 请把收音机打开(关掉)。Turn on(off)the radio, will you?

把声音关小些。Please turn down a little.

这台收音机音调很美。This radio has a fine tone.

我听到许多静电的叽叽声。I get a lot of static(squeaks).

让我看今日的广播节目。Let me see the radio programs today.

②电视现在在播什么？What's on TV now?

在播连续剧。There's a telecast of a drama.

你没办法收到更好的画面吗？Can't you get a better picture?

我们现在可以收到更好的影像。We can get a clear image on TV now.

今晚有什么节目？What's on the program for tonight?

今晚的节目有什么精彩的？What's the highlight of tonight program?

让我查一查报纸。Well, let me consult the newspaper.

我们收看北京台好了。Let's turn in Beijing TV.

我们的电视机需要修理。We need to fix the TV set.

对白是英语。The dialog is in English.

非常实战测验

●活学活用●

1. Mom：Do you have to keep changing the channel like that?

   Doris：_____

   Mom：Then why don't you just turn off the TV and go do something else?

   (A) It's really nice having cable TV.

   (B) I always watch this program at five.

   (C) But this show is so interesting.

   (D) I can't find anything worth watching.

【答案】▶(D)

【译文】▶妈妈：　你一定要那样不停地转台吗？

　　　　多丽丝：_____

　　　　妈妈：　那么，你何不就关掉电视去做别的事？

(A)装了有线电视实在太棒了。

(B)我总是在五点钟时观赏这个节目。

(C)可是这表演节目这么有趣。

(D)我找不到任何值得看的节目。

● 活学活用 ●

2. Moderator：_____

Cathy： Well, as far as I am concerned, they're terrible. Some police shows are too violent and the news is extremely superficial.

(A) What do you think of today's TV programs?

(B) What are the advantages of having children?

(C) How do you feel about the housing condition?

(D) What's your opinion of public transportation?

【答案】▶(A)

【译文】▶主席：_____

凯茜：嗯，就我而言，很糟糕。部分警匪片太暴力，而且新闻也极为肤浅。

(A)你觉得今天的电视节目如何？

(B)有小孩的好处是什么？

(C)你觉得住宅的情况如何？

(D)你对公共运输有什么意见？

【讲解】▶①*moderator* ['mɔdəreitə] *n.* 主席

②*as far as sb. is concerned* 就某人而言

③*superficial* [ˌsjuːpə'fiʃəl] *adj.* 肤浅的

④*transportation* [ˌtrænspɔː'teiʃən] *n.* 运输

● 活学活用 ●

3. Woman：I hope you don't mind, but I want very much to watch the game this coming Sunday.

Man： _____ but there's not very much I can do about it,is there?

(A)You are welcome,

(B)Well,I'm glad to hear that,

(C)I certainly do mind,

(D)Forget it,

【答案】▶(C)

【译文】▶女士：希望你不介意,但是我很想看这个星期天的比赛。

男士：_____可是我也不能怎么样,对不对?

(A)不客气,

(B)嗯,我很高兴听你这么说,

(C)我当然介意,

(D)算了吧,

现场会话 实战复习测验●

1. A：My children are always watching TV.

B：_____

(A)They would rather do their homework.

(B)TV is a good baby-sitter.

(C)You had better control the amount of TV they watch.

(D)No wonder they don't like to do their homework.

(E)Why don't you turn it off sometimes?

2. Interviewer：What do you think about the TV programs today? Do you think that all of them are good?

Mr. Lee： _____

(A)Yes,I do. Some of the programs are interesting,but others are rather boring.

(B) Yes, I agree with you. It is impossible to satisfy

everybody's desire.

  (C) Yes, I would say so. All the programs leave much to be
    desired.

  (D) No, I don't. Although I am a TV fan, I guess some of the
    programs are more interesting than instructive.

3. Mother: It's getting late. Turn off the TV, Bob, and go to bed.

  Bob: Can't I see just this program through? It'll be over in
     ten minutes.

  Mother: OK. _____ It may disturb our neighbors.

  (A) But turn it down.

  (B) Then you won't get enough sleep.

  (C) But turn it off for a while.

  (D) But when will you study for tomorrow's test?

4. Daughter: I was late for the English class this morning.

  Mother: You stayed up until midnight watching the game on
      T. V. _____.

  (A) You are often mistaken for it.

  (B) It serves you right.

  (C) I don't think it makes sense to keep good time.

  (D) It's advisable for you to sit up late.

5. Tony: I think some TV commercials are very creative and well-
    shot.

  Jane: _____

  (A) I couldn't agree with you more.

  (B) But some are doing a bad business.

  (C) Oh, I don't know that.

  (D) You mean the ones for Coca Cola and Aquarius?

解题关键分析

1.【答案】▶(C)

【译文】▶A: 我的小孩老是在看电视。

　　B：_____

　　　　(A)他们宁愿做功课。

　　　　(B)电视是个好保姆。

　　　　(C)你最好控制他们看电视的量。

　　　　(D)难怪他们不喜欢做功课。（该改成 No wonder
　　　　　　they haven't been doing their homework.）

　　　　(E)你为什么不偶尔把电视关掉呢？

　　　　(本句暗示电视原本一天二十四小时都开着,故不选)

2.【答案】▶(D)

　【译文】▶记者：您认为今日的电视节目如何？ 您认为所有节目
　　　　　　都很好吗？

　　　　李先生：_____

　　　　　(A)是的,我认为都很好。有些节目很有趣,有些节
　　　　　　　目则相当无聊。

　　　　　(B)是的,我同意您的观点。不可能满足每个人的愿
　　　　　　　望。

　　　　　(C)是的,我会这么说。所有的节目都有很多缺点。

　　　　　(D)不,我不认为如此。虽然我是个电视迷,但我想
　　　　　　　有些节目与其说有益,不如说很有趣。

　【讲解】▶①*leave much to be desired*　有很多缺点

　　　　　②*fan* [fæn] *n.*〔口〕(电视、电影、运动)迷

　　　　　③*instructive* [in'strʌktiv] *adj.* 有益的

3.【答案】▶(A)

　【译文】▶母亲：时间不早了。鲍勃,关掉电视,上床去。

　　　　鲍勃：不能让我看完这个节目吗？ 再有十分钟就结束
　　　　　　了。

　　　　母亲：好吧! _____可能会吵到邻居。

　　　　　(A)但是关小声点。

　　　　　(B)那么你就会睡眠不足。

　　　　　(C)但是先关掉一会儿。

　　　　　(D)但是你什么时候为明天的考试做准备?

　【讲解】▶turn down　关小声

4.【答案】▶(B)

　【译文】▶女儿:今天早上我英语课迟到了。

　　　　　　母亲:你熬夜到午夜看电视上的比赛。_____

　　　　　(A)你经常弄错。

　　　　　(B)你活该。

　　　　　(C)我认为准时没有意义。

　　　　　(D)你熬夜是明智的。

　【讲解】▶①*keep good time*　准时

　　　　　②*advisable* [əd'vaizəbl] *adj.* 明智的

5.【答案】▶(B)

　【译文】▶托尼:我认为有些电视广告非常有创意,而且拍得很

　　　　　　　　好。

　　　　　简:_____

　　　　　(A)我再同意不过了。

　　　　　(B)但有些是做不好的生意。

　　　　　(C)哦,这我就不知道了。

　　　　　(D)你是指可口可乐和水瓶座的广告吗?

　【讲解】▶①*commercial* [kə'mɜ:ʃəl] *n.* 商业广告

　　　　　②*shoot* [ʃu:t] *v.* 拍摄(过去式与过去分词为 shot)

　　　　　③*Aquarius* [ə'kwɛəriəs] *n.* 水瓶座(此指一种饮料名)

Going to the Movies
看电影

①
A: I hope we are not late. It's already half past two.

B: What time does the movie begin?

A: It starts at half past two.

B: Well, they usually run some previews before the main feature.

A: Then, the main feature won't start before two forty.

B: Right. Now, you'd better get the tickets.

甲: 希望我们没有迟到。已经两点半了。

乙: 电影什么时候开始?

甲: 两点半开始。

乙: 他们通常在正片前会放映一些预告片。

甲: 那么正片不会在两点四十分之前开始啰!

乙: 是的,好了,你最好去买票吧!

②
A: Where is the ticket office?

B: Right there.

A: Ok, I'll be back in a minute. Where do you want to sit?

B: I like to sit on the aisle.

A: I'll go and get the tickets now.

B: And I'll get us some drinks.

甲:售票处在哪儿?

乙:就在那儿。

甲:哦,我马上回来。你要坐哪儿?

乙:我喜欢坐在过道旁边。

甲:我现在就去买票了。

乙:我去买点喝的。

"和电影有关"的常用语句

①去看电影好吗?

How about(What do you say to)going to the movies?

好主意,我好久没看电影了。

That's a good idea. I haven't been to the movies for a long time.

②这戏院上演什么影片? What movie is on at this theater?

谁主演啊? Who is playing the leading role?

谁是导演啊? Who is the director?

③第一部是新闻片。 The first picture is a newsreel.

这部电影改编自有名的小说。

This is a film version of a well-known novel.

这部电影有一个半小时。

This movie runs for an hour and a half.

非 常实战测验 ●──────────────

● 活学活用 ●

1. A：Which movie are you going to see?

　　B：There's nothing good on at the moment. _____ Would

　　　you like to go to a concert?

　　　(A)Let's do something different.

　　　(B)Let's take a look at the menu.

　　　(C)Let's go there right away.

　　　(D)Let's go buy the tickets.

【答案】▶(A)

【译文】▶A：你要去看哪一部电影？

　　　　B：现在没有好片在上映。_____ 你想去听音乐会吗？

　　　　(A)我们来点不一样的吧。　(B)我们看一下菜单吧。

　　　　(C)我们立刻去那里吧。　　(D)我们去买票吧。

【讲解】▶①B说没有好片上映，而提议另一种不同的娱乐(听音乐

　　　　会)。

　　　　②*on*(电影)上映中

　　　　③*at the moment*　目前；此时

● 活学活用 ●

2. Susan：　Mother，can I go to the National Theater to see

　　　　　Gone with the Wind?

Mother：　_____

Susan：　What do you mean?

Mother：　You may go only if you have finished your home-

　　　　　work.

　　(A)It depends.

(B)I happened to see the movie today.

(C)I'll be glad to.

(D)What do you think of Clark Gable?

【答案】▶(A)

【译文】▶苏珊:妈妈,我可以去国家戏院看《乱世佳人》吗?

母亲:＿＿＿＿＿＿＿

苏珊:什么意思?

母亲:只要你做完作业,你就可以去。

(A)视情况而定。

(B)我今天刚好去看这部电影。

(C)乐意之至。

(D)你觉得克拉克·盖博怎样?

【讲解】▶***It depends.＝That depends.***(视情况而定。)

例:***It*** all ***depends***(on)what you will do next.

(一切全看你下一步如何做了。)

● 活学活用 ●

3. X:That was such an interesting movie! I hope you enjoyed it.

Y:I dozed off after the first thirty minutes. ＿＿＿＿＿＿＿

(A)It was very affecting.

(B)I must admit that it was boring.

(C)I found it informative.

(D)I've never seen such a sickening movie.

【答案】▶(B)

【译文】▶X:那部电影真是有趣! 我希望你喜欢。

Y:开演三十分钟之后,我都在打瞌睡。 ＿＿＿＿＿＿＿

(A)那部电影非常感人。

(B)我必须承认那部电影很无聊。

(C)我发现那部电影非常有教育价值。

(D)我从来没有看过这么使人作呕的影片。

【讲解】▶①*doze* [dəuz] *v.* 打瞌睡

②*informative* [in'fɔ:mətiv] *adj.* 有教育价值的

③*sickening* [sickening] *adj.* 使人作呕

现场会话 实战复习测验●

1. Tony：_____

   Peter：Very impressive.

   (A) How do you think of *The Last Emperor*?

   (B) What do you think of *The Last Emperor*?

   (C) Were you impressed by *The Last Emperor*?

   (D) Did you like *The Last Emperor*?

2. (Outside the theater.)

   Jane：What do you think of the film, then?

   Bill：Oh, I think it was great. Don't you think so, Pat?

   Pat：_____

   (A) No, I think it was great, too.

   (B) I prefer operas to films.

   (C) Well, I'm not used to thinking.

   (D) Mmm, I suppose. But I've seen better ones.

3. Janet：What do you think of the movie?

   Martin：Oh, I think it's terrific.

   Janet：So do I. A lot better than the soap operas on TV.

   Martin：_____

   (A) It's inferior to the lousy TV programs.

   (B) Out of the question!

   (C) The feeling is mutual.

   (D) That's the last movie I want to see.

4. Tony：Will you go to see the movie at the Great World tonight?

   Henry：_____

   (A) Yes, I am busy tonight.

(B) Good. I have to prepare for tomorrow's test.

(C) Yes, I saw it yesterday.

(D) What's on?

解题关键分析

1. **【答案】**▶ (B)

　　【译文】▶托尼：_____

　　　　　　彼得：令我印象非常深刻。

　　　　　　(A) 你是怎么想《末代皇帝》的？（应改为 How do you find...?）

　　　　　　(B) 你觉得《末代皇帝》如何？

　　　　　　(C) 你对《末代皇帝》印象深刻吗？

　　　　　　(D) 你喜欢《末代皇帝》吗？（回答(C)(D)的问题，应用 Yes 或 No）

　　【讲解】▶ *impressive* [im'presiv] *adj.* 令人印象深刻的

2. **【答案】**▶ (D)

　　【译文】▶（在剧院外）

　　　　　　简：　那么，你觉得这部电影如何？

　　　　　　比尔：喔，我认为很棒。帕特，你不这么认为吗？

　　　　　　帕特：_____

　　　　　　(A) 不，我也认为很棒。

　　　　　　(B) 我喜欢歌剧甚于电影。

　　　　　　(C) 嗯，我不习惯思考。

　　　　　　(D) 嗯，我也这么认为。不过我看过更好的。

　　【讲解】▶ opera ['ɔpərə] *n.* 歌剧

3. **【答案】**▶ (C)

　　【译文】▶珍妮特：你认为那部电影怎么样？

　　　　　　马丁：　噢，我认为满好的。

　　　　　　珍妮特：我也是这么认为。比电视上的肥皂剧好太多了。

　　　　　　马丁：　_____

(A)比那讨厌的电视节目还差。

(B)根本不行。

(C)有同感。

(D)这是我要看的最后一部电影。

4.【答案】▶(D)

【译文】▶托尼:你今晚要去大世界看电影吗?

亨利:_____

(A)是的,今晚我很忙。

(B)好,我必须准备明天的考试。

(C)是的,我昨天看过了。

(D)演什么?

School Life
学校生活

㈠

—**A**：How was the class?

—**B**：Pretty interesting.

—**A**：Were you on time for the class?

—**B**：You bet, I was.

—甲：课程如何?

—乙：很有趣。

—甲：你准时上课吗?

—乙：当然,是的。

㈡

—**A**：Are you having a test tomorrow?

—**B**：Yes. We're having a test in English.

—**A**：Good luck to you.

—甲：你明天要考试吗?

—乙：是的。我们要考英文。

—甲：祝你好运。

㈢

—**A**：Why are you so worried, Johnny?

—**B**：My sister doesn't study hard enough.

—**A**：Isn't she interested in school?

—**B**：School interests her, but homework doesn't.

甲：约翰，你为什么如此烦恼？

乙：我妹妹不够用功。

甲：她不喜欢上学吗？

乙：她很喜欢上学，但对家庭作业就不行了。

（四）

A：I'm worried about my school work.

B：What's the problem?

A：I think I'm going to fail the examinations.

B：Maybe you won't if you have more confidence.

甲：我很担心学校的功课。

乙：怎么了？

甲：我想我考试会不及格。

乙：如果你更有自信，也许就不会。

（五）

A：Do you really like English?

B：Yes, very much. I enjoy conversation classes.

A：Is Mr. Grant your English teacher?

B：Yes, he is.

A：He taught me English last year, too.

甲：你真的喜欢英文吗？

乙：是的，很喜欢，我喜欢上会话课。

甲：格兰特先生是你的英文老师吗？

乙：是的，他是。

甲：他去年也教我英文。

A: Do you enjoy your school life?

B: Yes,I do.

（六）

A: What are your favorite subjects?

B: English and history. And you?

A: My favorites are mathematics and physics.

甲：你喜欢学校生活吗?

乙：是的,我喜欢。

甲：你最喜欢的科目是什么?

乙：英文和历史。你呢?

甲：我最喜欢数学和物理。

A: What did you apply for,Bob?

B: I applied for a scholarship. Helen.

A: What school did you apply to?

（七）

B: I applied to Chicago University.

A: When are you supposed to go abroad for advanced education?

B: Next spring,if I can make it.

甲：你申请什么,鲍勃?

乙：我申请奖学金。海伦。

甲：你向什么学校申请?

乙：我向芝加哥大学申请。

甲：你什么时候要出国深造?

乙：明年春天,如果能够顺利的话。

1. ➡"点名"常用语句

①我将点名。A？B？ Now I'm going to call the roll. A？B？
到。Here, sir. Present, sir.
②有没有人缺席？ Is there anyone absent?
全部出席。All present.

2. ➡"老师上课时"常用语句

①我们来复习上一课。Let's review the last lesson.
②拿出课本。Take out your texbooks.
③不要打开书。Keep your books closed.
④打开书第十页。Open your book at page 10.
⑤翻回第十页。Turn back to page 10.
⑥你明白意思吗？ Is the meaning clear to you?
⑦注意听我的话。Listen to me carefully.
⑧跟我念。Repeat after me.
⑨一起说。Say it altogether.
⑩在这短语下面划线。Underline the phrase.
⑪不要看旁边。Don't look aside.
⑫注意看书。Keep your eyes fixed on your book.
⑬如能回答，举手。Raise your hand if you can answer the
question.
⑭放下手。Put down your hands.
⑮有没有疑问？ (Is there) Any question?

3. ➡ "下课"常用语句

①时间到了，我们到此为止。Well, time is up. We'll stop here.
②到此为止，星期五再见。So much for today. Good-bye until Friday.
③到此为止，明天见。I'll stop here. See you tomorrow.
④下课。Class dismissed.

非常实战测验 ●

● 活学活用 ●

1. Sally：What do you plan to do after the exam?

　Kathy：_____. How about you?

　Sally：I'll take some computer lessons.

　　(A) You can say that again!

　　(B) I'm all for it.

　　(C) Nothing special.

　　(D) I've changed my mind.

【答案】▶ (C)

【译文】▶ 萨莉:考完试你要做什么?

　　　　凯茜:_____。那你呢?

　　　　萨莉:我要上电脑(课)。

　　　　(A)你再说一遍。

　　　　(B)我完全同意这么做。

　　　　(C)没什么特别的。

　　　　(D)我已经改变心意了。

●活学活用●

2. Teacher：What's your excuse for being late today?

Student： I had a heartburn this morning and I went to see a doctor.

Teacher：_____ You have a different excuse each day.

(A)I wish I were as imaginative as you are.

(B)How come you always have the same excuse?

(C)What did the doctor say?

(D)Do you feel better now?

【答案】▶(A)

【译文】▶老师：你今天迟到的借口是什么？

　　　　学生：我今天早上胃痛(胃灼热)并且去看医生。

　　　　老师：_____ 你每天都有不同的借口。

　　　　(A)我希望我像你那么有想象力就好了。

　　　　(B)为什么你总是一样的借口？

　　　　(C)医生怎么说？

　　　　(D)你现在觉得好一点了吗？

【讲解】▶①*heartburn* ['hɑ:tbə:n] *n.* 胃痛(特别指胃酸太多或消化不良所引起)

②*stomach-ache* ['stʌməkeik] *n.* 胃痛(一般用语)

③*heart-ache* ['hɑ:teik] *n.* 伤心

④*imaginative* [i'mædʒinətiv] *adj.* 富有想象力的

⑤*How come+S+V...*？为什么？

⑥与现在事实相反的假设语气：

If＋S＋过去式 V...，S＋should/would＋V 原形…

If＋S＋were＋...，S＋should/would＋V 原形…

故本句中 wish 从句用 I were... 的形态来表示与现在事实相反。

● 活学活用 ●

3. Jack：I've been wanting to get a chance to discuss our homework with you.

  Mark：_____

  (A) Do you want me to go shopping with you?

  (B) So have I. Let's meet at seven o'clock tonight.

  (C) That's fine. I'll see you off.

  (D) Thank you. Then it's settled.

【答案】▶ (B)

【译文】▶ 杰克：我一直想找个机会和你谈谈我们的家庭作业。

  马克：_____

  (A) 你要我跟你一起去逛街吗？

  (B) 我也是。我们今晚七点见面。

  (C) 很好。我会送你。

  (D) 谢谢。就这样解决了。

【讲解】▶ I have been wanting... 我一直想要……

● 活学活用 ●

4. A：I'm really frustrated. Last semester I failed in two subjects.

  B：Take heart! _____

  (A) The world didn't come to an end.

  (B) You can kill two birds with one stone.

  (C) Better late than never.

  (D) Old dogs cannot play new tricks.

【答案】▶ (A)

【译文】▶ A：我真的感到挫折。上学期我有两科不及格。

  B：鼓起勇气来！_____

  (A) 又不是世界末日。

  (B) 你可以一石二鸟。

(C)迟做总比不做好。

(D)老狗要不出新把戏。

【讲解】▶①A 因有两科不及格,所以有挫折感,B 用"*Take heart*!"

安慰他,故只有答案(A)能配合。

②答案(A)有时也可说成:This is not the end of the world.

③*frustrated* [frʌ'streitid,'frʌ-] *a.* 受挫折的

●活学活用●

5. A:I can't believe it! I took the math exam, and I got the highest score in my class!

B:_____ I'm thrilled for you.

(A)It's a pity.   (B)That's great.

(C)No wonder.   (D)You can count on it.

【答案】▶(B)

【译文】▶A:我真不敢相信! 我参加数学考试,在班上得到最高分!

B:_____ 我为你感到高兴。

(A)真可惜。   (B)太好了。

(C)难怪。   (D)你可以依赖它。

【讲解】▶①A 对自己意外地在考试中得到高分,难以相信,而 B 也

为 A 感到高兴。

②*thrilled* ['θrild] *adj.* 兴奋的;激动的

③*count on* 信赖;指望

●活学活用●

6. Mike:What courses are you going to take next semester?

Dinana:_____ I have to talk to my advisor.

(A)It's not my fault.   (B)I haven't decided yet.

(C)What's your problem?   (D)No wonder.

【答案】▶(B)

【译文】▶麦克: 你下学期要选什么课?

黛安娜：_____我必须和指导教授谈一谈。

　　(A)不是我的过错。

　　(B)我尚未决定。

　　(C)你的问题是什么？

　　(D)难怪。

【讲解】▶①*take courses* 选课

　　②*advisor* *n.* 指导教授；新生之导师

═══════ ●活学活用● ═══════

7. May：Believe me，Sue，this program can help you with your
　　　geography course.

　　Sue：_____

　　(A)It's called *A Trip Down the Amazon*.

　　(B)Do you often watch public TV?

　　(C)Any idea about the program?

　　(D)Okay，you've talked me into watching it.

【答案】▶(D)

【译文】▶梅：相信我，苏。这个节目对你的地理课会有帮助的。

　　苏：_____

　　(A)它叫做《亚马逊河之旅》。

　　(B)你常看电视节目吗？

　　(C)对这个节目有什么意见吗？

　　(D)好吧，你已经说服我去看这个节目。

现场会话 实战复习测验●

1. A：I'm sorry I've been absent. I had a bad cold.

　B：Perfectly understandable.

　A：_____

　B：I understand. When I had one last month，I stayed home and

      rested for three days.

      (A)I coughed a lot.

      (B)I had a fever.

      (C)It took a long time to go away.

      (D)I went to see a doctor yesterday.

2. Teacher:How is it you are late for class again?

    Student:＿＿＿＿

      (A)By bus and then on foot.

      (B)Because I missed the bus.

      (C)It's far from school.

      (D)There are a lot of people on the bus.

3. John:In three years,how would you feel being a student in this high school?

    Mary:Pretty good. But I don't know what I'm going to be yet.

    John:＿＿＿＿You are the master of yourself.

      (A)Anything you want to be,you will be.

      (B)You won't be anything you want to be.

      (C)You shouldn't be studying here.

      (D)You must acknowledge you are not very talented.

4. Diana:What would you like to be after you've graduated?

    James:＿＿＿＿

      (A)I'll go abroad for advanced studies.

      (B)Selling cars.

      (C)A physician.

      (D)To get married.

5. Teacher:Tell me who gave the best answer?

    Pupil:＿＿＿＿(多选)

      (A)Well,I would if only I could remember the name of the person.

      (B)I don't know which is the best.

      (C)I would if I should remember it.

      (D)I dare say it was John.

(E)You must make out a right answer.

6. A：Don't cheat in the examination.

　B：_____

　　(A)I don't.　　　　　(B)I didn't.

　　(C)I won't.　　　　　(D)I haven't.

7. A：The final exam is coming. Aren't you nervous?

　B：_____

　　(A)No，I am well prepared for it.

　　(B)Yes，I am not nervous at all.

　　(C)No，I have been so nervous lately that I hardly get any sleep.

　　(D)Yes，and that's why I like the exams.

8. A：Why did our teacher give us so much homework?

　B：_____

　　(A)Because this part is unimportant.

　　(B)Well，he didn't want to keep us busy.

　　(C)He wanted us to be familiar with the materials he taught.

　　(D)I like his way of teaching.

解题关键分析

1.【答案】▶(C)

　【译文】▶A：我很抱歉我缺席。我感冒了。

　　　　　B：完全可以理解的。

　　　　　A：_____

　　　　　B：我了解。上个月我感冒时，我呆在家里休息了三天。

　　　　　(A)我咳嗽很厉害。

　　　　　(B)我发烧。

　　　　　(C)要花好长时间才好。

　　　　　(D)昨天我去看病。

2.【答案】▶(B)

　【译文】▶老师：你怎么上课又迟到呢？

学生：_____

    (A)乘车、步行。

    (B)因为我错过了巴士。

    (C)离学校远。

    (D)车上人多。

3.【答案】▶(A)

  【译文】▶约翰：在未来三年里，你对于身为这所高中的学生会有

        什么感觉？(此句问话暗示玛丽仍未进入这所高

        中，故用 would 表假设语态。)

      玛丽：我会感觉很好，但我还不知道将来要做什么。

      约翰：_____你是你自己的主人。

      (A)你想要成为什么，你就会成为什么。

      (B)不论你想成为什么，都无法如愿。

      (C)你不该在这里读书。

      (D)你必须承认你并非很有才能。

  【讲解】▶*acknowledge* [əkˈnɔlidʒ] *v.* 承认

4.【答案】▶(C)

  【译文】▶黛安娜：毕业后你想成为什么？

      詹姆斯：_____

      (A)我要出国深造。   (B)卖车。

      (C)内科医师。   (D)结婚。

  【讲解】▶*physician* [fiˈziʃən] *n.* 内科医师

5.【答案】▶(A)(D)

  【译文】▶老师：告诉我，谁的答案最好？

      学生：_____

      (A)这个嘛，假如我记得那个人的名字，我就告诉你。

      (B)我不知道哪一个最好。(原问句问的是 who，不

        是 which。)

      (C)如果到时我把它记住了，我就会告诉你。

      (D)我敢说是约翰。

      (E)你必须分辨出正确的答案。

  【讲解】▶*make out* 分辨

6.【答案】▶(C)

　　【译文】▶A:考试不要作弊喔!

　　　　　　B:_____。

　　　　　　(A)我不作弊。

　　　　　　(B)我没作弊。

　　　　　　(C)我不会作弊的。

　　　　　　(D)我从来不作弊。

7.【答案】▶(A)

　　【译文】▶A:期末考快到了。你难道不紧张吗?

　　　　　　B:_____

　　　　　　(A)我一点儿也不紧张。我早就准备好了。

　　　　　　(B)是的,我一点儿也不紧张。

　　　　　　(C)紧张,我最近紧张得睡不好。

　　　　　　(D)我很紧张,所以我才喜欢考试。

8.【答案】▶(C)

　　【译文】▶A:为什么老师给我们那么多功课?

　　　　　　B:_____

　　　　　　(A)因为这部分不重要。

　　　　　　(B)喔! 他不想让我们很忙。

　　　　　　(C)他想让我们熟悉他教的东西。

　　　　　　(D)我喜欢他的教法。

Weather

天 气

第**20**篇

情景对话精选

(一)

A: It's hot outside. Shall I turn on the air-conditioner?

B: All right
O. K. , that would be fine.

┌ **甲**: 外面很热，要我打开冷气机吗？
└ **乙**: 好的，可以。

(二)

A: The weather is good today. Let's go on a picnic.
an outing.
a trip.

B: That's a good idea.

┌ **甲**: 今天天气很好。我们去郊游。
└ **乙**: 好主意。

(三)

A: It's a nice
lovely
beautiful day today, isn't it?

B: Yes, it is fair and sunny.

┌ **甲**: 今天天气很好，不是吗？
└ **乙**: 是的，天气晴朗而且阳光普照。

有关"谈天气"的常用语句

①谈"今天天气"的常用语句：

❶Beautiful(Nice)day,isn't it?

❷It's a beautiful day,isn't it?

❸Isn't it a beautiful day?

②表"今天天气不错"的常用语句：Yes,it couldn't be better.

③其他有关"天气"的常用语句：

❶今天天气很冷啊？ Isn't it chilly today?

❷下午可能下雪。 It looks like snow this afternoon.

❸云越来越浓。 It's getting cloudy.

❹好热的天啊？ What a hot day!

❺今天天气如何？ How is the weather today?

非常实战测验

●活学活用●

1. X：Is it raining？（选错误答案）

　　Y：_____

　　　(A)It is at the moment.

　　　(B)It's simply pouring down.

　　　(C)Why don't you look out the window for yourself?

　　　(D)One never knows.

【答案】▶(D)

【译文】▶X：正在下雨吗？

　　　　Y：_____

　　　　　(A)现在正在下。

　　　　　(B)大雨正倾盆而下。

　　　　　(C)你怎么不自己看看窗外？

　　　　　(D)我们永远不会知道。

【讲解】▶*pour down* 倾盆而下

● 活学活用 ●

> 2. Martin：Hurry up！It's starting to rain.
>
> Jack：_____
>
> (A)I'm tired. I can't ride any faster.
>
> (B)Why?
>
> (C)Slow and steady wins.
>
> (D)Right！Let's take a rest.

【答案】▶(A)

【译文】▶马丁:快点儿！开始下雨了。

杰克:_____

(A)我好累,不能骑得更快了。

(B)为什么?

(C)稳健扎实必制胜。

(D)对！让我们休息一下。

【讲解】▶***Slow and steady wins（the race）.***

〔谚〕稳健扎实必致胜。

● 活学活用 ●

> 3. A：What's the weather like today?
>
> B：_____
>
> (A)Everybody likes it very much.
>
> (B)That's for sure.
>
> (C)I think it'll be really nice.
>
> (D)We'll never have weather like this.

【答案】▶(C)

【译文】▶A:今天的天气怎样?

B:_____

(A)每一个人都非常喜欢它。

(B)那当然。

(C)我想会相当不错。

（D）我们不会再有像这样的天气了。

【讲解】▶ *for sure*　确定地

现场会话 实战复习测验 ●

1. X：I don't want to spoil your plan for the sights of the city, but I think it's going to rain in about ten minutes.

Y：Yes,＿＿＿＿＿＿

（A）it looks threatening.

（B）it will clear up very soon.

（C）we don't want to see the town in a rainstorm.

（D）that would be pleasant.

2. Bert： Rain, rain, go away. Come again another day!

Kathy：Why are you singing that song?

Bert：＿＿＿＿＿＿

Kathy：Well, I don't think singing that song will make the rain go away any faster.

（A）I like the rain.

（B）I wish it could stop raining.

（C）I can't stop it from raining.

（D）I'm not sure if it's going to rain.

3. R：The weather forecast said that tomorrow would be cloudy in the morning but it would clear up.

J：I hope the weather forecast is right.

R：Look,＿＿＿＿＿＿

J：You're right; it's not raining as hard, either.

（A）there's a break in the clouds already.

（B）it's begun to rain.

（C）it's certainly so clear and there is no cloud in the sky.

（D）it's just a shower.

4. A：Do you think we will be able to go to the beach tomorrow?

B:_____ Have the plans changed?

A:No, but I am worried about the weather. It might rain.

B:It certainly seems fine now. There's not a cloud in the sky.

 (A)Certainly.   (B)Perhaps.

 (C)Why not?   (D)Pardon me.

解题关键分析

1.【答案】▶(A)

 【译文】▶X:我不想让你游览城市的计划泡汤,但是我想大约再
     过十分钟后会下雨。

    Y:是的,_____

    (A)看起来要变天了。

    (B)很快就会放晴了。

    (C)我们不要在暴风雨中看这座城市。

    (D)那会很愉快。

 【讲解】▶①*threatening* [ˈθretəniŋ] *adj.*(天气等)要转坏的

    ②*clear up*(天气)放晴

    ③*rainstorm* [ˈreinstɔm] *n.* 暴风雨

2.【答案】▶(B)

 【译文】▶波特:雨啊,雨啊,走开吧! 改天再来!

    凯茜:你为什么唱那首歌呢?

    波特:_____

    凯茜:嗯,我想唱那首歌不会让雨快点走开。

    (A)我喜欢下雨。

    (B)我希望它能让雨停。

    (C)我不能阻止下雨。

    (D)我不确定是否会下雨。

3.【答案】▶(A)

 【译文】▶R:气象预测说明天早晨是阴天,但天气会转晴。

    J:但愿气象预测是对的。

    R:看,_____

J：你对了；而且雨现在也没下那么大了。

(A)云已经走开了。

(B)开始下雨了。

(C)当然，天气这么晴朗而且天空没有云。

(D)只是一场阵雨。

4.【答案】▶(C)

【译文】▶A：你认为我们明天能去海滩吗？

B：_____计划改变了吗？

A：没有，但是我担心天气。可能会下雨。

B：现在看来，天气很好。天空连一朵云也没有。

(A)当然。　　　　(B)或许。

(C)为什么不能？　(D)对不起。

Micellaneous
综　合

第21篇

情景对话精选

一 ➡棒球

　A：Hello, Billy, where are you going?

　B：I'm on my way to a baseball game. Do you want to come along, Tom?

㈠　A：May I join you?

　B：Sure, by all means.

　A：Do you like baseball?

　B：I'm mad about it.

　甲：嗨，比利，你要去哪里？

　乙：我要去看棒球赛。你要一起去吗，汤姆？

　甲：我可以加入吗？

　乙：当然，一定要。

　甲：你喜欢棒球吗？

　乙：我迷死棒球了。

　A：May I ask your favorite sports?

　B：I like baseball.

㈡　A：Can you play baseball?

　B：Yes, a little bit, but not so well, though. How about you?

　A：I'm just interested in a good game. I prefer watching a baseball game to playing baseball.

甲：请问你最喜欢的运动是什么？

乙：我喜欢棒球。

甲：你会打棒球吗？

乙：是的，会一点，但不是很好。你呢？

甲：我只对精彩比赛感兴趣。我比较喜欢看棒球赛，而不喜欢打棒球。

二 ➡其他常考会话实例

A：Are you going to show up tomorrow?

㈠ — B：I'm still on the fence about it.

A：I sure wish you'd make up your mind!

甲：你明天来不来？

乙：我还在考虑。

甲：真希望你做个决定！

A：Does Hitchcock's picture suit your taste?

㈡ — B：I enjoy very much.

A：That makes two of us.

甲：希区科克的电影合你的口味吗？

乙：我很喜欢。

甲：我也一样。

A：How about these dishes?

㈢ — B：Well, I am not particular anyway. But I would prefer a plain home cooking.

A：Sounds inviting. I heard you are some cook.

甲：这几道菜如何？

乙：嗯，反正我也不挑剔。但是我还是比较喜欢家常便饭。

甲：听起来很吸引人，我听说你是位很棒的厨师呢！

（四）
A：I feel terrible lonesome, Joe. Can you fix me up with someone the weekend?
B：No sweat!

甲：我好寂寞，乔，周末为我安排个玩伴吧！
乙：没问题！

（五）
A：I got a dear-John-letter from her yesterday.
B：Are you kidding?
A：No, I am on the level.

甲：我昨天收到女朋友的绝交信了。
乙：真的吗？
甲：真的！

（六）
A：I'll go at it for my own good.
B：Now you are talking!

甲：为我自己好，我将全力以赴。
乙：这才像话。

（七）
A：I'm sure nervous about giving this speech.

B：Don't worry. Before you know it you'll be through.

A：What's keeping the M. C. ? I'd like to get this over with.

B：He'll be here in a jiffy.

甲：发表这次演说我真紧张。

乙：别担心，很快就会完的。

甲：主持人怎么还没到啊？我真想快点结束。

乙：他马上就会到。

（八）
A：I must get rolling, my date is waiting.

B：What's the big hurry? Is she your steady?

A：Don't get too personal, would you?

甲：我必须走了，我约的朋友在等我。

乙：干吗这么急?她是你固定的女朋友吗?

甲：不要打探别人隐私好吗?

(九)

A：I've finished this report. What do you say we knock off early for lunch and avoid the rush?

B：Suits me.

甲：我报告写完了。我们早点结束去吃午饭，免得等会儿人多，好吗?

乙：好啊!

(十)

A：Let's call it quits. What do you say?

B：It's up to you.

甲：我们就算了吧! 你意下如何?

乙：随你便。

(十一)

A：Unless you start making your bed every morning, you won't get your allowance. Do I make myself clear?

B：I guess you mean business, don't you?

甲：除非你开始每天早上铺床，否则你拿不到零用钱。我说的够清楚了吗?

乙：我想你是当真的，对不对?

(十二)

A：Where did you learn to play billiards so well?

B：I picked it up from a buddy in the army.

甲：你从哪学的，台球打的这么好?

乙：我是在部队跟一个朋友学的。

(十三)

A：Would you like to drop by the cafeteria with me?

B：Don't mind if I do.

A：Good. While we're eating I'll fill you in on some developments. By the way, lunch is on me.

B：I'm for that.

—甲：跟我一起到自助餐厅好吗？

—乙：我无所谓。

—甲：很好，用餐的时候，我会告诉你一些新的事物，顺便告诉你，午餐我请客。

—乙：我同意。

1. ➡"棒球场上"常用语句

①谁担任什么角色？ Who's playing whom?

比分是多少？ What's the score?

最后比分是四比三。 The final score was 4 to 3.

谁赢了？ Who won? /Who is the winner?

②现在是第几局？ What inning is this?

是全垒打。 It's a home run.

③谁是世界纪录保持者？ Who holds the world's record?

谁是冠军？ Who is the champion?

这场比赛的确精彩。 This is really a great game, isn't it?

2. ➡"理发店"常用语句

①先生，理发吗？ Haircut, sir?

是的，外加修面。 Yes, plus a shave.

好的，先生，要理哪种发型啊？ Very well, sir. How do you like your hair done?

不要太短，脑后不要推剪。 Not very short, I don't want the clippers at the back.

那后面要怎样剪呢？ How do you want it cut at the back?

剪刀理理就好。Use the scissors only.

②请坐这边。Please sit here. /Won't you take a seat?

现在轮到你了。It's your turn now.

3. ➡"道贺"常用语句

①恭贺恭喜。Congratulations(on your victory)! /Let me congratulate you(on your success).

②祝你生日快乐。Happy birthday! /Many happy returns(of the day)!

③圣诞(新年)快乐。Merry Christmas! /Happy New Year! /Best wishes!

④谢谢。彼此彼此。Thank you. /The same to you.

4. ➡"惊叹"常用语句

①老天啊! Oh,boy! /Oh,my! /Oh,dear!

②其他❶How nice!

❷Well done!

❸Oh, it's beautiful!

❹Oh,that's wonderful!

❺Isn't that exciting?

❻What a nice room!

5. ➡其他应注意的常用语句

①好的。All right. /Good.　我很乐意。With pleasure.

②当然。Certainly. /Of course. /Why,certainly. /Of course not.

③真的? Do you? /Is that right? /Really?

④我懂了。I see. /Oh, yes.

⑤对了。That's it. /That's right. /You're right.

⑥我认为不。I don't think so.　我认为如此。I think so. 恐怕不。I'm afraid not.　我不希望。I hope not.　我希望。I hope so.　我想我要。I think I will.

⑦这是真的。It certainly is (was). /It really is.

⑧也许。May be. /Let me see.　我没把握。I'm not sure.

⑨顺便说。By the way.

⑩我真高兴知道。I'm glad to hear that.

　真遗憾知道。I'm sorry to hear that.

⑪请。Please do.

⑫我也是。So am I(or So do I).

⑬那倒使我想起来了。That reminds me.

⑭好主意。That's a good idea.

⑮还用你说。You don't say!

●活学活用●

1. Guodong：How long did it take you to speak English so fluently?

　Huaming：Ten years. You have to practice it every day.

　————

　Guodong：Your're right about it

　　(A)I'd be glad to do it for you.　(B)Nothing really matters.

　　(C)So far so good.　(D)There's no shortcut.

【答案】▶(D)

【译文】▶国栋：你花了多长时间才把英语讲得这么流利？

华明：十年。你必须每天练习。_____

国栋：你说得对。

　　(A)我会高兴为你做此事。　　(B)没有什么真正重要的事。

　　(C)到现在，一切还不错。　　(D)没有捷径。

━━━━━ ● 活学活用 ● ━━━━━

2. Alice： Is there a garage sale in the neighborhood today?

　　Nancy： Yes. There's one next street. _____

　　Alice： Some old furniture, perhaps.

　　(A) What can I do for you?

　　(B) What do you plan to buy?

　　(C) What's the big idea?

　　(D) What's on your mind?

【答案】▶ (B)

【译文】▶ 爱丽丝：今天这附近有人在卖旧货吗？

　　　　南茜： 有，下一条街有一家在卖。_____

　　　　爱丽丝：一些旧家具，也许。

　　　　(A)我能为你做什么？

　　　　(B)你计划买什么？

　　　　(C)是什么了不起的主意啊？/那是怎么回事？/搞什

　　　　　　么名堂？

　　　　(D)你在担心什么？

━━━━━ ● 活学活用 ● ━━━━━

3. Kent： I've just found out that my dog is very ill and
　　　　　doesn't have long to live.

　　Linda： _____

　　Kent： I know he's old for a dog, but he's like a member
　　　　　of the family.

　　(A) I'm so tired of hearing this.

　　(B) I'm so relieved to hear that.

　　(C) I'm so sorry to hear that.

　　(D) What exciting news!

【答案】▶(C)

【译文】▶肯特：我刚发现我的狗病得很重,而且活不了多久。

琳达：_____

肯特：我知道对一条狗来说他已经很老,但他就像家里的
一分子。

(A)我很厌烦听到这事儿。

(B)我听到那消息,真是松了一口气。

(C)听到此事令我很难过。

(D)好令人兴奋的消息!

● 活学活用 ●

4. Mark：Is this your pen? I just picked it up from the floor.

Jim：_____My pen is right here.

Mark：Then I wonder whose it is.

(A)Well,thank you very much.

(B)Let me see...no,it can't be.

(C)Oh, it's so nice of you to say so.

(D)Hmm.... It might be John's.

【答案】▶(B)

【译文】▶马克：这是你的笔吗? 我刚从地板上捡起来。

吉姆：_____我的笔就在这儿。

马克：那么我就不知道这支笔是谁的。

(A)好,多谢。

(B)让我看看……不,不可能是。

(C)噢,真感谢你这么说。

(D)嗯……可能是约翰的。

● 活学活用 ●

5. Mom：Tom,hurry and do the dishes.

Tom：_____

Mom：Is it? I thought she did the dishes last night.

Tom:She did. But I did them once for her, and now she
     owes me a night.

  (A)It's not my turn.

  (B)It's Lois's turn tonight.

  (C)Ask Lois to do the dishes.

  (D)It's none of my business.

【答案】▶(B)

【译文】▶母亲:汤姆,快去洗碗盘。

    汤姆:＿＿＿＿＿＿＿

    母亲:是吗？我原以为她昨晚洗过了。

    汤姆:她是洗了。但我曾替她洗过一次,现在她欠我一个
      晚上。

    (A)不是轮到我洗。   (B)今晚轮到洛依丝。

    (C)叫洛依丝去洗碗。   (D)不关我的事。

【讲解】▶do the dishes　洗碗盘,洗餐具

━━●活学活用●━━

6. Karen:Mary enjoys playing the violin.

John:＿＿＿＿＿＿＿

Karen:Since she was a little girl.

  (A)Oh, she must be very good.

  (B)Does she? How long has she been playing it?

  (C)Was she good when she was young?

  (D)I wish I could play the violin too.

【答案】▶(B)

【译文】▶卡伦:玛丽喜欢拉小提琴。

    约翰:＿＿＿＿＿＿＿

    卡伦:从她是小女孩时开始。

    (A)噢！她必定十分擅长。

    (B)是吗？她拉小提琴有多久了？

(C)她年轻时就很擅长吗?

(D)真希望我也会拉小提琴。

● 活学活用 ●

7. Peter：I think I'm going to quit my present job.

John：Why? Don't you like it at all?

Peter：_____ but I can't get along with my boss any
more.

(A)I used to,　　　　　　(B)Not at all,

(C)Hardly,　　　　　　　(D)I believe so,

【答案】▶(A)

【译文】▶彼特:我想我要辞掉现在的工作。

约翰:为什么? 你一点也不喜欢这个工作吗?

彼特:_____但是我和我的上司再也相处不来。

(A)我以前很喜欢,

(B)我一点也不喜欢,

(C)我几乎不喜欢,

(D)我想是的,

【讲解】▶***used to***＋***V.*** 以前……

故 I used to＝I used to like it.

● 活学活用 ●

8. Tom：Jack was stopped by the police again for speeding
and his driver's license was taken away.

Frank：Good. _____

Tom：Ture. He is such a reckless driver.

(A)I'm sorry to hear that.

(B)That'll teach him a lesson.

(C)It's not fair.

(D)How unfortunate for him!

【答案】▶(B)

【译文】▶汤姆：　杰克又因为超速被警察拦下来，他的驾驶执照也被拿走。

法兰克：太好了! _____

汤姆：的确。他是一个如此鲁莽的驾驶员。

(A)我很遗憾听到这件事。

(B)那样可以给他一个教训。

(C)这不公平。

(D)他真不幸!

【讲解】▶①*reckless* [ˈreklis] *adj.* 鲁莽的

②**teach＋sb.＋a lesson**　给……一个教训

● 活学活用 ●

9. Mary： I've found the right apartment. It's nice and clean.

Susan： Is it expensive?

Mary： _____ Only five hundred dollars a month.

(A)Yes, it is cheap.

(B)Yes, I like it very much.

(C)No. That's the beauty of it.

(D)No. I agree with you entirely.

【答案】▶(C)

【译文】▶玛丽：我找到合适的公寓了，又好又干净。

苏珊：贵不贵?

玛丽：_____一个月才五百美元。

(A)是的，很便宜。

(B)是的，我很喜欢。

(C)不贵，那就是它的优点。

(D)不，我完全同意你的看法。

【讲解】▶*the beauty of* ～　……的优点

●活学活用●

Mom：What kind of dressing should we use?

Sam：I think Thousand Island will be.... Ouch!

Mom：____10____.

Sam：I cut myself while I was slicing this carrot.

Mom：____11____. It's bleeding pretty badly... Here's a tissue. Wrap it around the cut and hold it tight to stop the bleeding.

Sam：Thanks. I guess I forgot this was supposed to be a vegetarian salad.

Mom：____12____ while I get the antiseptic ointment and a bandage.

10. (A) What do you do?

　　(B) What did you do?

　　(C) What will you do?

　　(D) What will you have done?

11. (A) Pardon me?

　　(B) Oh, dear.

　　(C) What a surprise!

　　(D) I'm so glad to hear that!

12. (A) Go get the phone

　　(B) You do the dishes

　　(C) Wait a minute

　　(D) I'll call an ambulance

●本文翻译●

母亲：我们应该用哪一种沙拉酱呢？

山姆：我想千岛酱会……噢！

母亲：_____

山姆：我在切萝卜的时候切到了自己。

母亲：_____流了这么多的血……这里有卫生纸。用它来包住伤口，紧紧握住来止血。

山姆：谢谢，我想我忘了这应该是素食沙拉的。

母亲：_____我去拿消毒药膏和绷带。

● 重点突破 ●

❶ *dressing* ['dresiŋ] *n.* 沙拉酱

❷ *Thousand Island*　千岛酱

❸ *slice* [slais] *vt.* 切成薄片

❹ *tissue* ['tisju:] *n.* 卫生纸（＝tissue paper）

❺ *oh,dear* ＝oh,my god.

❻ *bleed* [bli:d] *vi.* 流血

❼ *wrap* [ræp] *vt.* 包裹

❽ *vegetarian* [ˌvedʒi'tɛəriən] *adj.* 素食的　　*n.* 素食者

❾ *antiseptic* [ˌænti'septik] *adj.* ;*n.* 杀菌的；消毒的

❿ *bandage* ['bændidʒ] *n.* 绷带

10.【答案】▶(B)

　　【译文】▶(A)你从事哪一行业？　　(B)你做了什么？

　　　　　　(C)你要做什么？　　　(D)你打算要做什么？

11.【答案】▶(B)

　　【译文】▶(A)对不起,你说什么?

　　　　　　(B)喔,我的天啊!

　　　　　　(C)真令人惊讶!

　　　　　　(D)我真高兴听到那个消息。

12.【答案】▶(C)

　　【译文】▶(A)去接电话　　　　(B)你去洗碗

　　　　　　(C)等一下　　　　　(D)我要叫救护车

【讲解】▶ *ambulance* ['æmbjuləns] *n.* 救护车

═══════ ● 活学活用 ● ═══════

Fran：Eeee!　How come the water's so cold?

Bill：___13___ We're out of gas.

Fran：___14___ Well,hurry up and order a new tank.

Bill：I have. But it probably won't be here for another hour
　　or so.

Fran：But I'm already in the shower!

Bill：Sorry— __15__ Or you could take a cold shower.

Fran：__16__ I'm back in my robe. I'll wait.

13. (A)Oh，take my word for it.

    (B)Oh，I'm frightened.

    (C)Oh，I forgot to tell you.

    (D)Oh，turn off the light.

14. (A)Good thing we have an electric water heater.

    (B)You told me that yesterday.

    (C)Now you tell me.

    (D)I'm glad we have an extra tank.

15. (A)why don't you order some gas?

    (B)the water isn't that cold.

    (C)just go ahead and shower.

    (D)looks like you'll have to wait.

16. (A)I just took a shower.

    (B)That sounds like a good idea.

    (C)No，that's all right.

    (D)O. K. ，I'll try it.

● 本文翻译 ●

弗兰：咦！为什么水会这么冷？

比尔：_____我们煤气用完了。

弗兰：_____嗯，赶快去订一罐来。

比尔：我已经订了。但是可能要过一小时左右才会送到。

弗兰：但是我已经在冲澡了啊！

比尔：抱歉——_____。或许你可以冲个冷水澡。

弗兰：_____我会穿着浴袍，我要等。

● **重点突破** ●

❶ *forget* ＋ *to* V 原形→忘记要做……
　forget ＋ *V-ing* →忘记做过……
❷ *tank* [tæŋk] *n.* (煤气或汽油)桶
❸ *robe* [rəub] *n.* 浴袍(＝bathrobe)

● **解题分析** ●

13.【答案】▶ (C)

　【译文】▶ (A)喔,你可以相信我的话。　(B)喔,我好害怕。

　　　　　(C)喔,我忘记告诉你了。　(D)喔,把灯关掉。

14.【答案】▶ (C)

　【译文】▶ (A)真好我们有电热水器。

　　　　　(B)你昨天已经告诉过我了。

　　　　　(C)现在你才告诉我。

　　　　　(D)我真高兴我们还有一罐煤气。

15.【答案】▶ (D)

　【译文】▶ (A)你为什么不订煤气呢?

　　　　　(B)这水并不是那样的冷嘛!

　　　　　(C)你就进去冲澡嘛!

　　　　　(D)看来你必须等着。

16.【答案】▶ (C)

　【译文】▶ (A)我刚刚才淋浴过。

　　　　　(B)那听起来像是个好主意。

　　　　　(C)不要,算了。

　　　　　(D)好吧! 我会试试看。

● **活学活用** ●

Lynn：How come you're home so late tonight? The food is cold.

Bob：You wouldn't believe the traffic I ran into! It took me an hour and a half to get here!

Lynn：　17

Bob：Tomorrow is the Dragon Boat Festival—this is start of the long weekend.

Lynn：Oh—so I guess lots of people are heading home.

Bob：　18　Can you get me a bowl of rice? I'm starved.

Lynn：Right away. And I'll heat up the food.

Bob：　19　I want to eat now!

17. (A)It's nice when you have the road almost all to yourself.

(B)Any idea why the traffic was so bad?

(C)Don't you wish it were that way every day?

(D)You must have met my friends.

18. (A)Apparently so.   (B)That's ridiculous.

(C)That's a good one!   (D)Try again.

19. (A)I guess I'm not that hungry after all.

(B)Good,and take you time.

(C)OK,that should only take an hour or so,right?

(D)No,don't bother.

● 本文翻译 ●

林恩：你怎么会这么晚才回到家？饭菜都凉了。

鲍勃：你不会相信我碰到的交通状况！我花了一个半小时才回到这里！

林恩：_____

鲍勃：明天是端午节——正好是这次周末长假的开始。

林恩：喔——所以我猜有许多人正赶着回家。

鲍勃：_____你可以帮我盛一碗饭吗？我好饿喔！

林恩：马上就好。我要热一下饭菜。

鲍勃：_____我现在就想吃了！

● 重点突破 ●

❶ *How come + S + V ...? = Why + S + V ...?*　为什么

❷ *run into*　遇到；碰到

❸ *starved* [staːvd] *adj.* 肚子饿的

❹ *heat up*　加热

17. 【答案】▶ (B)

　　【译文】▶ (A) 当你自己几乎拥有整条马路时真好啊！

　　　　　　(B) 你知道交通状况这么差的原因吗？

　　　　　　(C) 你不希望每天都如此吗？

　　　　　　(D) 你一定遇到我的朋友了。

18. 【答案】▶ (A)

　　【译文】▶ (A) 显然是如此。

　　　　　　(B) 那真是可笑。

　　　　　　(C) 那一个不错。

　　　　　　(D) 再试试看。

　　【讲解】▶ *ridiculous* [riˈdikjuləs] *adj.* 可笑的；滑稽的

19. 【答案】▶ (D)

　　【译文】▶ (A) 我想我毕竟还不是那么饿。

　　　　　　(B) 好的，而且你可以慢慢来。

　　　　　　(C) 好吧，那应该只花大约一小时的时间，对吧？

　　　　　　(D) 不用麻烦了。

　　【讲解】▶ ① *after all*　毕竟

　　　　　　② *take one's time*　慢慢来

========== ● 活学活用 ● ==========

(Tom and Jack are lost on their tour in England.)

Tom：Well, it looks like we're lost.

Jack：___20___

Tom：Who do you ask in a strange town?

Jack：___21___

Tom：Where can we find one?

Jack：See，there is one over there.

20.（A）Don't worry. All we have to do is ask.

（B）What should we see next?

（C）I'm scared. Let's go home.

（D）Yes，we just lost a tire.

21.（A）Who knows！

（B）You ask a policeman.

（C）There is a police station there.

（D）I don't see any police station.

●本文翻译●

（汤姆和杰克在英国旅行时迷路了。）

汤姆：噢，看来我们迷路了。

杰克：_____

汤姆：在陌生的小镇里你要问谁呢?

杰克：_____

汤姆：我们去哪里找个警察呢?

杰克：你看，那里就有一个。

●解题分析●

20.【答案】▶（A）

【译文】▶（A）别担心，我们只要问路就可以了。

（B）我们接下来要看什么呢?

（C）我很害怕，我们回家吧。

（D）是的，我们刚才丢了一个轮胎。

【讲解】▶All one has to do is(to)＋V 某人必须做的是……

21.【答案】▶（B）

【译文】▶（A）谁知道！

（B）问警察啊。

（C）那里有一个警察局。

(D)我没看到什么警察局。

【讲解】▶ You ask a policeman. 此句中, you 是指"任何人"。

例: You never know when you will die.

谁也不知道什么时候会死。

━━━ ●活学活用● ━━━

22. Tony: My brother's in hospital.

Suzy: Oh, _____

Tony: He has a heart problem.

(A) he's very sympathetic.

(B) that's very nice of him.

(C) is it anything serious?

(D) you really like to crack jokes.

【答案】▶ (C)

【译文】▶托尼:我的兄弟在住院。

苏西:喔! _____

托尼:他有心脏病。

(A)他很有同情心。

(B)他人很好。

(C)很严重吗?

(D)你真的喜欢开玩笑(说笑话)。

【讲解】①*in hospital* 住院　　　*in the hospital*　在医院中

②*Is it anything serious*? 有什么严重性吗?

━━━ ●活学活用● ━━━

23. Mary: My father quit smoking three months ago.

Sue: _____ I wish my Dad could do that, too.

(A) Don't worry about that. 　(B) I'm very grateful.

(C) By all means. 　　　　　　(D) Good for him.

【答案】▶ (D)

【译文】▶玛丽:我爸爸三个月前戒烟了。

苏：_____希望我爸爸也能做到。

  (A)别担心。

  (B)很感谢。

  (C)当然。

  (D)不错(做得好)。

【讲解】▶①*quit smoking* 戒烟

  ②*good for him* 不错；做得好

  ③*grateful* 感谢的

  ④*By all means＝Of course* 当然

●*活学活用*●

24. Peter：I live in a room with two roommates.

  Bob：Are they easy to live with?

  Peter：_____

   (A)Oh, yes. We get along fine.

   (B)Oh, no. They're very friendly.

   (C)Yes. They're always fighting.

   (D)Yes. It's nice to see them.

【答案】▶(A)

【译文】▶彼得：我和两位室友住在一个房间。

  鲍勃：他们好相处吗?

  彼得：_____

   (A)喔，是的。我们相处得很好。

   (B)喔，不。他们很友善。

   (C)是的。他们经常打架。

   (D)是的。很高兴看到他们。

【讲解】▶①*easy to live with* 好相处

  ②*get along* 相处

━━━━━ ●活学活用● ━━━━━

25. Patient：_____

Doctor：That's too bad. What's the matter?

Patient：Well, I've got a terrible headache.

(A) I need some rest.

(B) I really feel awful.

(C) I don't feel better today.

(D) I need your help right now.

【答案】▶(B)

【译文】▶病人：_____

医师：那太糟了。怎么回事了？

病人：喔！我头痛得很厉害。

(A) 我需要一些休息。

(B) 我真的觉得很不舒服。

(C) 我今天感觉不太好。

(D) 现在就需要你的帮助。

【讲解】▶①*feel awful* 觉得难过或不舒服

②*have got a terrible headache* 头痛得很厉害

③*feel better* 觉得比较好

━━━━━ ●活学活用● ━━━━━

26. Mother：Jack, back to your books.

Jack： I have studied for hours. I'm just taking a break.

Mother：_____

(A) You shouldn't order me around.

(B) You're great at finding excuses.

(C) You're very obdient.

(D) You're really slow to respond.

【答案】▶(B)

【译文】▶母亲：杰克，回去念书。

杰克:我已经念了好几个小时了,我只是休息一下而已。

母亲:_____

(A)你不该颐指气使。　　(B)你真会找借口。

(C)你很听话。　　　　　(D)你反应真慢。

【讲解】▶①*order sb. around*　指挥别人做这、做那

②*excuse* [iks'kju:z] *n.* 借口

③*obedient* [ə'bi:djənt] *adj.* 服从的;顺从的;孝顺的

● 活学活用 ●

27. Sue： Peter is very naughty! He put a frog in my drawer.

Mother： _____ He is still very young.

(A) Has he said anything like that?

(B) That's really something!

(C) How did it go?

(D) Don't get so upset.

【答案】▶(D)

【译文】▶苏： 彼得非常顽皮! 他把一只青蛙放在我抽屉里。

母亲:_____他还小。

(A)他说过那样的话吗?　(B)那真不错!

(C)情况如何?　　　　　(D)不要这么心烦嘛!

【讲解】▶*upset* [ʌp'set] *vt.* 令(人)烦乱

● 活学活用 ●

28. John： Tell me something about London.

David： It's an old city. There are many historic sites.

John： Does it have many good museums?

David： _____

(A) Oh, not much.　　　(B) It's a nice city.

(C) Some of them are here. (D) Well, a good many.

【答案】▶(D)

【译文】▶约翰:告诉我有关伦敦的事。

大卫:伦敦是座古老的城市,有许多历史古迹。

约翰:有很多好的博物馆吗?

大卫:_____

(A)噢,不多。

(B)它是个很棒的城市。

(C)他们有一些在这儿。

(D)哦,相当多。

【讲解】▶①约翰问是否有许多博物馆,大卫表示有很多。

②*a good many* 相当多的(通常用来指可数的名词)

③答案(A)应改为"*not many*"因为"*much*"是指不可数的名词。

④*historic sites* 古迹

━━━━● 活学活用 ●━━━━

29. Doctor：　　　We're ready now. Sorry to have kept you waiting.

Mrs. Freeman：_____Do you have all the test results?

Doctor：　　　Yes,I've got all of them now.

(A)Pleased to meet you.　(B)None of my business.

(C)That's all right.　(D)You bet.

【答案】▶(C)

【译文】▶医生:　　我们现在准备好了。抱歉让您久等。

弗里曼太太:_____你有全部的检验结果吗?

医生:　　是的,我全都拿到了。

(A)很高兴认识你。　　(B)与我无关。

(C)没关系。　　(D)当然!

【讲解】▶①*keep sb. waiting* 使某人等待

②*none of my business* 与我无关

③*You bet*. = You can be certain. 当然;包在我身上。

现场会话 实战复习测验 ●

1. Frank：An accident happened，but no one got hurt.

    John：＿＿＿＿

    (A) For heaven's sake!

    (B) That's too bad.

    (C) Oh，my!

    (D) Thank goodness!

2. Tom：When did you start jogging?

    Phil：When my doctor first suggested that I needed to strengthen my heart. How about you?

    Tom：When I had to be treated for a weak heart.

    Phil：＿＿＿＿

    (A) Practice makes perfect.

    (B) Haste makes waste.

    (C) Look before you leap.

    (D) Better late than never.

3. Joan：Sh，Sh，don't keep laughing that way.

    Peter：＿＿＿＿

    (A) Sorry，I just can't help it.

    (B) I don't see what's so funny.

    (C) Leave it to me.

    (D) Yes，it's nice.

4. Mary：In another half hour we'll be home.

    John：It'll be good to get back again.

    Mary：I always hate to see a vacation come to an end.

    John：＿＿＿＿

    Mary：I'll have a lot of dirty clothes to wash，too.

    (A) I'd better take a look at that washer for you.

    (B) Oh，come on. Don't be so silly.

(C) There's always so much to do. I'll bet the grass is a foot high.

(D) I'm tired from all this driving. It's going to be hard to go to work tomorrow.

5. Joe：There will be another violent demonstration tomorrow.

Sue：_____

Joe：Yes. The police will have a hard time keeping order.

(A) The fat is in the fire!

(B) The coast is clear.

(C) Things are looking up.

(D) For all I care.

6. (At the theater booking office)

Clerk：Can I help you?

Man： I want two tickets for tonight's performance, please.

Clerk：Do you want to sit in the stalls or in the circle?

Man： _____

(A) Yes, please. Thanks a lot.

(B) In the stalls, please, in the middle, if possible.

(C) Yes, I do. In the middle, if possible.

(D) I'd like to go to the circus.

7. Mary：Don't stay up too late.

John： _____

(A) All right, I don't.   (B) Don't worry. I won't.

(C) Of course I have to.   (D) Please don't bother.

8. Husband：Honey, I'm home! Have I got some news for you!

Wife： I hope it's good. _____ You look so excited!

(A) What's happened?

(B) What's matter with you?

(C) What's up?

(D) Take easy!

9. Father： Can you believe it? Our son failed all his exams.

Mother： _____

(A)You are not serious. It can't be true.

(B)That's silly. Cut it out!

(C)Excellent! I knew he'd fail.

(D)Everybody does once in a while.

解题关键分析

1.【答案】▶(D)

　【译文】▶弗兰克:发生一起车祸,但是没有人受伤。

　　　　　约翰:　＿＿＿＿＿

　　　　　　(A)千万!　　　　(B)太不幸了!

　　　　　　(C)我的天!　　　(D)谢天谢地!

2.【答案】▶(D)

　【译文】▶汤姆:你什么时候开始慢跑的?

　　　　　菲尔:当医生第一次建议我必须强化我的心脏时。那

　　　　　　　　你呢?

　　　　　汤姆:当我必须治疗心脏衰弱时。

　　　　　菲尔:　＿＿＿＿＿

　　　　　　(A)熟能生巧。

　　　　　　(B)欲速则不达。

　　　　　　(C)三思而后行。

　　　　　　(D)亡羊补牢,犹未晚矣。

　【讲解】▶①*Haste makes waste.*〔谚〕欲速则不达。

　　　　　②*Look before you leap.*〔谚〕三思而后行。

　　　　　③*Better late than never.*〔谚〕亡羊补牢,犹未晚矣。

3.【答案】▶(A)

　【译文】▶琼:　嘘,嘘,不要那样子笑。

　　　　　彼得:　＿＿＿＿＿

　　　　　　(A)抱歉,我实在忍不住。

　　　　　　(B)我不了解什么事这么好笑。

　　　　　　(C)把它留给我。

　　　　　　(D)是的,太好了。

读者调查表

亲爱的读者：

为进一步做好"新航道图书"的出版工作，更好地为广大读者提供服务，请允许我们占用您宝贵的时间，请您填妥这份表格并邮寄或传真给我们。

为了表示对您的诚挚谢意，所有真实填写并寄回该调查表的读者都将成为新航道书友会会员，我们将定期为您寄送有关新航道英语图书及培训的最新消息。另外，如果您有幸从最后抽取的 **50** 位幸运读者中脱颖而出，您还将获得新航道为您准备的考研英语、新四级、雅思、新概念英语、创新国际口语等价值 **500** 元的超值听课证。

感谢您的支持！您填写的数据仅用于读者调查和联系，我们将严格保密。

关于您的个人信息

姓名_____   性别_____   年龄_____   职业_____

学历：□ 小学   □ 中学   □ 大专、大学   □ 其它_____

邮寄地址_____邮政编码_____

联系电话_____   手机_____电子信箱_____

1. 您购买本书的书名_____

2. 您通过何种渠道得知新航道图书的相关消息？

    □ 网上书店   □ 逛书店   □ 媒体宣传   □ 讲座

    □ 朋友/同事推荐   □其它_____

3.　您对本书的评价：

（1）封面设计 □ 有品味、新颖　　□ 一般、还好　　□ 较差、不喜欢

（2）内容质量 □ 很好　　　　　　□ 一般、还好　　□ 较差

（3）文字版式 □ 不错　　　　　　□ 一般　　　　　□ 不好、不方便阅读

（4）图书定价 □ 较高　　　　　　□ 适中、可承受 □ 便宜

4.　您是否愿意收到新航道的新书快讯？

　　□ 是　　　　　　□ 否

5.　您是否有近期参加英语培训的计划，打算参加哪种培训？

　　□ 是　　　　　　□ 否　　　培训种类＿＿＿＿＿＿＿＿＿＿＿＿

6.　您是通过何种渠道购买到此书？

　　□ 新华书店　　□ 学校附近书店　　□ 网站　　□ 图书市场

　　□·书友会（请注明）＿＿＿＿＿＿＿＿＿＿＿＿＿＿＿＿＿＿

7.　您对本书的意见：

＿＿＿＿＿＿＿＿＿＿＿＿＿＿＿＿＿＿＿＿＿＿＿＿＿＿＿＿＿＿

8.　您对新航道还有哪些希望和要求：

＿＿＿＿＿＿＿＿＿＿＿＿＿＿＿＿＿＿＿＿＿＿＿＿＿＿＿＿＿＿

回函请寄：北京海淀区中关村南大街 12 号农科院科海福林大厦新航道书友会

邮编：100081　　　　　　　网址：www.newchannel.org

电话：010-62138899-660 / 661　　传真：010-62117166

4.【答案】▶(C)

【译文】▶玛丽:再过半小时,我们就到家了。

约翰:又回到家是很棒的一件事。

玛丽:我总是讨厌看到假期结束。

约翰:_____

玛丽:我也有好多脏衣服要洗。

(A)我最好替你看看那台洗衣机。

(B)喔,好啦! 别傻了。

(C)总是有好多事情要做。我敢打赌草已经长到一英尺高了。

(D)开车让我好累。明天去上班会很困难。

【讲解】▶①*come to an end* 结束

②*washer* [ˈwɔʃə] *n.* 洗衣机

5.【答案】▶(A)

【译文】▶乔:明天会有另一场暴力示威。

苏:_____

乔:是啊。警察维持秩序将会很困难。

(A)事情严重了。

(B)没有危险。

(C)事情正在好转。

(D)我才不在乎。

【讲解】▶①*demonstration* [ˌdemənsˈtreiʃən] *n.* 示威

②*The fat is in the fire.* 事情严重了。

③*The coast is clear.* (眼前)没有危险。

④*look up* 好转

⑤*for all I care* 我不在乎

6.【答案】▶(B)

【译文】▶(在戏院售票处)

职员:我能帮您忙吗?

男士:请给我两张今晚表演的票。

职员:您要正厅前排的座位还是特别座?

男士:_____

(A)是的,非常谢谢你。

(B)请给我正厅前排的座位。如果可能,要中间的。

(C)是的,我要。如果可能,要中间的。

(D)我想去看马戏团。

【讲解】▶①*booking office*〔英〕售票处(=〔美〕ticket office)

②*stall* [stɔːl] *n.*〔英〕(戏院)正厅前排座位

③*circle* [ˈsəːkl] *n.*(戏院二楼成圆弧形之)特别座

④*circus* [ˈsəːkəs] *n.* 马戏团

7.【答案】▶(B)

【译文】▶玛丽:别熬夜熬得太晚。

约翰:_____

(A)好的,我不。　　　(B)不要担心,我不会的。

(C)当然,我必须熬夜。(D)请不要麻烦。

【讲解】▶*stay up* 　熬夜

8.【答案】▶(C)

【译文】▶丈夫:甜心,我回来了! 我有一个消息要告诉你!

妻子:我希望是好消息。_____你看起来好兴奋。

(A)发生了什么事?

(B)怎么啦?

(C)怎么啦?

(D)放轻松点!

【讲解】▶Have I got some news for you. 为强调用法 = I have got...

9.【答案】▶(A)

【译文】▶父亲:你相信吗? 我们的儿子考试没有一科及格。

母亲:_____

(A)你不是当真的吧,这不可能是真的。

(B)太荒谬了,别再说了!

(C)太棒了! 我就知道他会不及格。

(D)每个人偶尔都会这样。

【讲解】▶*cut it out* 　停止;别说下去

新航道图书目录

书　名	定　价	作　者
雅思系列		
剑桥雅思考试全真试题集 3 经典课堂	39.00	雅思梦之队 编著
剑 4 全攻略	12.00	雅思梦之队 编著
雅思考试高分作文	29.00	Mark Griffith 编著
雅思考试核心词汇 21 天速听速记（配磁带 5 盘）	书 19.00/磁带 35.00	曲冰　李鑫 编著
雅思考试口语练习（配磁带 4 盘）	书 18.00/磁带 28.00	Nick Stirk 编著
雅思考试口语突破	33.00	Mark Griffiths 编著
雅思考试听力理解（配磁带 8 盘）	书 32.00/磁带 56.00	张皓 编著
雅思考试阅读理解	33.00	刘洪波 编著
雅思考试综合应试指南	32.00	熊莹 编著
雅思口语真经	12.00	李鑫　John Gordon 编著
雅思阅读真经	29.00	刘洪波 编著
雅思词汇真经	22.00	刘洪波 编著
雅思阅读真经 2	29.00	刘洪波　Nick Stirk 编著
考研系列		
2007 考研英语核心词汇笔记	29.00	胡敏主编
2007 年考研英语词汇 21 天速听速记	19.00	胡敏主编
2007 年考研英语读真题记单词	待定	胡敏主编
2007 考研英语阅读理解精读 200 篇	45.00	胡敏主编
2007 考研英语阅读理解精读 120 篇	待定	胡敏主编
2007 考研英语阅读真题全方位突破	待定	胡敏主编
2007 考研英语真题长难句突破	待定	胡敏主编
2007 考研英语语法突破	待定	胡敏主编
2007 考研英语高分作文	待定	胡敏主编
2007 考研英语英译汉四步定位翻译法	待定	胡敏主编
2007 考研英语完型填空与阅读选择搭配题	待定	胡敏主编
2007 考研英语十年真题点石成金	待定	胡敏主编
2007 考研英语模拟冲刺卷	待定	胡敏主编
大学四级系列		
大学英语四级词汇 21 天速听速记（配磁带 5 盘）	16.00/磁带 35.00	曲冰 编著
大学英语四级核心词汇精讲精练	19.00	马宁 编著
大学英语现代文背诵篇章	22.00	谭慧 编著
大学英语写作教程新编	29.00	Barbara Harris Leonhard 著
大学英语自学指南	待定	Nick Stirk
大学英语新四级词汇真经	15.00	刘洪波主编
大学英语新四级 710 分写作 21 天突破	待定	张艳华主编
大学英语新四级 710 分口语 21 天突破	待定	张艳华主编
大学英语新四级 710 分听力 21 天突破	待定	张艳华主编
大学英语新四级 710 分阅读 21 天突破	待定	张艳华主编

书　名	定　价	作　者
读故事系列		
胡敏读故事记单词——小学英语词汇	12.00	胡敏主编
胡敏读故事记单词——高中英语词汇（配磁带 3 盘）	书 18.00/磁带 21.00	胡敏主编
胡敏读故事记单词——大学英语四级词汇（配磁带 4 盘）	书 22.00/磁带 28.00	胡敏主编
胡敏读故事记单词——大学英语六级词汇（配磁带 3 盘）	书 22.00/磁带 21.00	胡敏主编
胡敏读故事记单词——考研英语词汇	19.00	胡敏主编
胡敏读故事记单词——雅思词汇	29.00	胡敏主编
胡敏读故事记单词——TOEFL 词汇	32.00	胡敏主编
胡敏读故事记短语——常用英语短语（配磁带 5 盘）	29.00	胡敏主编
胡敏读故事记短语——基础英语短语（配磁带 3 盘）	书 12.00/磁带 21.00	胡敏主编
读故事记单词新 GRE 核心词汇（附赠 MP3 光盘）	52.00	胡敏主编
突围英语丛书		
励志英语语法	29.00	胡敏 郝福合编著
这样学习英语最有效	18.00	胡敏编著
这样学习英语写作最有效	18.00	张耀飞 钟爱德编著
这样学习英语单词最有效	22.00	陈震 编著
这样学习英语短语最有效	25.00	张耀飞 编著
这样学习英语口语最有效	22.00	李奇 编著
这样学习英语语法最有效	18.00	威利 编著
这样学习英语阅读最有效	20.00	王伟 编著
澳大利亚留学全程攻略	29.00	刘洪波 曲冰 编著
TOEFL 托福全真题高分作文	26.00	胡敏 编著
口语系列		
标准英语口语操练手册(2CD＋书)	19.00	John Gordon 编著
最新国际英语口语词典（配磁带 5 盘）	书 25.00/磁带 35.00	卢琳 罗飞等 编著
英语情景口语 100 主题	38.00 元	Mark Griffith Carol Rueckert 编著
创新国际英语教程学生用书（一）（配磁带 2 盘）	书 39.00/磁带 14.00	Hugh Dellar
创新国际英语教程学生用书（二）（配磁带 2 盘）	书 39.00/磁带 14.00	Hugh Dellar
创新国际英语教程学生用书（三）（配磁带 2 盘）	书 39.00/磁带 14.00	Hugh Dellar

总部地址：北京市海淀区中关村南大街 12 号农科院内科海福林大厦

网　　址：www.newchannel.org

发 行 部：010－62195842 62138899－667

客户服务：010－62116766/6866

邮　　编：100081